DOUBLE EAGLE

OTHER WORKS BY THOMAS KING

FICTION
Medicine River
Green Grass, Running Water
One Good Story, That One
Truth and Bright Water
A Short History of Indians in Canada
The Back of the Turtle
Indians on Vacation
Sufferance

DREADFULWATER MYSTERIES
DreadfulWater
The Red Power Murders
Cold Skies
A Matter of Malice
Obsidian
Deep House

NON-FICTION
The Truth About Stories
The Inconvenient Indian

POETRY
77 Fragments of a Familiar Ruin

CHILDREN'S ILLUSTRATED BOOKS
A Coyote Columbus Story, illustrated by William Kent Monkman
Coyote Sings to the Moon, illustrated by Johnny Wales
Coyote's New Suit, illustrated by Johnny Wales
A Coyote Solstice Tale, illustrated by Gary Clement
Coyote Tales, illustrated by Byron Eggenschwiler

GRAPHIC NOVELS
Borders, illustrated by Natasha Donovan

DOUBLE EAGLE

A DreadfulWater Mystery

THOMAS KING

HarperCollins*Publishers*Ltd

Double Eagle
Copyright © 2023 by Dead Dog Café Productions Inc.
All rights reserved.

Published by HarperCollins Publishers Ltd

First edition

No part of this book may be used or reproduced in any manner whatsoever without the prior written permission of the publisher, except in the case of brief quotations embodied in reviews.

HarperCollins books may be purchased for educational, business or sales promotional use through our Special Markets Department.

HarperCollins Publishers Ltd
Bay Adelaide Centre, East Tower
22 Adelaide Street West, 41st Floor
Toronto, Ontario, Canada
M5H 4E3

www.harpercollins.ca

Library and Archives Canada Cataloguing in Publication

Title: Double eagle / Thomas King.
Names: King, Thomas, 1943- author.
Description: Series statement: A DreadfulWater mystery ; book 7
Identifiers: Canadiana (print) 20230460445 | Canadiana (ebook) 20230460852
ISBN 9781443472128 (hardcover) | ISBN 9781443472135 (softcover)
ISBN 9781443472142 (ebook)
Subjects: LCGFT: Novels. | LCGFT: Detective and mystery fiction.
Classification: LCC PS8571.I5298 D68 2023 | DDC C813/.54—dc23

Printed and bound in the United States
23 24 25 26 27 LBC 5 4 3 2 1

For Christopher.
My favourite and, as it turns out, only brother.

DOUBLE EAGLE

1

Thumps DreadfulWater and Moses Blood dozed in the shade of a large cottonwood and listened to Cooley Small Elk and Claire Merchant chase Claire's six-year-old back and forth between the house and barn.

Thumps slipped the camera out of his jacket pocket, turned it on, set the aperture. Through the viewfinder, he watched Ivory try to turn cartwheels in the grass. The effort was there. The technique would come later.

"You could help, you know."

Thumps looked up to find Claire standing over him.

Moses kept his eyes shut. "I think she means you."

"I mean the both of you," said Claire.

"I'm taking pictures," said Thumps. "Recording the moment for posterity."

"Don Corleone chased his grandson through his garden," said Moses, "and look what happened to him."

Claire folded her arms across her chest. "How you feeling?"

"The doctor says I'm getting old," said Moses, "but this is not a surprise."

"What'd he say about your heart?"

"Said it was congenial."

"I think he might have said 'congestive.'"

Moses smiled. "He cautioned me against chasing little girls in tall grass."

Cooley came over with Ivory tucked under his arm, twisting and wriggling like an eel in a net.

"Put me down!"

Cooley looked at Claire.

"Take her into the mountains," said Claire. "Leave her there for the wolves to eat."

"No mountains!" shouted Ivory. "No wolves!"

Cooley tossed Ivory into the air. "I could drop her in the river."

"Excellent idea," said Claire.

"No river!"

"Maybe that one would like something to eat," said Moses.

"Chocolate cake!"

"How about watermelon?"

"Watermelon and chocolate cake!"

The remnants of lunch were still on the blanket. There was no chocolate cake left, because there had been no chocolate cake to begin with, but now that Ivory had mentioned it, Thumps found himself wanting a piece as well.

"Looks like we're out of watermelon," said Cooley. "How about a carrot?"

"No," said Ivory.

"Potato salad?"

"No."

"How about I chase you some more."

"Can't catch me," shouted Ivory. And off she went, racing through the grass like the wind.

Cooley stayed put and watched her go. "Gives you a new appreciation for mothers."

"I'm going to sit here," said Claire. "And I'm not going to move."

Thumps followed Ivory with the rangefinder, let the autofocus do the work. It was so much faster than his field camera.

"That one is quick," said Moses. "She will be a strong woman."

"If I don't kill her first," said Claire.

Ivory came racing back, crashed into Cooley on the fly, bounced off the big man, tumbled backwards into the grass.

"Hey," she cried out. "You're supposed to move."

"I'm a tree," said Cooley. "Trees don't move."

"You're not a tree."

"I certainly am." Cooley held out his arms. "These are my leafy branches."

"Maybe you want Thumps to chase you," said Claire.

"I'm hungry. I want chocolate cake."

"Carrots," said Claire. "And potato salad."

"Then," Ivory said, striking a pose, her hands on her hips. "I want a horse."

MOSES LIVED ON fifty acres of bottomland that fronted the river. There was a small house, a barn, a chicken coop, along with a small herd of derelict trailers put out to pasture.

An oasis. Of sorts.

"Had a preacher come out one time," said Moses. "Told me my place reminded him of the Garden of Eden."

"There's a strip club over in Great Falls by that name," said Cooley. "But I'm guessing he meant the other one with the naked couple and the snake."

"Every so often," said Moses, "I'll find a snake in the woodpile. But they all swear they're not related to the one with the apple."

"And you believe them?"

"They all sound very sincere and have honest faces."

Thumps leaned back, closed his eyes, let his skin soak up the sun. Fall was his favourite time of the year. Warm days, cool nights. The land laid out like a painting. Greens and golds in the light. Deep blues and purples in the shadows.

And a high sky filled with clouds.

Claire sat down next to Thumps, leaned against his shoulder. "So, this is what men do."

"I wouldn't answer that if I were you," said Moses.

"It wasn't a question," said Claire. "Mind you, I can see the appeal. Sit around all day. Watch the sky. Let someone else do the work."

"I wouldn't answer that one either."

"That also wasn't a question," said Claire.

"No point in asking me," said Moses. "I'm senile."

Thumps kept his eyes closed. "Ditto."

"You two should take your act on the road," said Claire. "But while we're waiting for Second City to call, maybe you could do something useful."

"Remind your woman that I'm senile," said Moses.

"I'm going to be at Buffalo Mountain for the next couple of nights," said Claire.

"This about the gold show?"

Claire shook her head. "Scoop and her genome project."

"Ah," said Moses. "Gnomes and their gold. There was a movie on Netflix about that."

"Genomes," said Claire. "The Four Grandmothers' Genome Project."

"Had a big dragon in it." Moses chuckled. "The gnomes try to steal the dragon's gold, and the dragon burns down a village. It doesn't end well."

"Maybe we can have dinner."

"Sure."

"I'm too old to eat dinner," said Moses. "I used to do that, but I don't anymore."

"What about Ivory?"

"You remember her uncle? Melton?"

"Sure."

"He and his fiancée are coming to the resort. They're going to take her for the weekend."

"Melton getting married?"

"Her name is Ona."

"So just the two of us."

"My treat," said Claire. "I could use your two cents on the repatriation of Deep House and Antelope Flats."

"Courts have already ruled on that."

"Three times," said Claire. "Only now the state and their corporate friends want to do a multi-use feasibility study, want to explore the possibility of a joint conservancy with the tribe and the state managing the Flats as a protected wilderness area *and* explore the possibility of using Deep House as a recycling and waste management site."

"By which they mean a public park and a dump."

"By which," said Claire.

"That's not going to happen."

Claire smiled. "You said the same thing about that idiot when he ran for president."

Ivory started shrieking and calling for help. Cooley was dangling her over the river.

"Make sure you drop her in deep water," shouted Claire.

"No deep water!"

"That's why children are on the earth," said Claire. "To ensure we appreciate the quiet of old age and death."

"This is true," said Moses.

"I thought you were senile," said Claire.

"I have occasional moments of lucidity," said Moses.

Claire turned to Thumps. "We could have dinner, talk. Might think of other things to do as well."

Moses put his hands to his ears. "All this intimate chit-chat is embarrassing me."

"What happened to senile?"

"No one is that senile," said Moses. "Maybe you two should go for a walk."

On the far side of the river, Thumps could see a figure running across the high ground.

Scoop Macleod.

She moved quickly down the slope and out across the flat, her shadow racing ahead of her, as she turned toward the river.

"How are things working out with Scoop?" asked Thumps.

"She makes good soup," said Moses.

"Do we know who her family might be?" said Claire.

"Not yet," said Moses, "but my little grey cells are working on it."

"You should grow a moustache," said Thumps. "Get a nice homburg. A cane and pince-nez."

Moses patted Thumps's hand. "You could be my Captain Hastings."

"Sure," said Thumps. "You could solve all the mysteries, and I could stand around looking perplexed."

"That photograph any help?" said Claire.

"Not yet," said Moses, "but my little grey cells are working on it."

Scoop hit the river. Thumps got several shots of her splashing across the shallows and climbing the near bank. She waved as she jogged into the yard.

"Going to get changed," she shouted, and disappeared into the cluster of trailers.

"She's had a tough life," said Claire. "Don't know that we're going to make it any easier."

"Sometimes," said Moses, "having a safe place to rest is the first step."

"We don't know who she is," said Claire. "She doesn't know who she is. We don't even know where she was born."

"She's one of the ghost children," said Moses. "Mostly they disappear and are never seen again."

"But this one came home," said Claire.

"Yes," said Moses. "This one came home. She just doesn't know it yet."

Ivory was wrapped around one of Cooley's legs, was hanging on, as the big man lumbered through the grass.

"Any of you seen a little girl?" he asked.

"I'm right here," said Ivory. "And I'm not little."

"I had her," said Cooley, "and then she ran off."

"I'm right here!"

Cooley looked down at his feet. "There seems to be something nasty stuck to my shoe."

"I'm not nasty. I'm not stuck."

"Honey," said Claire, "come bother Thumps."

"Dog," said Ivory.

"She still calling you that?" said Cooley.

"Evidently."

"She can say *Thumps* well enough," said Claire. "But she doesn't appear to want to."

"Dog is fine."

"She'll probably grow out of it," said Cooley.

"I'm going home," said Claire, "and taking Ms. Monster with me."

"I'm not Ms. Monster," said Ivory.

"Unless one of you big, strong men want to look after her for the day."

"I have to take Moses home," said Cooley.

"That's right," said Moses. "He has to take me home."

"Don't look now," said Claire, "but you're already home."

"Ah," said Moses, "another troubling indicator of decline in the hippocampus."

Thumps could feel all eyes on him. "I guess we could spend some time together."

Claire gave him her hawk stare, the one she reserved for federal officials, men in general, and rodents.

"And what would the two of you do?"

Thumps shrugged. "Take her to breakfast at Al's."

Claire looked at her watch. "Little late for that."

Thumps shrugged. "Take her home. She could play with Freeway and Cookie. Spend some time with me in the darkroom."

"As well as take her to the park and let her play on the slide over and over and over again? As well as try to put her down for a nap, while she screams at the top of her lungs? As well as give her a bath, while she dumps water on the floor with her tub toys? As well as try to get her to eat something besides pancakes and potato chips?"

"Only one good answer to that one," said Moses.

Claire squatted down next to her daughter. "How about it, honey. You want to go with Dog?"

Ivory looked up at Thumps. Her lower lip began to quiver. "No!"

"And that's what love looks like," said Claire.

"I would have taken her."

Claire lifted Ivory off her feet. "You want a big, squeezy hug and some sloppy kisses?"

Ivory cuddled up against Claire, buried her face in her breasts. "No," she said. "I want a horse."

2

It had been a perfect afternoon on the river bottom with Moses and Cooley, Claire and Ivory, and as Thumps drove back into town, he felt a wave of well-being and good will break over him, something that didn't happen all that often, something that was a bit of a shock to the system.

The moment lasted longer than usual, and as he turned onto Main Street, he found himself thinking that he might stop in at the Aegean, see how Archie Kousoulas was doing. He hadn't seen the man in over a week, and Archie would probably have a good story or two to share.

But stopping in to see Kousoulas was not without its cost. There wasn't an enthusiasm the little Greek didn't embrace. And each time Archie set out to save the world, he would wind up at Thumps's door, insisting that Thumps join him in his newest *cause du jour*.

On sober second thought, it would be better to drop by the sheriff's office. Duke Hockney had survived his prostate operation. He had recovered physically, but the mental part had been slower. Maybe he was still a little depressed. A friendly face, some kind words couldn't hurt.

Yes, Hockney had a knack for dragging Thumps into harm's way. Yes, the man made the worst coffee on the planet. Yes, he could be as big a bully as Archie.

As he pulled up in front of the sheriff's office, Thumps realized that, in the end, neither was a good choice, that the only real difference between the two was that the sheriff's office might have doughnuts and the bookstore would not.

The office was warm and cozy. Duke's old percolator was bubbling away, with its disturbing smelter noises and alarming smelter smells. There was a Dumbo's doughnut box on the filing cabinet. Deanna Heavy Runner, one of Duke's deputies, was standing next to the cabinet, a cup in her hand. Sheriff Duke Hockney was at his desk, his service revolver out and pointed at the monitor.

Deanna gave Thumps a nod. "Doughnuts are all gone."

Duke thumbed back the hammer. "You're just in time." And he pulled the trigger.

Thumps jerked back, closed his eyes.

"It's okay," said Deanna. "He took the bullets out."

Thumps opened his eyes. The monitor was still standing.

Duke cocked the gun again. "I can always put them back in."

"What happened to the doughnuts?"

Deanna gave a little grunt. "He ate them all."

"When I'm angry," said Duke, "I get hungry."

"Computer problems?"

"Amazon," said Deanna.

"Black hole of the modern world." Duke pulled the trigger a second time, the hammer coming down on another empty cylinder. "You have Amazon?"

"Amazon what?"

"The online retailer," said Deanna.

"No."

"How about Amazon Prime Video?" said the sheriff.

"Nope."

"Then you win first prize," said Duke.

"First prize is a cup of coffee," said Deanna. "Second prize is two cups."

"Pass."

"What are you talking about," said Duke. "It's perfect."

Deanna held her cup up. "Remember the tar baby from Brer Rabbit?"

"You're drinking it," said Duke.

"No," said Deanna, "I'm holding it. Suspicion of assault and impersonating a hot beverage. As soon as I figure out the rest of the charges, I'm taking it into custody."

Duke waved her off. "I have a comedian for a deputy."

"So, what happened with Amazon?"

"He can tell you the sad tale. I have to get over to the courthouse." Deanna grabbed her hat, set the cup on the edge of Duke's desk. "Put this in the holding cell. I'll interrogate it later."

Thumps waited to see if Deanna was going to come back and beat a confession out of the percolator. Then he settled in the chair in front of Duke's desk.

"So?" he said. "Amazon?"

Duke reloaded the revolver. "Amazon Prime streaming whatever. Has a bunch of programs that Macy likes, says network television is nothing but reality crap."

Duke slipped the gun back into its holster.

"So I say, 'Sure, get the streaming whatever.' And she does."

"And?"

"Maybe I will shoot the damn thing."

"No shooting. Use your words."

"Couple of weeks back, Amazon froze our account. Said there was suspicious activity. Macy tells me to call Amazon, straighten it out. Get the programs up and running again. Easy peasy."

Thumps could see a *but* on the horizon.

"But?"

"Turns out you can't call Amazon. There's no Amazon customer service number."

"So, email them."

"No email."

"Chat line?"

"Nope." Duke pulled the gun out of the holster and laid it on the desk next to the keyboard. "No nothing. You know Christopher Reno?"

Thumps didn't recognize the name.

"Moved into the old Prentice building on Fifth. Computer consulting, repairs, that sort of thing. Has the contract with the county."

"Okay."

"So, I stopped by, and Chris tells me that Amazon doesn't have a customer service centre. They don't want to talk to customers. They just want to sell shit. And if they lock your account, it will never get unlocked."

"That doesn't make sense."

"Chris says it's the new reality. You can buy, but you can't talk. Said the only way I can get around it is to get a new email account and a new credit card number and start all over again."

"That's ridiculous."

"In the meantime, the corporate assholes sit back and rake in the dough."

Thumps glanced at the old coffee percolator. Maybe Deanna was wrong about the coffee. Every so often, if he caught a cup just after it was brewed, it was only terrible.

"One of Amazon's executives decides to come through Chinook, I'll go out of my way to show them the ins and outs of customer service."

"What's Macy going to do?"

"Books," said Duke. "We got a good library, and if there's a problem, we can just go over and have a nice chat with Berri or Lorraine. Unlike Amazon, you can talk to librarians."

"Okay." Thumps got out of the chair. "Good talk. Enjoy your books."

"Sit down."

"I have to get home."

"You know I'm looking to shoot something, don't you? And right now, my options are you and the monitor."

"I can't believe you ate all those doughnuts."

Duke looked at his watch. He got to his feet, took his hat off the hook.

"How about I give you a ride home? Think of it as customer service."

"Every time I get in the car with you," said Thumps, "we wind up with a dead body."

"The exciting life of law enforcement."

"And I have my own car. And I'm going home. I only stopped by to cheer you up."

"Cheer me up?"

"The operation? The depression?"

"You want to cheer me up," said Duke, "meet me at Dumbo's."

"You want more doughnuts?"

"I ran out," said Duke. "Someone ate the ones I had."

"You don't need more doughnuts."

"Sticks and stones," said Duke. "Sticks and stones."

THE LAST TIME Thumps had been to Dumbo's, the doughnut shop had been a dog-shit brown clapboard with all the appeal of a landfill. But when he pulled into the parking lot, the building waiting for him was clean and bright with a stucco facade in light earth tones, the soffits and window frames in a soft green accent.

Thumps stood by his car, unsure if he was in the right place. "What the hell happened?"

"Pretty impressive, eh?"

"Morris sell the business?"

"Nope," said Duke. "He got *Bustervated*."

"He got what?"

"*Bustervated*," said Duke. "Don't you watch any TV?"

"*Bustervated* is a TV show?"

Duke straightened his hat. "Alan Buster. One of those reality shows. Buster takes beat-to-shit businesses and fixes them up. Or as Alan likes to say, Bustervates them."

"Morris let someone touch his building?"

"The renovations were free," said Duke. "Show paid for them. Win-win."

"Did they Bustervate the inside as well?"

"Come on." Duke headed across the lot. "Let's see what's behind door number two."

The old interior had been a collection of yard-sale tables with plastic tablecloths, mismatched chairs with wobbly legs, a sketchy recliner behind the register. A Budweiser clock on the wall. Rumour was that Morris slept in the recliner and was responsible for the damp, nasty smells that filled the café.

The new interior was bright and shiny and smelled like a forest. An artificial forest to be sure, but a forest nonetheless.

"What happened to the shitty furniture and the recliner?" said Thumps. "And the stink?"

"All gone," said Duke. "Bustervated."

"Sheriff Hockney. You're back."

The woman who popped up behind the counter was somewhere in her late twenties. Short, sturdy, with bright red hair and freckles. Round glasses in neon blue.

"Ms. Whelan," said the sheriff, "like to introduce you to my special deputy, Thumps DreadfulWater."

"I'm not his special deputy."

"You're the photographer," said Whelan. "Yeah?"

"Thumps, this is Fancy Whelan." Duke waited a beat or two for effect. "Morris's niece."

"Niece?"

"Uncle Morris is my mum's brother."

"Morris has a mother?"

"That was the first question out of my mouth as well," said Duke.

"Uncle Morris can be a bit intense," said Fancy.

Thumps did a quick sweep of the doughnut shop. In case Morris was hiding in the shadows, ready to rush out and assault him with his views on race and gender.

"If you're looking for Morris," said Duke, "you can relax."

"He's not here?"

"Nope," said Duke. "He's gone."

"Gone? As in . . . ?"

Fancy's smile was brilliant. "No, no, Uncle Morris is still amongst the living. He's off having a good time."

"Morris Dumbo?"

"Hard to believe," said Duke. "But there it is."

"Off on a cruise, he is," said Fancy. "Five weeks around Asia and Indonesia and the like."

Thumps waited for the rest of the story.

"Seems our Morris has a girlfriend," said Duke. "Difficult as that is to believe."

Thumps would have said impossible.

"Yesenia Ramos," said Fancy. "She looks a lot like Salma Hayek."

Thumps tried nodding.

"You know, *The Hitman's Bodyguard*? *Hitman's Wife's Bodyguard*?"

"Thumps doesn't watch much TV," said Duke.

"Those are movies."

"Doesn't get to the movies much either," said the sheriff.

"I have this thing with faces," said Fancy. "For instance, you look a bit like James Coburn."

"Me?"

"And the sheriff has a bit of Michael Caine to him."

"My wife thinks I look like John Wayne."

"Nah," said Fancy. "Don't see it."

"Morris's girlfriend," said Duke, "is Puerto Rican."

Thumps tried to think of something to say.

"Morris and a Latina," said Duke. "It does defy belief."

"She was the makeup artist for the show," said Fancy. "She and Uncle Morris hit it off."

Thumps found his voice. "Morris is a racist."

"True love," said the sheriff. "A wonder to behold."

"He's also a sexist."

"The two of them hit it off over puzzles," said Fancy. "The big ones. Thousand pieces and up."

"Puzzles?"

"Uncle Morris is a pepper for puzzles." Fancy flashed her smile. "That's what Yez calls him. Her little pepper."

"I think Thumps could use a cup of coffee," said Duke. "And a doughnut."

"What kind would you have an eye on?"

"Thumps is diabetic," said Duke.

"Old-fashioned, then," said Fancy. "Unglazed."

Thumps and Duke found a table by the window. Thumps tried to remember if the old place had had windows that had simply been cleaned or whether the windows he was looking out were brand spanking new. Whatever the case, the light coming in brightened the interior in a way that he would have never imagined possible.

"I got a theory," said the sheriff.

"About?"

"Morris. I figure that he's been lonely a long time."

"Lonely."

"And if you're lonely, you tend to get nasty and unpleasant." Duke set his hat on the chair next to him. "Then someone comes along, smiles at you, and the sun comes out."

"Her little pepper?"

Fancy came over with a tray. "Here you are. Chocolate-coated for the sheriff. Unglazed old-fashioned for the special deputy."

"Photographer."

"Speaking of which." Fancy took a cellphone out of her pocket. "Here's the happy couple."

There was Morris, standing next to a statue of an enormous cat, dressed in a Hawaiian shirt and walking shorts. With a smile on his face.

"Most of us would have bet that the man *couldn't* smile," said Duke.

The woman standing next to him was short and round with spiked hair and tattoos running down her arms. She was snuggled up against Morris's shoulder, her arm around his waist.

"A few more pounds than Hayek," said Fancy, "but you can see the resemblance."

"Morris looks a little like that guy from *The Deer Hunter*."

"Christopher Walken? Maybe the mouth and chin. I'm thinking he's more a Steve Buscemi," said Fancy. "Around the eyes."

Thumps tried the doughnut. As good as ever. At least some things didn't change.

"Going to be challenging getting used to a new Morris," said Duke.

"In the meantime," said Fancy, "you're stuck with me."

"I'll swing by early tomorrow," said the sheriff. "Grab two dozen assorted."

"Two dozen?"

"Going to give those assholes at Amazon one more try," said Duke. "I'm anticipating the worst."

"Then I'll throw in a couple extra of the chocolate," said Fancy. "Yeah?"

Thumps waited for Fancy to disappear into the kitchen before he turned on Duke. "All right," he said. "What's up?"

"Nothing. Just having coffee and a doughnut with a friend."

"Bullshit."

"A somewhat potty-mouthed friend."

"Count of ten, I get up and go home."

Duke shrugged. "I was thinking that you were probably missing law enforcement."

"Not one bit."

"You used to be a pretty good cop," said Duke. "You don't just walk away from that."

"Yes, you do."

"And I was thinking that you might like to have another kick at the can. For old times' sake."

"No kick. No old time anything."

Duke leaned on the table, lowered his voice. "What do you know about gold? Specifically gold coins."

"The exhibition up at Buffalo Mountain?"

"Might need a hand," said Duke. "Me still being on the mend from the operation and all."

"The operation was a year ago."

"You don't heal as fast as you get older." Duke tapped the table with a finger. "So, what do you think?"

"About?"

"Morris. The new-look doughnut shop. A girlfriend. Fancy."

"I like Fancy."

"You figure we might have misjudged Morris all these years? Maybe he's mellowed with age."

"That's whiskey," said Thumps, "not people. People generally get worse as they get older."

"We do get set in our ways." Duke licked the sugar off his lips. "So, I'll pick you up tomorrow, first thing."

"No, you won't. I'm going to sleep in. Then I'm going to have breakfast at Al's."

"Okay, after you feed your face, meet me at the Aegean."

"After I eat, I'm going to go home, print some photographs, have lunch, take a nap, go for a walk, take a nap, have dinner, go to bed."

"Bookstore, bookstore, bookstore." Duke got out of the chair, brushed off his pants. "Come on. I want to show you something."

THE PARKING LOT was empty. Except for the two cars. Duke ambled over to the cruiser, leaned against the door, crossed his arms, tipped his hat back.

Thumps wasn't feeling particularly patient. "Okay," he said, "what are we doing?"

"Enjoying the remains of the day," said Duke. "Western sunset. You only get so many. You do much thinking about death and dying?"

"Shit," said Thumps. "The cancer back?"

"I mean one day, you're alive, and the next you're not. Like throwing a switch or closing a door that never gets opened again."

"Duke . . ."

"No," said Duke. "I'm okay. It's Macy."

"Macy?"

"After the operation, I had to stay home for a couple of weeks. Sometimes you don't notice things unless you're there to notice them."

"You talking about . . ."

"It wasn't much at first. A little confusion. She couldn't find her keys. I'd tease her. Stupid. Then one day, I found her standing at the counter, staring off into space. As though her mind had gone on a trip and left her body behind."

"She been to a doctor?"

Duke nodded. "They're not sure yet. Could be some kind of dementia or it could just be an imbalance in her electrolytes."

"So, it could be nothing."

"Or she might wake up tomorrow and not recognize me."

It wasn't much of a sunset. The sky was empty, a cold glow on the horizon, the dark settling in behind.

"What are you going to do?"

"What I can." Duke pushed off the cruiser, unlocked the door. "Which isn't much. So, I'll keep working. Maybe shoot a bad guy or two. Take my mind off the little surprises of life."

"You're just trying to make me feel sorry for you," said Thumps, "so I'll go along with whatever you want me to do."

Duke smiled, opened the door, slid in behind the wheel. "How am I doing?"

3

The bungalow was dark, and as he parked at the curb, Thumps reminded himself once again that he should leave a few lights on, so the house wouldn't look as though it had been abandoned.

He was halfway up the walk when he saw his next-door neighbour. Virgil "Dixie" Kane was a large, pleasant man with a ready smile and an open heart. He lived alone with a Komondor named Pops. Pops was almost as large as Dixie, not so much a dog as a sack of laundry. With legs.

"How's it going?"

Thumps gave a little wave. "Great."

"Pops was getting worried about you," said Dixie. "Normally, you're home before this."

Thumps looked at the sky. No stars. No moon.

"Freeway was concerned as well."

"Nice thought," said Thumps. "Wrong cat."

"Cookie too," said Dixie. "Freeway wanted me to call you on your cell. But you don't have a cell."

Pops came off Dixie's porch, crossed the yard, lumbered onto Thumps's porch, and began banging his tail on the front door.

"I was thinking about that today," said Dixie. "About how you're getting further and further behind."

"Behind?"

"The digital age."

Freeway and Cookie popped up at the window to see what all the commotion was about. Pops beat his tail harder.

"Here." Dixie held up something in his hand. "This is the newest cell. Thing does everything. It has a three-lens camera. You can get your email anywhere in the world. You can even watch stuff like sports and movies on it."

Thumps had used a cell from time to time. The sheriff had made him carry one for brief periods, and he had to admit that it was amazing what the phones could do.

"But the reality," said Dixie, "is that if you don't have a cell these days, you can't do much of anything. They're like credit cards. That's what the world runs on. Cellphones and credit cards."

"I pay cash."

"Sure," said Dixie, "that works in old black and white movies, but the fact of the matter is cash is obsolete. No one wants cash anymore."

"Al's is cash only."

"Not anymore," said Dixie. "Now you can buy your breakfast there with a credit card."

Thumps felt a tremor run through his body. It was easy to hold the line on needless technological innovations so long as there were others who were willing to stand on the line with you.

"And," said Dixie, "if you want any of the great TV streaming services or if you want to order something from Amazon, you have to have a credit card and an email account."

"Amazon."

"Lot of people don't like Amazon," said Dixie, "but they control a large part of the market for just about everything."

Pops was at the window now, licking the glass, while Cookie pawed at him from her side. Freeway settled on the sill, looking bored.

"It's our own fault," said Dixie. "All we want is comfort and convenience. And this is what we get."

"Amazon."

"Correctamundo," said Dixie, "a corporate monster with the moral centre of a cow flop."

Dixie slipped the phone into a pocket.

"You planning any trips?"

"Trips?"

"You used to go on photography trips in the early fall. The pandemic probably slowed you down, but I figure that you might be looking to get away this year."

"Maybe."

"I bring it up in case you need someone to look after your kitties." Dixie gestured to the animal variety show on the porch. "You know, all you have to do is ask."

"Appreciate that." Thumps stepped onto the porch, opened the door.

"And you should think about a cellphone," said Dixie. "It's not the world we might have imagined, but it's the one we deserve."

FREEWAY AND COOKIE jumped him when he got to the kitchen, whining and weaving themselves around his legs. Thumps checked their water bowls.

Full.

Food bowls?

Each morning, he mixed dry and wet food together. Freeway had developed a technique for sucking the wet up and leaving the dry to rot. Cookie tended to eat everything, but Thumps was sure that it was only a matter of time before the son learned his mother's bad habits.

"You need to eat the dry food as well as the wet."

Freeway sat down next to her bowl and stared at him. Cookie began licking his bowl, pushing it across the floor so Thumps could see that it was empty.

"I could feed you dry only until you decide to co-operate."

Freeway didn't move, held her position.

"We're going to try this one more time," said Thumps, "and then we're going to look at some changes."

He was talking to himself, talking to hear himself talk. Maybe this is what happened to people who lived alone with cats. Freeway let out a long, mournful yowl.

"First you have to eat everything on your plate."

This had been one of his mother's admonitions. And it hadn't been all that effective with him. Liver? Really? What kid wants to eat liver? Velvet steak, his mother had called it. And chipped beef on toast? Who was the sadist who thought that one up?

Thumps went to the cupboard, took down a can of cat food.

"This is the last time," he said, waving the can in Freeway's face. "The very last time."

As he opened the can, he wondered if wet dog food smelled as bad as wet cat food.

Dixie and Pops.

Thumps and Freeway.

As he spooned the cat goop into the bowl, he was struck and somewhat dismayed by the similarities he and his neighbour shared. Two men living alone with animals.

Sure, he had Claire. Some of the time. And Dixie might have a part-time someone as well. And now that he thought about it, his mother had been in much the same situation. Abandoned by her husband, she had lived the rest of her life alone. She hadn't had an animal for company.

She had had Thumps.

Was that better?

Thumps wandered into the bathroom to brush his teeth. As he stood at the mirror, he began to count up the other people he knew who lived alone. Moses Blood, Cooley Small Elk, Claire Merchant, Archie Kousoulas, Ora Mae Foreman, and Alvera Couteau for starters. More than he had realized. A bit of a shock.

Of course, there were Duke Hockney and his wife, Macy, Beth Mooney and Gabby Santucci, Chintak and Nandini Rawat, Stas and Angie Black Weasel.

Thumps rinsed his mouth in the sink. Maybe this was fallout from the digital world. More cellphones, fewer relationships. Credit cards and security codes, greater isolation.

The bed was cold and empty. Well, beds generally were until you crawled into them. Would he be happier if Claire was here? Would he enjoy life more if Ivory was in his life full-time? Or were two cats as much human contact as he could manage?

The Obsidian Murders, the deaths of Anna Tripp and her daughter, Callie, were still with him, as was the spectre of Harold Shipman's attempt to kill Claire and Ivory. That might have something to do with his lying in bed alone. That sense that he was toxic, dangerous to the people around him.

He had just gotten comfortable under the covers when the cats came in, licking their faces and smelling of liver and fish. They jumped onto the bed, curled up against his back and neck.

Maybe, Thumps thought as he drifted off, this is as good as it gets.

4

Thumps stood outside Al's and let the morning sun warm his face. Early fall was the best season on the high prairies. Winter would be along soon enough, but aside from depression, there was little to be gained with that kind of thinking.

Today was the day he had, and today was glorious.

Through the plate-glass window, Thumps could see Alvera Couteau working at the grill, could see Wutty Youngbeaver, Jimmy Monroe, and Russell Plunkett on their usual stools. Chintak Rawak was sitting with Stas Black Weasel. There were several stools free, and one of them was his.

Al's had started life as a dead-end alley that ran between the Fjord Bakery and Sam's Laundromat. The city council didn't know what to do with the property until Al came along. She bought the space for a dollar, turned it into a long, narrow café, and started serving breakfast from six in the morning to just after one in the afternoon.

It wasn't Caffè Florian in Venice or Café Central in Vienna or Café Gerbeaud in Budapest. But neither was it a clone of a Make-America-Corporate chain. A Second Cup or a Tim Hortons or a Starbucks.

A turtle shell with the word "Food" written on it and glued next to the front door was the only sign that the place existed. Inside was a long lime-green counter with a run of scruffy red and chrome stools on one side and plywood booths on the other. The stools were for the regulars.

The booths were for the tourists who wandered in off the street and stayed. There was a grill at the front and a window.

And that was that.

The place smelled of coffee and grease, toast and warm bodies. The air was heavy and moist, and each time Thumps stepped into the café, there was the momentary sensation of being shoved underwater.

"Hey, Thumps." Wutty Youngbeaver turned on his stool. "You ready for my new fall adventure?"

Thumps smiled.

"Good news," said Jimmy. "Wutty has finally learned how to count."

"Wasn't funny then," said Wutty. "Isn't funny now."

When Wutty first started his tourist business, he made a mistake in his count. He counted himself, and when the group got to Red Tail Lake for lunch, he counted again. But this time he didn't count himself and went into a panic thinking that he had left one of his customers behind at Deep House.

Russell started chuckling. "What comes after fifteen?"

Wutty raced back to the canyon to rescue his lost lamb, slipped on a boulder, and wrecked his leg. Russell and Jimmy figured out the problem with the count, and although Wutty's leg had healed, his ego was still tender.

"Seventeen," said Jimmy. "Seventeen comes after fifteen."

"Wasn't funny then," said Wutty. "Isn't funny now."

Thumps kept moving until he found his favourite stool. Al picked up the coffee pot and dragged it down the counter.

"I suppose you want coffee."

"I do."

Al glanced back at Wutty and Jimmy and Russell. "I figured they'd waste a month or so giving Wutty a hard time about that little slip, but I was wrong."

"Good stories are hard to give up."

Al filled Thumps's cup. "That they are."

"Breakfast, please," said Thumps. "The usual."

"You're supposed to ask me about Lucy."

Thumps looked around to see if the kitten was in sight. "How is Lucy?"

Al beamed like a mother with a baby. "Little dickens is all attitude."

"Good to know."

"Took out four mice overnight," said Al. "Left a pile of feet and tails by the refrigerator."

Thumps tried to push the image out of his mind.

"And whenever I sit down, she's in my lap." Al wiped the counter with her towel. "Purrs up a storm."

Thumps nodded. "Good to know."

"Speaking of families," said Al, "how are things going with you and Claire?"

Thumps's stomach began to growl. "You think I can get breakfast before lunch?"

"Hear that genome woman is living out at Moses's place."

"Scoop Macleod," said Thumps. "Yeah, Moses is letting her stay in one of the trailers."

"Hear her and Claire are becoming good buddies." Al wiped at the counter. "Could be a problem."

"Problem?"

"You know what us women are like."

Thumps leaned forward on his elbows. "I know what I like. I like to eat breakfast."

"We like to compare notes."

"Notes?"

"On men."

It was warm in the café, but Thumps could feel a chill settle on him. There were no notes to compare. He was sure of that. Nothing outside the mundane. Yet even as he assured himself that all was well, he began a quick review.

Attentiveness? Check.

Respect? Check.

Patience? Check.

Passion? Well, that was a joint project, wasn't it.

Kindness? Check.

Check, check, check.

"You know, we pay more attention to you guys than you pay to us," said Al.

"I don't know that that's true."

Al cupped her hands over her ears. "What kind of earrings am I wearing?"

"You don't wear earrings."

"Lucky guess."

"Breakfast?"

Al picked up the coffee pot and headed back to the grill. "Well, why didn't you say so?"

Claire didn't wear earrings, at least not most of the time. And she didn't go in for makeup. Except on special occasions. Her eyes were brown, her hair was black. Mostly. Her birthday. When was her birthday? Her favourite colour? Her favourite food? Her favourite song? Were those things still important?

Shit.

"Mr. Thumps. Please forgive the interruption of your contemplations."

Thumps looked up to find that he was surrounded. Chintak Rawat on one side. Stas Black Weasel on the other.

"We have a hypothetical question," said Rawat, "that touches on religion and nature."

"All religion is affront to nature," said Stas.

Chintak was a pharmacist. He had purchased Chinook Pharmacy when Harry Lomax retired. It had not been easy for Harry's customers to make the transition from old-world immigrant to subcontinent immigrant, but Rawat had outwaited the firestorm of prejudice with kind words and good service.

"If there is such a thing as the divine," said Rawat, "would it be found more readily in a church or in a river?"

"A river with many fish," said Stas.

Stas Black Weasel was the proprietor of Blackfoot Autohaus. A Russian who married Angela Black Weasel and took her name. Stas's surname was Fukin, a perfectly good name in Moscow or St. Petersburg, but not so good, Stas discovered, in rural Montana.

Or anyplace in North America, for that matter.

Al came by with the pot. "Seems Rawat has won a fishing trip for two."

"Rawat is taking me," said Stas. "Very kind."

"To the wilds of Canada," said Rawat. "Where we will live off the land and commune with nature. The pharmaceutical association to which I belong has a raffle every year at its annual meeting."

If you needed drugs or over-the-counter medical advice, you saw Rawat. If you needed your BMW or your Mercedes tuned up, you went to Stas.

"This one of those fly-in fishing camps?"

"Indeed," said Rawat. "Five days of splendid contemplation."

"Swatting mosquitoes?" Thumps shook his head. "Avoiding bears?"

"Yes," said Stas. "Also drink, sing, piss on fire."

"The holy trinity of male bonding," said Al.

"And shooting." Stas slapped his chest. "Russians and Americans together. There should be shooting."

Thumps had been in these kinds of conversations before with Rawat and Stas. It was akin to following Theseus into the labyrinth blindfolded.

"Churches," said Rawat, "demand blind faith and an untrammelled imagination."

"Yes," said Stas, "must have ability to believe anything, no matter how crazy."

"Whereas fishing," said Rawat, "requires only patience and an optimistic heart."

"Church or fishing," said Stas. "This is very Russian question."

Thumps tried humming the opening riff from "Rumble," in an attempt to drown out the conversation.

"The existence of the divine is a constant source of vigorous debate," said Rawat.

"But if it exists," said Stas, "would want me to get back to work. Fix cars."

"And it would want me to help keep people healthy," said Rawat. "So, I shall say no more about it."

THUMPS WATCHED THE two men make their way to the door, and suddenly his world was quiet and at peace. Al strolled down the counter, a large plate in one hand, the coffee pot in the other.

"Never a good idea to sit between those two."

"Wouldn't mind some salsa." Thumps turned the plate around, so the sausages were at the top of the hour. "Sheriff come by?"

"He looking for you?"

"Maybe."

"Last time I saw Duke," said Al, "he looked depressed."

"He always looks depressed." Thumps peppered the eggs and the potatoes. "What's this I hear about you and credit cards?"

"You got big ears."

"Is it true?"

"You want salsa?"

"I do."

"Then keep your big ears to yourself."

"Ears are zipped. Eating my breakfast in silence."

"Smart move." Al filled Thumps's cup. "That Lucy. She's one mean little shit."

5

Thumps sat on the stool, cleaned up the remains of breakfast with a bit of toast. The café was quiet now. Maybe he'd just sit here until Al threw him out. He wasn't all that anxious to go home. If he went down to the darkroom, he'd have to scrub the trays and change the chemistry.

Never a pleasant task.

And the house was empty. Sure, there were Freeway and Cookie, but two cats in an empty house didn't make it any less empty. The promise of solitude had a certain appeal, but the more he retreated into himself, the more it felt as though he were falling down a well.

With no bottom.

On the other hand, he didn't want to go to the Aegean either. The prospect of having to deal with Archie and Duke at the same time was not much of an improvement. Both men would want him to do something, and in all likelihood, it would be something that Thumps would prefer to avoid.

Still, there was an enthusiasm to the way the little Greek approached life that tended to cheer him, and if Duke had already stopped by Dumbo's this morning, there would be doughnuts.

Archie was in his office, at his desk. Duke was on the sofa. A box of doughnuts was on the library table in the middle of the room.

"Come for the adventure," said Duke, "stay for the doughnuts."

"Thumps doesn't eat doughnuts." Archie glowered over his glasses. "He's diabetic."

"'Moderation is a fatal thing. Nothing succeeds like excess,'" said Thumps. "Mark Twain."

"That's Oscar Wilde," said Archie. "If you're going to kill yourself with sugar, at least get your source correct."

Duke put one leg up on the sofa. "Didn't that St. Augustine guy have something to say on moderation?"

"'To many,' intoned Archie, "'total abstinence is easier than perfect moderation.'"

Thumps fished an unglazed old-fashioned out of the box. "That's because they didn't have Dumbo's doughnuts in Hippo."

Archie held up a hand, opened a drawer. "Before you eat that," he said, "I have a transplant form somewhere in here for donating your organs to needy people who will take better care of them."

Thumps took a slow, deliberate bite of the doughnut.

"And the parts they can't use will be donated to science," said Archie. "Or fed to wild dogs in Australia."

Duke stretched out on the sofa, tipped his hat over his eyes. "Let me know when you two are done, so we can get to the matter at hand."

Thumps took a second bite. "There is no matter at hand."

Archie's head snapped around. "I thought you said he was on board."

Duke folded his arms on his chest. "Let's say he's rowing his way out to the ship."

It was, Thumps realized, worse than he had imagined. The thing that Duke had in mind appeared to be the same thing that Archie had in mind.

"No rowing, no ship."

"Have another doughnut," said Duke.

"I don't have time for this," said Archie. "Are you in or out?"

"Out," said Thumps.

"In," said Duke.

"Okay," said Archie. "I get the tiebreaker. You're in."

"Whatever it is," said Thumps, "you two can manage it yourselves."

"No can do," said Archie. "I'm on the board."

Thumps waited.

"The Intermountain Numismatics Association," said Archie. "This year, I'm in charge of exhibitions."

Thumps rolled his eyes. "As in Buffalo Mountain?"

"Exactly," said Archie. "Do you know how many exhibitions the association has held in this area?"

"You can't go wrong guessing none," said Duke.

"That's right," said Archie. "None. Now do you see my problem?"

Thumps shook his head. "No."

"This is a big deal," said Archie. "And it has to go off without a hitch."

"Okay."

"Gold coins." Archie snatched the glasses off his face, set them on the desk. "*Gold* coins."

Thumps realized that he had eaten the first doughnut. What the hell. Okay, maybe he *would* have another.

"Archie thinks there's going to be trouble."

"So, hire security."

"We have security," said Archie. "I need someone who can work under the radar."

Thumps looked in the box, but he didn't see another unglazed old-fashioned.

"Like a secret agent?"

"A bit dramatic," said Archie. "What I need is someone who can mix and mingle. Someone who can keep their eyes and ears open. Someone who can assess any potential threats."

The chocolate-coated doughnuts looked good. Maybe he'd try one of those next.

"I need someone I can count on."

"Sheriff's your man," said Thumps. "He's got a badge. He's got a gun. He's got a car with flashing lights and a nifty siren."

"I'll pay you." Archie put his glasses back on. "What are your rates?"

"One hundred an hour," said Thumps. "Prints are extra."

"I don't want a photographer."

"That's what I am."

"I want a friend to help out a friend," said Archie. "Is that too much to ask?"

"One fifty an hour."

"Hell of a deal," said Duke.

Archie put his head in his hands. "It's always a mistake to have the two of you in the same room. Okay, how about this. Come up to Buffalo Mountain, look at the set-up, tell me if you see anything untoward."

Thumps waited.

"And I'll give you two free meals at the restaurant."

"Three free meals," said Thumps. "For two."

"That's my buddy," said Duke.

"I'm not feeding you," said Thumps.

"Okay. Two free meals for two. But you can't order the octopus."

"Three free meals for two," said Thumps, "and you can keep your octopus."

Archie pushed out of his chair and went to the bookshelves. Back and forth he went, including a trip up the rolling ladder to fetch a book from the top shelf.

"Read these." Archie stuffed the books in a bag. "A crash course on gold coins."

"I'd rather read *War and Peace*."

"I'm staying at the resort for the duration of the show. Unit 824." Archie headed into the store, stopped in the doorway, turned back. "Meet me there. This is important."

Duke waited until Archie was out of the room. "He thinks something's hinky."

"Such as?"

"He won't tell me. Figures the mystery will lure me up there."

"And you want him to lure me."

"You need the exercise," said Duke. "It will help with your depression."

"I'm not depressed."

"You live alone with two cats," said Duke. "End of story."

"I am only doing this because of Macy."

"I know." Duke swung his legs off the sofa, stood, rolled his shoulders. "And don't even think about taking one of the chocolate-coated. Those are mine."

6

The decision to go to Buffalo Mountain had little to do with Archie and the gold-coin exhibition and everything to do with Claire. If properly managed, the two of them could have a vacation of sorts. Swim in the large indoor pool, walk the trails, even take a turn in the casino.

Or they could just lie around in her condo and do nothing. Much.

Yes, Claire would have to spend time with Scoop and the genome project. And in those moments when he was left to his own devices, he could take a quick peek at whatever it was that was causing the little Greek distress. He'd check the security, make reassuring noises, and disappear before Archie could drag him into deep water.

All in all, a perfect plan. More or less.

But first, he had to go home, grab his toiletries, a change of clothes, and his new camera. He had finally broken down and stuck a toe in the digital age. Nothing too serious, a street camera, a trial run at the future.

Lynn Langfield had talked him into a Fuji X100V, a small, fixed-lens rangefinder.

"It looks like some of the old cameras from the '50s," Lynn told him, "so the shock won't be all that great."

Thumps had to admit that the camera was handy. And quiet. He could hardly hear the shutter. Lynn had volunteered to process the shots, put them up on his computer, show Thumps how easy digital photo processing was.

"I'll print some of your shots," said Lynn, "show you what a good computer and printer combination can do."

"So, if I go digital, I'll have to buy a computer and a printer? What's that going to cost?"

"Let's not get ahead of ourselves," said Lynn. "Don't want to scare you off right out of the gate. Let's sneak up on this."

"Okay."

"Look, if it doesn't work out, I'll buy the Fuji back. You'll lose some money, but it won't be the end of the world, and you can chalk up the difference as a rental fee."

The one thing that didn't change between film and digital, Thumps discovered, was the extent of the *accoutrements,* a lovely French word that referenced all the additional stuff you needed to make the camera whole and complete.

His film cameras didn't require a battery. The Fuji did. In fact, Thumps had to buy two batteries, so there would always be one fully charged at any time. And a battery charger. No film, but he needed an SD card. The strap came with the camera, but a case was extra. And if you wanted to deck it out with a festive look, you could get an anodized button in red or gold to brighten the shutter release.

"The best part of digital," Lynn said, "is that it will get you out of the darkroom. Place is a death trap."

Thumps couldn't argue with him about that. After a session in the basement, his clothes would smell for days afterwards, and the cats, who were always on the lookout for a warm lap, would shun him until the stink of the chemicals had disappeared.

THERE WAS A car parked at the curb in front of his house. Thumps didn't own the space on the street, but over the years, he had come to think of it as his own. Not that many cars parked there. His two next-door neighbours had garages off the alley. Dixie always parked his car at the back. Mura Tanaka was eighty-seven and didn't have a car.

The car at the curb was an expensive number, built for speed and agility. Thumps parked in front of it, kept a couple of car lengths separation, so no one would be tempted to compare the two.

There were lights on in the house, and the front door was ajar. Thumps stepped inside, stood in the kitchen, waited. The house was quiet, but he could hear the washing machine going, and just for a moment, Thumps wondered if he had walked into the wrong house. There had been a song about a guy who did exactly that.

"Charlie, the Midnight Marauder."

The Limeliters or The Kingston Trio.

It happened during a power outage. A subdivision where all the houses looked the same, so the mix-up was an easy mistake to make. Charlie had gone to the bedroom, had kissed a woman he thought was his wife. She ran out into the night screaming, and Charlie was arrested. It wasn't really his fault. Still, Charlie was put in jail for a year, which didn't make a lot of sense, until you realized that the songwriter had to rhyme the word *fear* with the line "put him away for a . . ."

Month or *suspended sentence* just wasn't going to do it.

"Hello."

Nothing.

Thumps tried to think of the very small group of people who would feel free to wander into his house and do their laundry. Only one name came to mind.

CISCO CRUZ WAS standing next to the washing machine, a towel wrapped around his waist. A banana in one hand.

"Pancho!"

"Shit, Cruz. I could have shot you."

Cruz aimed the banana at him. "You don't have a gun."

"I know where to get one."

"Does your washing machine always make this much noise?"

Now that Cruz mentioned it, the washing machine *was* clomping along more than usual.

"What'd you put in it?"

Cruz shrugged. "Usual."

"Such as?"

"Underwear, socks, couple pairs of jeans." Cruz shifted from one leg to the other.

"Where are your shoes?"

"Runners," said Cruz. "An old pair."

"You put runners in my washing machine?"

"It's an old machine," said Cruz. "The old machines can handle shit like that."

There was a black T-shirt neatly folded on the dryer.

"You going to wash that separately?"

"My T? Are you crazy?"

The washing machine shifted into a spin cycle. Thumps could hear Cruz's runners banging off the sides of the drum.

"You wash a good T-shirt, you take out all the colour."

"It's black."

"There a good dry cleaner in town?"

"You dry clean your T-shirts?"

"You don't?"

The washing machine was on the move, the vibrations walking it across the floor. Thumps braced his leg against the front to keep it from trotting off into the kitchen.

"Runners?"

"Runner/boot combination. Ballistic fibre. Vibram soles. Probably the steel toes that's making the noise."

Thumps closed his eyes, took a deep breath, let it out, and opened his eyes. Cruz was still standing there in his towel.

"What are you doing here?"

"What happened to that vaunted western hospitality," said Cruz.

"Howdy, partner. Good to see you. How you been doing? Sit a spell and tell me what you've been up to."

"What are you doing here?"

The washing machine was slowing down, the banging less pronounced. Maybe the appliance would survive the close encounter with the footwear from hell.

"It's sort of a secret."

"How about you sort of tell me." The thought was sudden. And it struck Thumps full in the face. "You're staying here?"

"What? Here? With you?" Cruz shook his head. "No way. I just stopped in to say hello. You weren't home, so I figured I'd do some laundry while I waited."

Cisco Cruz had popped up in Thumps's life on a number of occasions, and after all this time, he knew no more about the man than he had when he first met him. Archie called him "the ninja assassin," which was hyperbolic and somewhat derogatory, but Thumps wasn't sure that it was entirely inaccurate.

"You came all this way to do your laundry?"

"Our laundry," said Cruz. "We're on vacation."

"We?"

"Zarina and me."

"And this Zarina is a . . . secret agent?"

Cruz was all smiles. "*Cabrón*, she's my fiancée."

"She's here?"

"Relax, Pancho. It's just you and me."

The washing machine came to a staggering stop, dinged its little bell. Cruz gave it a pat.

"I'm going to toss this load into the dryer and get dressed," said Cruz. "Why don't you make us lunch."

"Sure," said Thumps, "you want caviar or goose pâté with your chateaubriand?"

Lunch was toasted tomato-cheese sandwiches with a side of leftover spaghetti and coffee. Thumps put a border of red grapes around the edge of the plates for accent.

"Beats burgers at that giant squirrel place," said Cruz.

"So, you have a fiancée."

"How are you and Claire?"

"A fiancée as in you plan to get married?"

"Got to settle down sometime," said Cruz. "Zarina works in Seattle. Hates the place. Rain, rain, rain. Wants to get into the country."

"And you said, 'Hey, I know just the place.'"

Cruz held his arms out. "Open spaces. Big sky. Land in all directions, friendly people, cheap real estate. Check, check, check, and check."

"You know I don't believe you." Thumps picked up a grape and bit it in half. "When do I get to meet this mysterious fiancée?"

"Any time," said Cruz. "Maybe we could double date. Me and Zee. You and Claire."

"Sure."

"We're staying at Buffalo Mountain. Hit the hot springs, take a run at the casino. Just enjoy ourselves."

"Buffalo Mountain doesn't have a hot springs."

Cruz took a bite of the sandwich. "The hell you say."

"Why are you really in town?"

"You are one suspicious burro. You got to learn to trust. Relax. Enjoy life."

"Says the ninja assassin."

Cruz pointed the sandwich at Thumps. "Is that Greek buddy of yours still calling me that?"

"He thinks you work for one of the alphabet agencies," said Thumps. "He thinks you kill people for a living."

"Man's got one vivid imagination," said Cruz. "*Doble O Siete*, that's me."

Thumps stroked the side of his cup. It was pleasantly warm to the touch. "So, what exactly do you do for a living?"

"Between engagements right now. You hear of something, let me know." Cruz pushed his plate to one side. "In the meantime, it's rest and relaxation and Zee."

The bell on the dryer went off.

"There's my signal to *adios* your *hacienda*." Cruz stood and stretched. "Think about that double date. Be fun. Just like high school."

Cruz disappeared into the laundry room and reappeared with a bag slung over his shoulder.

"You need bananas," he said, as he got to the door. "And you're out of orange juice."

7

Thumps spent more time than necessary packing for Buffalo Mountain and Claire. Should he take a swimming suit? Absolutely. Evening wear? Would he need a suit? Did he have a suit? Yes, but it was that vintage thing that Archie had given him. The double-breasted, dark-blue pinstripe with lapels the size of vulture wings. Walking into the dining room dressed up like a 1940s gangster might work if the style had come back when Thumps wasn't looking, but he wasn't willing to bet on it.

Business casual. That was the safe choice. Sports coat, slacks, dress shirt, shoes other than runners or boots. Socks any colour other than white.

Along with hiking boots. Cold weather jacket. Wool toque. Gloves. His new camera, extra battery and SD card. Just how many shots could one of the cards hold? Toiletries. Should he take his pillow with him? In his experience, motels and the like had lousy pillows. Would he look foolish standing at reception with Mr. Fluffy in hand?

And how many nights? That would depend on Claire. One for sure. It could be as many as three. He didn't have much to do. The cats wouldn't miss him. He could stay for a week, so long as he could get Dixie to feed Freeway and Cookie, and clean their litter boxes.

THUMPS TOOK HIS time on the drive to Buffalo Mountain. So, Cisco Cruz was back in town. With a fiancée in tow. At least that was the story the man was trying to sell. Thumps was guarded in his reaction to the news. Other people he could name would find the notion of a domestic Cisco Cruz incredible. And if he wasn't in town with a fiancée and the promise of settling down, why was he here? The man didn't show up unless there was some game afoot. Each time he had come to town, someone had died.

Not a ringing endorsement for a potential neighbour.

Thumps wondered if the law of averages might be at play here. After so many calamities, maybe this time would be different. Maybe Cruz would prove to be a benign presence. They had gotten along well enough in the past. Thumps didn't have that many friends. Another one wouldn't hurt.

The problem was going to be breaking the good news to Duke and Archie. Both men would view Cruz's return with alarm and suspicion. There was a history there not easily dismissed. Maybe this Zarina would be the oil to smooth the troubled waters.

Thumps turned off the main road, began the winding climb up to the resort and the casino. He parked the car at the far end of the lot, sat behind the wheel, waited for divine intervention. A cataclysmic omen in the heavens, perhaps. A flaming text message burned into his windshield.

So far, it had been a day of bad ideas. Helping Archie was a bad idea. Helping Duke was a bad idea. Cisco Cruz in town was a bad idea. Leaving his house was a bad idea.

Which he didn't need to compound by getting out of the car.

Yet here he was. Out and about in the world. With little protection from obligation and community.

THE DINING ROOM was mostly empty, the dinner crowd still an hour away. He searched the tables. No Claire, no Archie, no sheriff, no Cruz. So far, so good.

"You're late."

Thumps had no idea where Roxanne Heavy Runner had come from, how she had materialized out of thin air. The woman was part magician.

"She's been waiting."

And part aircraft carrier.

"Claire didn't specify a time."

"That a suitcase?"

"Clothes."

Roxanne loomed over him. Thumps could feel the temperature in her shadow drop several degrees.

"Hope you brought a suit."

"You bet."

"That a pillow?"

Thumps liked Roxanne. In much the same way that tourists at an animal park liked seeing lions from the safety of a bus. With Roxanne, you always knew where you stood. There was nothing subtle about the woman. You were either safe or in danger of being eaten alive.

"Leave your junk with me," she said. "I'll have it sent to Claire's condo."

"Okay."

"Don't suppose you brought her something nice."

Thumps tried a smile. "Is the sheriff around?"

"The sheriff?"

"He has doughnuts."

"Doughnuts are not going to get it done."

Roxanne tapped Thumps on the chest. To his credit, he stayed on his feet.

"I keep telling her to check out those dating sites. Don't hurt to walk the aisles, see what's on the shelves."

"Good advice," said Thumps.

Thumps didn't think that Roxanne disliked him, and he didn't think she went out of her way to hurt his feelings.

"It's not your fault," said Roxanne. "She wants to shop at the mini-mart, that's her business."

Thumps reckoned that it was just an unfortunate by-product of her scorched-earth approach to life.

"So, you're going to help her."

It was a statement, not a question.

"I am."

Roxanne took the suitcase and the pillow. "'Cause right now, looks like you're all she's got."

"I suppose I should go and find her."

"I suppose you should."

ACCORDING TO ROXANNE, Claire Merchant was to be found in the Blackfoot Room. Thumps wasn't sure how many meeting rooms Buffalo Mountain had, but he found seven others before he stumbled onto the right one.

Claire wasn't there. In fact, no one was in the room except Scoop Macleod, who was sitting at a table by herself.

"Mr. DreadfulWater."

"Thumps."

"You've come to sign up?"

There were brochures on the table, pens laid out in a fan, a small poster on a portable stand of a happy girl with braids. As well as a box of cheek swabs in sterile packages.

"Looking for Claire."

"Just missed her," said Scoop. "Pull up a chair. You can be my decoy."

"Decoy?"

Scoop tore a form off a pad, slid it in front of Thumps. "People see you in here, they may decide to stop by as well."

"The Human Genome Project?"

"No," said Scoop. "They wrapped that up in 2003. The HGP was interested in the base pairs that make up human DNA. I'm looking at relationships within Indian communities."

"Lot of communities."

Scoop rubbed her head. "You have no idea."

"Moses said you're looking for relatives."

"Couple of centuries of cultural genocide. You know how many aboriginal children were taken from their families? You know how many just disappeared into the child welfare system? You know how many have no idea who they are or where their home communities might be?"

Thumps sat back, away from the sorrow in Scoop's voice, the sound of loss.

"Yeah, I have to be careful," said Scoop. "I start in, and I put people off."

"You won't put me off."

Scoop smiled. "I already have."

"Lot of resistance?"

"The people who support the project think I'm an angel, that I'll flap my wings and every aboriginal community in North America will be miraculously made whole."

Scoop sat back in the chair, rubbed at an eye.

"The rest call me Auntie Snoop," said Scoop. "Sticking my nose where it doesn't belong. Stirring up shit. Trying to force square people into round holes."

"Rock and a hard place."

"There was an old woman out in the Dakotas who told me I was no better than the Whites who had caused the problem. She said it was too late for the ones who had been lost, that there was no room, that they had no business trying to come home."

"Moses wouldn't agree," said Thumps.

"He's great," said Scoop. "I was hoping I might be related to him."

"But you're not?"

"Happy ending like that only happens in bad movies." Scoop leaned forward on her elbows. "Did Moses tell you my story? Left at the Igloo in Fort Macleod, Alberta? Bounced around foster care until I was eighteen?"

"No."

"The double scoop," said Scoop. "That's what the Igloo is noted for.

Family came back from burgers and ice cream to find me on the front seat of their crew cab. Surprise."

"Fort Macleod?"

"That's right. Scoop Macleod. Story has all the makings of a romantic comedy, don't you think?"

Thumps turned the form around, so he didn't have to read it upside down.

"You're wondering why I was never adopted."

"Somebody missed out."

"I was six or seven when I figured out that it was never going to happen." Scoop touched the small birthmark on her cheek. "Nobody wants defective goods."

Thumps picked up one of the pens. "Do I qualify?"

"Absolutely." Scoop put on a pair of blue gloves, took one of the swabs out of the box. "Sit back. Open your mouth."

THE DINING ROOM was busy now. Thumps expected to find Claire holding court at one of the tables. The return of Deep House and the surrounding land had been a tangle of state, federal, and band council jurisdictions, and over the years that the controversy had been winding its way through the courts, little had changed. Federal and state authorities wanted oversight and the tribe wanted the both of them tied to horses and dragged out of town for cause.

There was, Thumps discovered, no limit to the number of times you can ask the courts the same question and expect to get a different answer, no limit to the amount of public money that people in power were willing to waste in order to maintain that power.

"Thumps."

Thumps felt his heart sink.

"You're just in time." Archie waved at him from a table with five other people. Three men and two women. As well as the sheriff. "Come. Come. Meet everyone."

Thumps took his time. If there was any justice in the world, Claire would suddenly appear and rescue him.

"Folks," said Archie, "you've met the sheriff. This is his special deputy, Thumps DreadfulWater."

"'I shot the sheriff,'" sang the younger woman. "'But I did not shoot the deputy.'"

No luck. No Claire. No salvation.

"This," said Archie, "is the irrepressible Emily Hunter of Hunter Gold."

"Of the Chicago Hunters," said Hunter.

"Along with Otto Myers of Myers Coin and Stamp in Salt Lake City." Archie moved his hand around the table. "Atticus Poe, Katheryn Souto, and Nicodemus Eliopoulos."

"Nico," said Eliopoulos. "You must call me Nico."

When Thumps was a cop in Northern California, he had been intrigued by last names and what they might suggest about a person's family background. He was reasonably sure that Eliopoulos was Greek. Myers might be Jewish. Souto was a Portuguese name. Hunter and Poe were British.

And while Hunter looked the part—chestnut hair, hazel eyes, fine features—Poe did not. He was a tall, light-skinned Black man who might well have been from Kenya or Jamaica or the plantations of Georgia, anywhere that imperialism and colonization had flourished.

"Mr. Eliopoulos owns Omega Coin and Stamp, with offices in Toronto and Athens. Ms. Souto comes to us from Golden Gate Bullion in San Francisco, and Mr. Poe is the proprietor of Central Park Currency in Manhattan."

Thumps smiled.

Emily Hunter swung her legs out from under the table and crossed them at the knees.

"Are you providing security for the exhibition?"

Thumps wondered if women were able to control just how far up their thighs a dress would ride. They could walk in heels, so he guessed that anything was possible.

"No," said Thumps. "I'm actually a photographer."

Myers made a sharp, barking sound.

"You take pictures of . . . money?" said Souto.

"Landscapes," said Thumps. "I mostly do landscapes."

Eliopoulos was a short man with a broad chest and thick legs. Curly hair that was more grey than black. When Thumps was growing up, he had waited patiently for hair to appear on his face. It never did. Eliopoulos looked as though he had to shave twice a day.

Archie moved quickly. "But he used to be in law enforcement. And he helps the sheriff whenever there is a particularly difficult situation."

"That's true," said Duke. "At times, he can be handy."

Poe held his cup aloft. "Maybe he can save us from this dreadful espresso."

"It is a bit sour," said Eliopoulos. "If you want good espresso, you have to make it yourself."

"Don't know why we need security at all," said Myers. "Not much to steal."

Otto Myers reminded Thumps of the giant beetles you see on the Discovery Channel. Short and compact. Thick through the middle with thin legs and a neckless head that came to a point.

"I'm going to take a nap," said Souto. "All this fresh air is exhausting."

Katheryn Souto was somewhere in her sixties. Tall and stately, a heritage building that had managed to survive the ravages of urban renewal.

"And I'm going to the casino." Hunter uncrossed her legs. The effect was much the same. "What about it, Mr. Poe? You want to join me?"

"It would be ungentlemanly to say no," said Atticus.

"Yes, it would," said Hunter.

Everyone stood on cue.

"If you have no objection," said Myers, "I'll follow you to the casino."

"Fedya and Pauline," said Hunter. "1949. Robert Siodmak. *The Great Sinner.*"

"From the novel *The Gambler* by Fyodor Dostoevsky," said Poe. "Do you like old movies?"

Thumps had already decided that Emily Hunter looked to be an easy woman to misjudge. And that you did so at your peril.

"Perhaps Special Deputy DreadfulWater would like to accompany us," said Hunter. "To protect us from outlaws and wild Indians."

"Thumps is Indian," said Duke, "but he's no longer all that wild."

"I can be pretty wild," said Myers.

"Besides," said Archie, "Thumps is working, and he's married."

THUMPS WAITED UNTIL the coin dealers had left before he turned on Archie.

"I'm not married."

"You'll thank me later," said Archie. "Hunter would eat you alive."

"And if she didn't," said Duke, "Claire would finish the job."

Archie clicked his tongue. "You looked at her thighs."

"No, I didn't."

"I looked at her thighs," said Duke. "And I *am* married."

"Come on you two." Archie herded Thumps and Duke to the elevators. "We have serious business to discuss."

THE CONDO WAS on the eighth floor, a corner unit with a view of White Goat Canyon and the river. Thumps walked the living area. There were bookshelves filled with books, several of Thumps's photographs on the walls, a large globe on a table.

"You bought a condo?"

"Business investment," said Archie. "Bought it when they first came on the market. It's already appreciated about twenty percent."

"And you never bothered to tell me?" said Thumps.

"Or me," said Duke.

"And if you had known?" said Archie.

Thumps looked at Duke. Duke looked at Thumps.

"Exactly," said Archie. "The two of you would have wanted to 'borrow' the place, and I'd have lost my sanctuary."

"But now we know," said Duke.

"He's going to throw us off the balcony before we leave and can spread the word," said Thumps.

"If only." Archie went to the kitchen, took a fruit plate out of the refrigerator, turned on the coffee machine. "But the fact of the matter is, I need your help."

8

Archie brought the fruit platter and the coffee to the table, along with small plates and flatware.

"Help yourself," he said. "I need your A game."

Thumps looked at Duke. "What happened to the two dozen doughnuts?"

"They weren't for me," said Duke. "Macy's book club is meeting at our place today."

"But you must have saved a chocolate-coated or two."

"Maybe."

"And you didn't bring me an unglazed old-fashioned?"

Archie tapped a spoon on the table. "Can we focus?"

"I'm saving Thumps from himself."

"Admirable," said Archie, "but the important things first. What do you two bandersnatches know about gold coins?"

Thumps shrugged. "They're made out of gold."

"Not funny," said Archie.

Duke took a section of orange. "Oh, I don't know," he said, "I've always found Thumps frightfully amusing."

Thumps helped himself to a couple of grapes. "*Frightfully?*"

"It could be nothing," said Archie.

Duke poured himself a cup of coffee. "I find when people start off a sentence like that, they already know that something is wrong."

Archie puffed out his cheeks. "Let's try this again. What do you two know about gold coins?"

"Well, I, for one, know shit," said Duke.

"Ditto," said Thumps.

"Except that they're worth more than silver coins," said Duke.

"My grandfather was a small-time collector," said Archie. "Gold mostly. Some silver. He tried to get me interested, but I was into sports and girls."

"Imagine some of it still rubbed off," said Duke.

"He left me his collection," said Archie. "I still have it. A few nice pieces. About fifteen years back, I got involved with the Intermountain Numismatics Association. It's fun. We get together once a year or so. Talk coins. Share stories."

Duke took a strawberry. "I had an uncle who was in the merchant marine. He'd send me stamps from around the world. My mother got me a book to stick them in."

Archie closed his eyes and waited.

"Don't really know what happened to those stamps."

"Let me guess," said Thumps. "You're worried that the exhibition is going to be robbed."

Archie opened his eyes. "This is a nice show. Not a big show. No really valuable coins. Mostly at the shallow end of the pool, a few deep-water. Two- to three-thousand-dollar range. Six or so could go as high as fifty thousand."

"Fifty thousand for a coin?"

"That's nothing of real value?" said Duke. "I'm in the wrong profession."

"If we had a 1909 S ten-dollar gold eagle or a 1927 Saint-Gaudens double eagle in uncirculated condition with a sharp strike, then we'd be talking serious money."

Thumps was intrigued. "As in a hundred thousand?"

Archie smiled. "As in two million."

"But we don't have any of those," said Duke.

"No," said Archie, "we don't have any of those."

"So, what do we have?"

"Half a million total," said Archie. "No more than that."

"Still a decent score," said Thumps. "Bad guys steal for a lot less."

"I'm not worried about a robbery," said Archie. "Security is solid."

Thumps took a moment to work it out. "There's something wrong with our guests?"

Archie got up and walked to the sliding doors that opened onto the balcony, then turned back.

"Let's say you're a Major League Baseball scout. It's your job to go around the country to all the first-rate baseball programs to look for talent. You're in Los Angeles. The Fayetteville Woodpeckers are playing in North Carolina. Are you going to drop everything and catch the first plane to Atlanta?"

"Who are the Fayetteville Woodpeckers?"

"Exactly," said Archie.

"Low-end show," said Thumps. "High-end dealers."

"Simplistic but accurate," said Archie. "Therein lies my problem."

Duke took a second strawberry. "The folks we met shouldn't be here."

"You see why I'm worried."

"Have to admit it," said Duke. "Old Archimedes does look worried."

"One or two whales might be an anomaly," said Archie. "Maybe Atticus Poe always wanted to see the Wild West. Maybe Katheryn Souto wanted to get out of the City by the Bay."

Thumps pushed his cup off to one side. "But five whales beaching themselves on our shores all at the same time is something else."

Archie took off his glasses, rubbed his eyes. "And I have no idea what that something else is."

Thumps and the sheriff left Archie to stew in his two-bedroom, deluxe suite with its river view.

They were in the elevator before Duke broke the silence.

"What do you think Archie paid for that place?"

"No idea."

"What do you think it's worth now?"

"You thinking about buying?"

"Maybe." Duke pressed the button for the main floor. "You remember back when I had that little blip."

"You mean your prostate operation?"

"Jesus, DreadfulWater. Keep it down."

"We're in the elevator."

"You have to practise discretion if you want to be discreet."

"You find that inside a fortune cookie?"

"Can we stay on point?"

"Right," said Thumps. "Little blip."

"Remember I thought about retiring?"

Thumps checked the floor indicator. The elevator wasn't moving fast enough.

"I'm thinking about it again."

Six, five, four, three . . . Thumps watched the indicator lights, as the floors counted down.

"I thought you couldn't retire. Because of Macy. Because of the medical coverage."

"Deanna is too new for the job," said Duke. "And I don't want to leave the office in the hands of some political clown city council tosses in from left field."

"I'm a photographer."

"Hell, DreadfulWater, we both know that's not a living. If it weren't for your pension, you'd be on the street."

The elevator reached the main floor. The doors opened.

"I have to head back into town," said Duke. "Just think about it. That's all I'm asking."

THUMPS HEADED FOR the front desk. He didn't glance over his shoulder to see if Duke was following him, but he did make use of the reflections in the glass and the surface of the granite veneer to make sure that he had escaped the sheriff alive and intact.

The woman at the front desk was all smiles. The tag on her jacket said "Lainey."

"Hi, do you have a reservation?"

Yes, he wanted to say, *it's where a rapacious and deceitful government dumped me after they stole my land.*

Instead, he said, "No, but I have a friend who is staying here."

Lainey waited.

"And I was wondering if he checked in."

"Name?"

"Cisco Cruz."

Lainey looked at the monitor. "He hasn't checked in yet."

"But he is staying here."

"You're a friend of Ms. Merchant's, aren't you?"

"I am. Mr. Cruz is a friend of hers as well."

"He hasn't checked in," said Lainey, "and he doesn't appear to have a reservation."

Of course he doesn't. Thumps tried to keep the annoyance off his face. Why did he think that Cruz was going to play straight with him? After all this time, he should know better.

"Could you check to see if there's a reservation for a Duncan Renaldo?"

"Is that Mr. Cruz's alias?"

"Sort of."

Lainey worked the keyboard. "We do have a Duncan Renaldo staying with us."

"Could you tell me where he's staying?"

"We're not supposed to give out that information."

Thumps turned away from the desk for a moment. Then he turned back. "Hypothetically speaking, if Ms. Merchant wanted to send flowers and a fruit basket to Mr. Renaldo's suite . . ."

"Hypothetically speaking?"

"Absolutely."

Suite 626. Rented to Mr. and Mrs. Duncan Renaldo for four nights. Thumps stood outside the door and tried to think up a good opening line. Something clever and cutting with just the right measure of annoyance.

He had just raised a hand to knock when the door opened.

"You must be DreadfulWater."

The woman standing in the doorway was not Cruz. She was very much not Cruz. Cruz was dark with dark hair, dark eyes and dark clothes. Much of the time, the man reminded Thumps of a storm cloud. Or a shadow.

The woman standing in the doorway was all bright skies and open meadows. Blond with soft, pale skin and eyes the colour of sunlit shallows.

"You better get in here before someone sees you."

"You must be Zarina."

"What exactly did Cruz tell you?"

"Hey, Pancho." Cruz appeared from a back room. Black pants, black T-shirt fresh from the dry cleaner. "Took you long enough."

"Duncan Renaldo? Really?"

"You don't argue with your mother," said Cruz. "She loved that show."

Thumps turned his attention to Zarina. "So, you . . . you two are . . ."

Thumps didn't get the rest of the sentence out. The bright skies and open meadows disappeared, and a tornado appeared on the land.

"Did you tell *everyone* we're married?"

"Of course not."

"He said you're engaged," said Thumps.

"I *implied* that we were engaged."

"God, but you're a child."

"This is Zarina Benoit," said Cruz. "Zee for short. Cajun out of New Orleans. She only looks sweet."

"I am sweet," said Benoit. "So long as no one screws with me."

Thumps could see that this was going to go south quickly. "So, you two aren't engaged."

"Cruz said you were a little slow," said Benoit, "but you seem fast enough to me."

"I said he was methodical," said Cruz.

Thumps held up both hands. "Okay, so if you're not engaged, it means that the two of you are working together."

Cruz looked at Benoit and then at Thumps. "Could be."

"And just how long have you two *cooyons* known each other?"

"Too long," said Thumps. "And long enough to know when I'm being played."

"So, Cruz told you we're engaged," said Benoit. "What else did he tell you?"

"Why don't we just cut to the chase?" said Cruz.

"No," said Benoit, "I want to hear this."

"He said you two were engaged . . ."

"Implied," said Cruz.

"And that you were in town looking at real estate, that you were thinking about settling down here."

"I'm FBI," said Benoit. "Cruz is . . . something else."

"Well," said Cruz, "there goes all the mystery."

"I've already filled the sheriff in."

Thumps could feel the start of a headache. "The sheriff knows about you?"

"It's protocol to check in with local law enforcement."

"How long has he known?"

Cruz shook his head. "Uh-oh, looks like Sheriff Duke isn't sharing with the rest of the children."

"Why would he?" said Benoit. "Mr. DreadfulWater is a photographer."

"But now that you two know what's going on, and the sheriff knows what's going on, how about telling me what's going on?"

"You really want to know?" said Cruz. "Much of the time, you don't."

"It's need to know," said Benoit.

"I bet Duke will tell you," said Cruz. "If you ask nice."

Thumps sat down on the sofa, made himself comfortable. "I don't need Duke. I've got most of it figured out already."

Benoit looked at Cruz.

"I didn't tell him a thing."

"Actually, what he did was lie to me," said Thumps. "He always lies to me. He enjoys lying to me."

"*Ese*, that's cruel."

"So, if you're FBI," said Thumps, "what is Cruz? CIA? NSA? Secret Service? Stop me when I'm close."

"I'm going to have to ask you to keep all this to yourself."

"So, the question is," Thumps continued, "what would bring federal law enforcement to a small town in rural Montana. There's no Indian uprising."

"We don't do that anymore," said Benoit.

"Pipeline protest in the Dakotas?" said Thumps.

"Mostly not anymore."

"The only thing of note that's happening in our little piece of the world is a gold-coin show, which, according to local authorities, is not all that exciting."

"Gold coins are valuable," said Cruz.

"So, why are you two here?"

"Not a question I can answer," said Benoit.

"So, if it's not our natural wonders and it's not the gold-coin exhibition, maybe it's the five major-weight coin dealers who are in attendance. Dealers who, like yourselves, shouldn't be here at all."

Benoit ran a hand through her hair. "I'm going to take a nap." She turned and headed into the back rooms. "Show Mr. Dreadful-Water out."

Cruz walked to the door, opened it. "So, what do you think of her?"

Thumps smiled. "She'll turn you into a chew ball."

9

The tête-à-tête with Cisco Cruz and Zarina Benoit left Thumps annoyed and grumpy. Cruz had lied to him. And not for the first time. Thumps suspected that the man had a natural talent for deceit that he had perfected through practice.

Whereas Benoit had probably taken courses in prevarication at Quantico as part of her training.

Duke had lied to him as well. Or to be more exact, he hadn't shared. If Benoit had checked in with the sheriff as soon as she hit town, then Duke knew that Cruz was in Chinook as well.

Mind you, Thumps also hadn't shared. Not that it was really his fault. He had *planned* to tell the sheriff about Cruz. He just hadn't found the right moment.

But all that aside, Thumps realized his current unease had more to do with Duke's suggestion that he give up photography and get a real job. To be sure, hiking about the high prairies, taking pictures of mountains and meadows, lakes and rivers, with towering clouds all around was restorative. But the operating costs, chemicals, paper, matting, framing, gallery fees, offset by the meagre returns, made photography a difficult profession to defend.

Okay, impossible.

But that wasn't the point. For Thumps, landscape photography had been a refuge from the realities of law enforcement. And when the aftermath of the Obsidian Murders stripped him and left his life in ruins, it was photography that saved him, that kept him afloat until he had made safe harbour.

Still, Duke was closer to the mark than he realized. Film photography was problematic. The darkroom was not a healthy place. Most of the chemistry was a contact poison of one sort or another. The effects of developers, stop baths, fixers, the pantheon of toners all tended to be long-term and cumulative. All contained toxins that attacked the liver and lungs.

Perhaps his diabetes had its origins in his basement.

Maybe digital was the answer. At first glance, it appeared cleaner, safer. No chemistry, no fumes. Just a computer and computer programs. Which would be endlessly maddening and complicated. Instead of printing a physical show and standing the costs of a real-life exhibition, he could put his images online, whatever that meant, whatever that entailed.

But who would want to buy a bunch of zeros and ones?

Or he could give up photography completely.

He was never going to be a star in the photographic heavens. *National Geographic* wasn't going to come knocking on his door. Maybe he should consider something more practical. Farming, for example. Or ranching. Take Duke up on his offer and come full circle back to law enforcement.

He wasn't getting younger. The road ahead wasn't getting wider.

THUMPS TOOK THE stairs to the seventh floor, part of a momentary urge to get back into shape. When he got to the door, he checked his pulse. A little fast. He glanced at his watch. Where had the last hour gone? Claire hadn't mentioned a specific time. So he couldn't really be late. At least not officially late.

Claire answered on the second knock.

"There you are," she said. "Not eaten by a bear after all."

"Am I late?"

"Let's say you're not early."

Claire was dressed in jeans and a cotton work shirt that was too big for her.

"Too late to kiss Ivory good night?"

"Yes," said Claire. "It is."

It was the tone. Flat and empty.

"You okay?"

"No," said Claire. "I'm not."

Thumps searched her face for a clue as to what to ask next.

"Have you been crying?"

Claire went to the sofa. "Yes," she said. "I have."

"Ivory all right?"

"Yes, she is."

Thumps sat on the sofa next to her. "You should probably tell me," he said. "You know how good I am at guessing."

"You're terrible at guessing."

"I'm terrible at guessing."

"I ordered some food," said Claire. "Beef bourguignon. It's on the kitchen counter."

Thumps waited. He might not be all that good at guessing, but he could wait with the best of them.

"The bourguignon is very good." Claire's eyes filled with tears. "It's the chef's specialty."

Thumps stopped waiting. "Where's Ivory?"

Claire nodded. "Not here," she said, softly.

"Claire . . ."

Claire pulled her knees up against her chest, wrapped her arms around her legs. "Melton and Ona were going to stay at the resort, so they could spend some time with Ivory."

"I remember."

"Instead, they decided to take her with them to Standoff. Wanted to show her the reserve. Melton's family wants to see her."

"But they're going to bring her back."

Claire didn't move.

"They have to bring her back," said Thumps. "You adopted her. She's yours."

"Adoption hasn't been finalized," said Claire. "Cross-border white tape has slowed it down."

"She's six years old. You're the only mother she's ever known."

"She's Melton's niece," said Claire. "She's blood."

"Jesus."

"Have some bourguignon."

"What did Melton say?"

"Said that Ona wanted the three of them to spend some time together. She comes from a family of ten, likes kids a lot, wants to have a bunch. That's what he said."

"Did he actually say he was taking Ivory back?"

Claire hugged her legs tighter, began a slow rocking motion. "Eat the fucking bourguignon."

THE BOURGUIGNON WAS good. In fact, it was excellent. Thumps used a finger to clean the plate.

"Why don't I talk to Melton."

"You mean *mano a mano*?"

Thumps could see this hadn't started well. "What I mean is . . ."

"I know what you mean," said Claire. "And if I need blunt-force trauma, I'll turn you loose. But in this instance, it will be the women who decide."

"Okay."

"But right now, I'm going to bed. I've got meetings tomorrow first thing."

"You want company?"

"You mind if we don't . . ."

"No," said Thumps. "The sofa looks comfortable."

Claire nodded. "Turn the lights out. And keep the sound on the TV down."

When Thumps got up the next morning, Claire was already gone. He hadn't heard her go, guessed she had dressed quickly and slipped out in silence. He had planned to take her to breakfast, bolster her spirits with encouragements and predictions that things would work out, and that Ivory would come home in good order.

Instead, here he was in a luxury condo, in his underwear, with no one to talk to but himself. He had just gotten dressed and was headed for the door when the phone rang. It wasn't his condo, so it couldn't be for him. It would be for Claire.

Then again, maybe it was Claire calling to talk to him. Maybe she wanted him to join her for coffee. Or whatever.

"Thumps?"

Thumps let his breath out in one long stream.

"Eight twenty-four," said Archie. "In case you forgot."

Thumps held the phone away from his face and stared at it.

"Stop staring at the phone," said Archie. "Chop, chop."

"How did you know I was here?"

"Claire told me. She said you were depressed and needed cheering up."

"I'm not depressed."

"Duke is here," said Archie. "He has doughnuts."

10

Duke and Archie were at the table. Archie had his laptop up and running. There was a box of Dumbo's doughnuts next to the sheriff's elbow, looking for all the world like a witness in protective custody.

"Are there any left?"

"You're diabetic," said Archie. "You don't need doughnuts."

Thumps frowned. "You ate them all?"

"No," said Duke, "I didn't eat them all, and I resent the insinuation."

Thumps lifted the lid of the box. There were two doughnuts left.

"What the hell are these?"

"Black licorice," said Duke, "and sweet corn and blueberry."

"Black licorice?"

"Fancy is trying out a couple of new ideas," said Duke. "Wants my expert opinion."

"I don't think you're going to have to eat them to form an opinion," said Thumps.

"I thought maybe you could try them and let me know what you think."

Thumps closed the lid, slid the box to one side. "I'm diabetic."

"And if I said I had a second box?"

"I'd say you're bluffing."

"He is bluffing," said Archie. "Grab some coffee. We have work to do."

"I'm busy," said Thumps.

"How can you be busy?" said Archie. "You don't have a job."

"I'm giving Claire a hand with a serious matter."

"Serious? The exhibition opens tomorrow evening." Archie twisted in his chair. "That's serious."

Thumps could feel his eyes start to droop. The sofa in Claire's living room hadn't been as comfortable as it looked. A nap would be nice.

"So, I have background on our dealers."

"Archie's pretty good with that computer of his," said Duke. "When you're sheriff, you should sit down with him, let him show you what you can do with a keyboard and an internet connection."

"You expect me to help you for a black licorice doughnut?"

"Okay," said Duke. "There's an unglazed old-fashioned in the cupboard by the sink. You're such a baby."

THUMPS RELAXED WITH his coffee and doughnut, while Archie ran down the dealers.

"Five of the biggest dealers in the country," the little Greek began. "All descend on a regional coin show with nothing of import on display. There isn't a coin in the bunch that would get any of them out of bed before noon."

"So, they didn't come for the exhibition."

Duke reached for the box of doughnuts, raised the lid, and looked in. "Archie thinks they're here to transact some kind of illegal business."

"Which might explain why Cisco Cruz and Zarina Benoit are in town."

The effect on Archie was immediate.

"Cruz? The ninja assassin?"

"He doesn't like to be called that."

"He's in town?"

"Jesus, DreadfulWater," said Duke, "you really know how to screw the pooch."

"And who's this Zar . . . Zar . . ."

"Zarina Benoit." Thumps took a leisurely bite of the doughnut. Delicious. "She's an FBI agent."

Archie turned on Duke, his head snapping around like an alligator grabbing a chicken.

"Need to know," said Duke. "Need to know."

"Lovely." Archie took off his glasses and looked at the ceiling for divine intervention. "Just lovely. The first time the Intermountain Numismatics Association is holding its first show in the Chinook area, and suddenly we're knee-deep in international intrigue."

"A bit hyperbolic," said Duke.

"That's because nothing's happened yet." Archie held out both hands. "Here's the fan, and here's the shit. We're just waiting for someone to find the switch."

Thumps waved the old-fashioned in the air. "Nothing to say that the two are connected."

Archie kept his hands where they were. "You don't *know* why Cisco Cruz and the FBI agent are in town?"

"No idea," said Duke. "I know they're here, but they won't tell me why."

"How can they *not* tell you?" said Archie. "You're the sheriff."

"There's that," said Duke.

"How about we do a little demanding?" said Archie.

"Sure," said Duke. "Point out that you're a taxpayer and entitled to know how your tax dollar is being spent."

"Or you could tell us what you have on the dealers," said Thumps, "and we can figure it out for ourselves."

"What he said," said Duke.

"All right." Archie turned back to his computer. "Listen up. I'm only going to do this once."

For the next hour, Archie regaled Thumps and the sheriff with the personal and professional background of each of the dealers. Partway through, Thumps began to sag again, and he wondered if another doughnut would help restore his energy.

"Emily Hunter is the young hotshot. Family business. Great-grandfather started the company. Business was supposed to be passed down the male line. You know, first son, first son, first son, ad nauseam."

"But?"

"After the great-grandfather, it was nothing but girls." Archie was all smiles. "Best laid plans."

"Couldn't have been easy," said Duke.

"Women in the coin business? In early- and mid-twentieth century." Archie shook his head. "Must have driven the patriarchy mad. Even worse, the women were good at it. Emily's grandmother, her mother, her older sister, all lined up in the mouth of the beast like shark's teeth."

Thumps wasn't sure about the simile.

Archie made a swimming motion with his hand. "And Emily Hunter is the great white."

Duke took the black licorice out of the box, turned it over, gave it a sniff. "What about the guy from Salt Lake? The one who looks like a beetle."

"Otto Myers," said Archie. "Collected coins as a kid. Turned it into a business that was always one month away from going under."

"But?"

"If at first you don't succeed," said Archie, "marry money."

Duke nodded. "Hell of a business plan."

"Otto's wife is part of a large and wealthy Mormon family. Her father took a liking to his new son-in-law, set him up in business, and suddenly Myers is out of the minors and into the major leagues."

Duke put the doughnut back in the box, licked his fingers, grimaced.

"Which brings us to Katheryn Souto," said Archie.

"And the City by the Bay," said Thumps.

"Correct," said Archie. "Golden Gate Bullion was her husband's business. Built it into a very successful enterprise. Did a great deal of business in the Far East. Japan in particular. And Indonesia."

"I hear they got a lot of money in that part of the world."

"Unfortunately, Harold Souto died in a traffic accident. Katheryn tried to sell the business, but then decided to keep it going. Turned out, she has a real knack for it. Has more than tripled the company's holdings in the last ten years that she's been in charge."

Thumps gestured to the box. "How was it?"

"Dee-licious," said Duke. "Give it a try."

"You didn't eat it," said Thumps. "You just licked your fingers."

"Four-year-olds," said Archie. "I'm dealing with four-year-olds."

"Tell you what," said Duke. "You take a bite, and I'll take a bite."

"How about you take a bite, and then I'll take a bite."

"Enough." Archie took the doughnut out of the box, broke off a piece, and put it in his mouth. "There," he said, "everyone happy."

"How's it taste?" said Duke.

"Like black licorice," said Archie. "Can we get back to business?"

"Who's next?"

"Nicodemus Eliopoulos," said Archie. "This one I know."

"Ah," said Thumps. "The Greek."

"Cretan," said Archie. "There's a difference. Family is from Chania. Nico went to university in Athens, worked at the Bank of Greece for about ten years, then went off on his own. Very smart. Very astute. Likes to play the fool. No one knows just how rich he is, but rumours say he has one of the best gold-coin collections in the world."

"You two related?"

"What? Because I'm from Greece and he's from Greece?"

"Very smart. Very astute," said Duke. "Likes to play the fool. What do you think, DreadfulWater? That remind you of anyone?"

"Which brings us to Atticus Poe," said Archie. "Born and raised in New York City. Single mother from Barbados. Got interested in coins as a kid. Has a small shop in Manhattan. Reputation for high-end integrity and high-end merchandise. Bit of a recluse. Does most of his business virtually."

Archie pushed away from the laptop. "So, that's the lineup."

"Which leaves us with the original question," said Duke.

"What are they all doing here," said Thumps.

"And," said Duke, "why are Cruz and the FBI here?"

Archie looked at Thumps. Tapped his fingers on the table. Hard.

"What?"

"He's your friend," said Archie.

"Cruz isn't going to tell me."

"Maybe he'll give you a hint." Archie broke the sweet corn and blueberry doughnut into three unequal pieces and gave the two larger parts to Thumps and the sheriff. "If there's trouble on the way," he said, "I need to know."

11

Thumps rode the elevator with Duke. The sheriff worked his mouth as though he was trying to suck something out from between his teeth.

"Who the hell would think that sweet corn and blueberry would make a good doughnut?"

"Same person who came up with black licorice."

"What am I going to tell Fancy?"

"'O, while you live, tell truth and shame the devil.'"

"You know, I could just shoot you and call it self-defence."

Thumps settled into the corner. "You think Archie is right?"

"You mean about the dealers? Maybe. The whole bunch showing up like this does seem a bit unexpected."

"Along with Cruz and Benoit."

"All at the same time."

"Yep," said Thumps. "All at the same time."

The doors opened. Thumps followed Duke to the foyer.

"I have to get back to town. Taking Macy to the doctor. I'll leave the doughnut report to you."

"I'm not telling Fancy we don't like her new doughnuts."

"Everyone appreciates constructive criticism," said Duke. "She may even give you a free doughnut."

"When was the last time you told a woman you didn't like her cooking?"

"I could deputize you," said Duke. "Give you a badge. Might even give you a gun."

"Send her an email," said Thumps. "You have a computer."

The sheriff set his hat on his head, gave it a pat to tamp it down. "Talk to Cruz. Tell him if he doesn't fill us in, I'll have him renditioned to a black site at Walt Disney World in July."

"Probably not a good idea to annoy the FBI just for shits and giggles."

"So what?" said Duke. "You want to be popular all your life?"

Claire was at her meetings. Archie was in his condo. The sheriff was on the way back to his office. Cruz and Benoit were out of sight, out of mind.

Lovely.

Thumps stood in the foyer of the resort and went through his options for a slow, stress-free day. A day that was going to begin with breakfast. The close encounter with the black licorice doughnut had temporarily suppressed his appetite, but now it had recovered and was back with a vengeance.

The resort had a breakfast buffet. It wasn't Al's, but it would have to do. Best of all, he could charge it to Archie, a reasonable expense against what the little Greek was asking him to do.

Thumps stood at the beginning of the line, plate in hand, and contemplated the selections. Scrambled eggs, bacon, sausages, fried potatoes, pancakes, as well as oatmeal, muffins, and several pitchers of juice.

Now that he could see it up close, the buffet didn't look all that appetizing. There was little you could do, Thumps allowed, with food left to perish in hot trays.

The eggs had an acrylic sheen to them. The bacon was overcooked. The sausages were corpse grey. The pancakes had begun to curl up at the edges. The muffins looked edible, and there were bananas, white and orange cheese cubes arranged on a cutting board, red and green grapes in a basket, and half a fresh pineapple sitting in a bed of ice.

Next to a large bowl of something that looked like pink pudding.

"Mr. DreadfulWater."

A line had formed behind him when he wasn't looking. Atticus Poe, Katheryn Souto, and Nicodemus Eliopoulos. Plates in hand.

"I prefer à la carte," said Poe, "but *cum Romae ut Romani faciunt fac.*"

"Oatmeal," said Souto. "And fruit. Thank god, they have oatmeal."

Nico probed the pink glop with a spoon.

"It's yogurt, Nico," said Souto. "Don't play with the food."

Thumps picked up a sausage with the tongs. There was a frilly skirt of fat stuck to the sides and bottom.

"This is what happens when you travel," said Poe.

"Atticus lives in Manhattan," said Souto. "He thinks it's the food capital of the world."

"It is," said Poe.

"Obviously," said Souto, "he's never been to San Francisco."

"But we are here," said Eliopoulos, "so we must make the best of our situation."

"Can we join you?" said Poe. "We know each other too well and would appreciate spending time with someone who hasn't heard all our stories before."

"Atticus is dying to tell you about the time this guy tried to rob him, and he knocked him out with a gold bar."

"A one-kilo gold bar," said Nico. "Very impressive."

"And I didn't knock him out," said Poe. "I just stunned him."

THUMPS FELT A bit like a scoutmaster leading a troop on a hike, everyone singing the "Heigh-Ho" song from *Snow White* as they went.

"Table in the corner," Souto sang out. "Away from the sunlight."

"The woman is part vampire," said Poe.

"San Francisco can be quite foggy," said Nico. "In Greece, we have more sunshine."

"Sunshine," said Souto, "is overrated."

Thumps settled himself, his back to the panoramic window. Poe sat directly across from him. Souto and Eliopoulos to either side.

Souto made a face. "How in the world can you ruin oatmeal?"

"Call the sheriff," said Poe. "Someone has murdered my eggs."

"My food is fine," said Nico. "But I come from a poor family."

"Yes," said Souto, "we know."

"Eight children," parroted Poe, "all raised by your mother and grandmother."

"We ate what they cooked," said Nico. "No questions. No complaints."

"Eat when you can," said Souto. "Eat what you find. Did I get it right?"

"Yes, yes," said Nico. "But it is more *peistikos* in Greek."

"How about you, Mr. DreadfulWater?" said Souto. "What's your story?"

Thumps tried the eggs. Poe was right. They were definitely dead. Rigor had set in.

"Single mother," said Thumps. "Just the two of us."

"Good," said Souto. "Now, shall we move on to politics or religion?"

Offhand, Thumps could think of two approaches. Be circumspect, sit back, let things play out, or pull the pin on a grenade, drop it into the conversation, see what happened.

"So," he said, opting for the more explosive of the two, "what brings you all out to this part of the world?"

"Ah," said Poe. "You've been talking to Mr. Kousoulas."

"Or more accurately," said Souto, "Mr. Kousoulas has been talking to you."

"He is Greek," said Nico. "Like me. We tend to be anxious."

And sometimes the grenade is a dud.

"Let me guess," said Souto. "He thinks it's unusual for major dealers, such as ourselves, to show up for a regional show such as this, that our appearance *en masse* is a portent of disasters to come."

"That's because we didn't," said Poe. "Come for the exhibition, that is."

"Most of us don't go to the shows anymore," said Souto. "Too crowded. Too busy. Been there, done that, got the T-shirt."

"Much of our business is one to one, internet, dealer to dealer."

"So, we don't see much of each other," said Nico, "unless we make the effort."

"Hence Chinook," said Poe. "Quiet, out of the way. Gives us a chance to catch up, do a little business, see a part of the world we haven't seen."

"We do it every two to three years," said Souto. "Very ad hoc."

"Have you explained all this to Archie?"

"Of course," said Poe. "It's not the first time we've caused a stir."

"Duluth three years back. Pine Bluff five years before that." Souto finished her oatmeal, wiped her mouth. "I think we rather enjoy it."

"Buying and selling coins is not the most exciting of professions," said Nico. "Any attention is appreciated."

Thumps cut into his sausage. It did look like something he might find in Beth Mooney's morgue.

"So, this is a . . . vacation?"

"Oh no," said Nico. "This is a business trip. A deduction. We take it off our taxes."

Thumps left the sausage where it lay. "You seem to have lost a couple of folks."

"Hardly," said Souto. "Otto has gone to the casino. Evidently, they have a free continental."

"He is a cheap man," said Nico.

"And Hunter is off jogging," said Poe. "She has this idea that sweating and annoying the muscles in her body will keep her young."

"We're getting together this evening," said Souto. "Will you be joining us?"

"Me?"

"Aren't you security?" said Souto. "Aren't you here to keep us from robbing the place?"

Once you got past the crusty part of the eggs, they were okay. Not exactly good, but Thumps was hungry. And Nico was right. Eat when you can. Eat what you can find. Good advice in any language.

"I hope we're not a disappointment," said Poe. "Conspiracy theories are so much more interesting than real life."

"Have you ever been to a gold-coin exhibition, Mr. DreadfulWater?"

"No," said Thumps. "This will be my first."

"It's not all that exciting," said Souto.

"It is boring," said Eliopoulos. "Unless you're a dealer. And then it is *very* boring."

Souto stood, placed her napkin on the table. "I am going to have a long soak in the tub and then a nap."

"I will join Otto in the casino," said Nico. "A little blackjack, I think. Of course, I have a limit."

"I've rented a car," said Poe. "I'm hoping to roam about and see where the deer and the antelope play."

"And you, Mr. DreadfulWater?" said Souto. "What's on your dance card?"

THUMPS STOOD IN the parking lot in the late morning sun and watched the river cut through the gorge. He had taken photographs of the big S-turn the river made as it worked its way down White Goat Canyon, before it plunged over the edge of the Bozeman Fault. But he hadn't tried any landscapes with his new digital camera. It had been fine for candids, and he could see where it would be very handy if he ever got into street photography.

The camera was in his trunk. Thumps rescued it from the bag, turned it on. He still couldn't get over how light and quick it was. Or the quality of the image you got without the need for large negatives and nasty chemicals.

Thumps walked to the railing, took several shots of the water as it rushed by. Then he turned and began taking random shots. The condos, the cars in the parking lot, the forest.

He was composing a shot of two large crows sitting on a dumpster when he saw the car come out of the forest, past the casino, and up the road, stopping at the entrance of the resort, like a yacht slipping into an anchorage.

A black stretch limo.

Thumps had seen stretch limos before, but he had to think long and hard to remember the last time he had seen one in this part of the world. Thumps began a slow stroll back toward the car, his camera at his side, his finger on the shutter release. The camera would focus by itself.

All he had to do was point and press.

A spy. Suddenly, he was a spy on a mission.

He had to admit he was enjoying this. Normally, he would have his field camera set up, a rig so obvious that no one would mistake him for a secret agent. He was halfway across the parking lot when the door to the limo opened and a man got out.

Click, click, click.

In many ways, the man matched the car. Large and imposing. Dark jacket, dark slacks, heavy face, full head of black hair.

Click, click, click.

He was flanked immediately by two men who could moonlight as sumo wrestlers.

Click, click.

Evidently, the drive in the limo had been an extended one. Mr. Big stood next to the car and slowly stretched from side to side. Thumps kept his arm extended, the camera firm to his thigh.

Click.

He was about to turn back to his car when a woman came up the path and jogged over to the limo.

Emily Hunter.

Whoever Mr. Big was, Hunter knew him. And he knew her. He started to give her a hug, but she held him off. Thumps could almost read her lips.

Sweaty.

Click, click, click, click.

One of the bodyguards snapped his head around, as though he had heard the shutter. Thumps turned away, quickly brought the camera up to his eye, took several photos of the casino dome all aglow in the mountain light.

But there was no need to pretend to be a tourist. Mr. Big was on the move. He pushed his way through the front doors, the two men trailing in his wake. Hunter jogged in place for a moment, stopped, then checked her pulse.

Thumps was back at his car when he heard footsteps behind him.

"I thought that was you."

"Morning."

"So, are you a photographer today," said Hunter, "or an undercover agent?"

"Photographer."

"Did you get any good shots of Boris?"

"Boris?"

"The missing piece of the conspiracy."

"Okay."

"Will you be joining us tonight?" said Hunter.

"I don't think so."

"You should come. It's where we're going to unveil our plan for the domination of the world."

Thumps brought the camera up to his eye, framed Hunter in the viewfinder.

"You really know how to embarrass a girl," she said, pushing the hair out of her face and turning away. "When I control the world, the first thing I'll do is destroy that photo."

Thumps held the camera so Hunter could see the monitor.

"I normally do landscapes."

"Yes," she said, "I can see that."

Hunter turned and jogged back up to the resort. "Think about this evening," she shouted over her shoulder. "We can be quite entertaining."

Thumps considered taking a couple more shots of the woman, and then thought better of it. The little camera was making him shutter happy. With film, you had to plan your shot, practise economy. Even with a thirty-five-millimetre roll, there were only thirty-six exposures.

Thirty-seven if you didn't wind the leader onto the spool all the way and the first frame didn't get fogged in the loading.

With digital, you could snap off hundreds of shots without even thinking. Thumps suspected that this profligate impulse could be addictive. Blast away, sort through the bodies, find the survivors. Take a hundred shots. One or two of them should be alive and well.

Holding the little camera at his side, as though it were a purse, and shooting blind had been somewhat exciting, and he was anxious to check the file to see where the adventure had taken him.

THUMPS PULLED OUT of the parking lot. The limo was still parked at the entrance. He slowed, noted the licence plate number, and almost missed the panel van parked by the side of the building.

Zarina Benoit.

She was behind the wheel, in sunglasses, a hat, trying to look inconspicuous. Thumps stopped as he came abreast. Benoit ignored him. Thumps stayed where he was. Finally, Benoit rolled down her window.

"Go away."

"Are you watching Boris?"

"Damn it, DreadfulWater," said Benoit. "Stay out of this."

"Why?"

"Cruz told me you were a boy scout."

"Just don't like being lied to." Thumps put the car in park, took his foot off the brake.

"Get used to it," said Benoit. "Now get the hell out of here before you blow my cover."

"Tell Cruz we need to talk."

In the rear-view mirror, Thumps saw one of the bodyguards come out of the resort and get into the limo.

"I could honk my horn. Introduce everyone."

"All right, I'll tell Cruz," said Benoit. "I'll let him kill you."

Thumps rolled up the window, pulled the car into gear, let it float down the road and into the trees. In addition to making him distrustful, being lied to also made him extremely curious.

12

Lynn Langfield was behind the counter, talking with an older woman. "So if you want high resolution, you'll want a camera with a decent pixel count."

"And that will guarantee that all my photographs are sharp?"

Thumps wandered the store, took his time peering at the cameras in the glass cabinets. Nikon, Canon, Sony, Fuji, Olympus, Panasonic. Sad.

The world he knew, the world of film, of mechanical cameras and manual lenses, was gone. All replaced and made digital.

Did anyone still remember the old TV show *The Six Million Dollar Man*?

So, what he was looking at were not cameras per se, they were computers. But then most things were computers nowadays. Televisions, cars, cellphones. Digital instruments performed surgeries. Computer-controlled drones dropped bombs. Thumps had heard rumours that the advent of digital pets was on the horizon.

Thumps smiled. A digital Freeway. There would probably be a menu that controlled temperament with separate settings for levels of affection.

"No," said Lynn. "High resolution will give you excellent dynamic range. Much of what we perceive as sharpness is a combination of proper focus, correct aperture and speed, and high-quality lenses."

"And my photographs tend to be dark."

"That's a matter of exposure."

Lynn took out a business card, wrote on the back. "Here's a camera that I think will do the trick."

"And what kind of film does it take?"

THUMPS WAITED UNTIL the woman was out the door and on the street.

"Tough sell."

"Norma Woodbridge," said Lynn. "She comes in once a week. I think she's lonely."

Thumps gestured to the rows of cameras. "You ever ask yourself why we need so many, when they all do the same thing?"

"Consumerism," said Lynn. "What keeps me in business. So, how do you like the new camera?"

"It's handy," said Thumps. "Just don't know if it's going to work for me."

Lynn held out his hand. "You got some shots on the card?"

"A few."

"Then let's see what we have." Lynn opened up his laptop, took the SD card out, stuck it in a reader. "Okay . . . That's nice . . . This Ivory?"

"It is."

"That a cartwheel?"

"Most of it."

Lynn worked the mouse. "And some grab shots."

"No-look photography," said Thumps.

"A little wide."

"I couldn't get any closer."

"Unless we do this . . ."

Suddenly, the limo and Boris—no last name—filled the screen.

"You pick up a bit of noise punching in like that," said Lynn, "but you can clean it up in post."

"Post?"

"Is that a Mercedes stretch?"

"It is."

"The guy reminds me of Tom Selleck in that cop show." Lynn squinted. "Is that a stick pin?"

"A what?"

"There, on his jacket." Lynn touched the mouse and Boris's lapel came into focus. "They were all the rage the last half of the nineteenth century and the first half of the twentieth. Lot of the old movies you see from that period had guys with stick pins."

"What do they do?"

Lynn shrugged. "Nothing. Ornamental. Like a watch fob or a ring. Most of them were made out of fourteen-carat gold, so they wouldn't bend. Some had enamelwork on the end. Some had diamonds. Some just had an initial."

The enlargement was coarse and grainy. Thumps could just make out the end of the stick pin. It looked like a tulip.

"So," said Lynn, "what do you want to do with these images?"

"Could I get a couple of prints of Ivory? Maybe a couple of the guy and the limo as well?"

"Four by six okay?"

"Perfect."

"The guy have something to do with a case? Do I get to charge the sheriff?"

"Afraid not," said Thumps. "It's just something I'm working on."

"Then it's free," said Lynn. "One of these days you're going to walk through that door and buy a state-of-the-art digital camera."

Thumps chuckled. "I will, will I?"

"You will," said Lynn. "Then I'll load you up with lenses and batteries and SD cards and all the high-profit-margin accessories I can think of, and in a year or two, when another dozen newer and better cameras hit the market, you'll discover that all your equipment is obsolete, and you'll be as miserable as the rest of us."

"Sounds depressing."

"You have no idea," said Lynn.

THE SHERIFF'S OFFICE was at the end of the block. Thumps took his time. When he got to Wild Rose Realty, he stopped, stood outside for a while looking at the houses on display in the window. It took him a moment to realize that all the listings were marked Sold.

Ora Mae Foreman was behind her desk, looking for all the world like the queen of the Nile. Off to the left was a young woman at a smaller desk, and off to the right was a young man.

Ora Mae waved him in.

"Well," she said, "if it isn't the Lone Ranger."

Thumps cocked his head. "Probably more of a Tonto."

"You know why the Lone Ranger never took off his mask?"

Thumps had played this game any number of times with Ora Mae. "Because if he did, everyone would see that the Ranger was really a Black man."

"A handsome Black man," Ora Mae corrected, "who would sweep me off my feet, and we'd ride off together into the sunset."

"Except you're . . ."

"A lesbian?" Ora Mae raised her arms above her head and stretched from side to side. "You worried about shocking the children?"

Thumps shrugged.

"Boys and girls," said Ora Mae, "this wild savage is Thumps DreadfulWater. Mind your manners and don't startle him with loud noises."

Thumps looked from the young woman to the young man. For as long as Ora Mae had owned Wild Rose Realty, she had worked alone.

"You expanding?"

"Tara," Ora Mae tipped her head toward the young woman, "and her twin brother, Derron. My sister's kids," said Ora Mae. "So I can beat them like a dusty rug."

"And I'm her favourite niece," said Tara.

"I'm her favourite nephew," said Derron.

"I'm the oldest."

"I'm the smartest."

"Family," said Ora Mae. "Nothing much to be done about it."

The bulletin board on the wall behind Ora Mae's desk was covered with photos of houses and condos. Most of them had a "Sold" stamped across their face as well.

"Business looks to be good."

"Business is red hot," said Ora Mae. "House prices have jumped twelve percent in the last two quarters. You want to know what your charming bungalow on a sought-after street is worth?"

"Last year you called it a sad sack of a dump in a bad location."

"That was last year." Ora Mae tapped her fingernails on the desk. "Wait. Are you working for that nice sheriff, again?"

"Maybe."

"'Cause every time you do, you wind up in a shitpile of hurt."

"I'm just checking on a couple of things for him."

"You going to arrest Auntie Ora Mae?" asked Tara.

"Can we watch?" said Derron.

Thumps smiled. "You're going to have a good time with these two."

Ora Mae gave a grunt.

Thumps turned toward the door. "Just out of curiosity," he asked, "what is my charming bungalow on a sought-after street worth?"

Ora Mae considered him for a moment, the way a bird considers a worm. Then she wrote a figure on a notepad, tore off the page, and handed it to him.

"Really."

"Course, all that don't mean shit unless you're planning on pulling up stakes."

Thumps stared at the figure in front of him.

"However, if you're finally coming to your senses and thinking about selling and getting a nice place for you and Claire and Ivory, then it would be a sideways move, financially. You wouldn't make any money, but you wouldn't lose much either."

"I'd lose money?"

"There's my commission."

Thumps shoved his hands into his pockets. "I think if we were going to get together, I'd probably move out to the reservation."

Ora Mae went back to tapping her fingernails. "Great place. Wide-open spaces. Clean air. Quiet."

"That it is."

"Home on the range," said Ora Mae. "Where the buffalo roam."

Thumps waited.

"Course, it's no place for a kid. Young girl like Ivory needs friends. A movie theatre. Shops to shop in. A good school."

"She'd have a horse on the reservation. You can't have a horse in the city."

"Sure," said Ora Mae, "but you can't go galloping across the prairies all day and call it life." Ora Mae opened a drawer. "Here are four properties. Take a drive by. See if anything catches your eye."

"Don't think Claire is ready to move in with me."

"How old's Ivory now?"

"Six, going on thirty."

"Give Claire another couple of months of twenty-four seven with a growing child, and she'll be yours for the taking. Woman will be begging for another adult to share the load."

"Unless she's as easy to raise as me," said Tara.

"Or me," said Derron.

Thumps could see the storm clouds gathering in Ora Mae's eyes.

"Which is why my sister sent her demon spawn out here. To brighten my lonely life."

Thumps looked at the description of the first property. A large two-storey with a garage. Four bedrooms, two baths. At the end of a dead-end street, a location that was described as quiet and secluded.

"You can't live by yourself forever."

"You do."

"I'm a woman. I can handle singularity."

"And a man can't?"

Ora Mae and the twins smiled in unison. The effect was chilling.

"Get out of here, cowboy," said Ora Mae. "Come back when you're ready to talk business."

SHERIFF DUKE HOCKNEY was sitting in the sheriff's office, sitting at the sheriff's desk, in the sheriff's chair, staring at the computer monitor.

"If you're looking for doughnuts, you're too late."

"Don't want a doughnut."

"But there's some coffee," said Duke. "Fresh made."

Thumps glanced at the old percolator. There was a stain running down one side that looked like dried blood. As though the pot had been seriously wounded in a shootout.

"Any luck with that Amazon thing?"

"Easier time talking to Elvis."

Thumps had hoped to find a sympathetic way to address the elephant in the room. Something organic and smooth. Something that spoke to his thoughtful and caring nature.

"Weather's been good, don't you think?"

"Christ, DreadfulWater," said Duke, "you can stop being sensitive. Ask the question."

"How's Macy?"

Duke sat back in his chair. "Talked to the doctor. Supposed to be some new drugs that might help."

"That's good news."

Duke shook his head. "None of which are covered by my health plan."

"Talk to Rawat. He might have some ideas."

"I did. He suggested that Macy and me make a run for the Canadian border."

"A pharmacist with a sense of humour."

"Don't think he was joking," said Duke. "Gave me a lecture on the sorry state of universal health care in the lower forty-eight and how we keep voting against our best interests."

"I know that lecture," said Thumps.

"He's going to try to help me with the costs of some of the medications," said Duke. "Find something generic. Not even sure we can afford that."

"Sorry."

"And then there's the other problem." Duke sat up, leaned forward on his elbows. "Remember I told you that Lance and Jenny were on their honeymoon."

"When's he coming back?"

"That's the problem." Duke drummed his hands on the desk. "Seems that his new bride doesn't like Lance being a cop."

"When you said the coffee was fresh, exactly what did you mean?"

"Made it today. You want a cup?"

Thumps got to his feet, grabbed a cup off the filing cabinet. "No," he said, "but I've got a feeling I'm going to need one."

The coffee could put a rocket into space, but it didn't have that burnt asphalt taste that was the hallmark of Duke's brewing techniques.

"Tara's father owns the Chevrolet dealership here in town and the rental car agency at the airport. Going to teach Lance the business."

"Pays better than being a cop?"

"What doesn't," said Duke. "Plus, it's nine to five, and nobody shoots at you."

Thumps took another sip. Okay, some asphalt. Just at the edges.

"But it means you're going to need another deputy."

"I know," said Duke, "you're a photographer."

Thumps put the cup on the desk. "I'll give you three months. See how it goes."

Duke sat up in the chair. "You'll be my deputy?"

"It's a bad idea," said Thumps, "but yes."

"I don't have to bribe you, twist your arm, threaten to arrest you?"

"You want me to change my mind?"

Duke opened a drawer and took out a large manila envelope, slid it across the desk.

"What's this?"

"Your badge," said Duke. "Contract that you'll need to sign, a cellphone so I can find you, keys to the office, and my old Glock. You'll have to buy your own ammo."

Thumps stared at the envelope for a moment. "You *expected* me to say yes?"

"I'm a trained investigator," said the sheriff. "It's what I do."

"Jesus."

"What is it that Ivory calls you?" said Duke. "Dog? That's it, isn't it. Deputy Dog."

"Don't push it."

"No," said Duke, "I like it."

"Shut up and tell me what you need me to do."

"How about we start with something simple," said the sheriff. "How about you ride herd on the gold? Archie tends to overreact, but better safe than sorry. We'd look pretty silly if someone did hit the exhibition."

Thumps took the photographs out of his pocket, handed them to Duke.

"This guy showed up this morning at Buffalo Mountain."

"Stretch limo." Duke gave a low whistle. "Don't see many of those in town. We know who he is?"

"Boris somebody," said Thumps.

"No last name?"

"Nope."

"Our Emily Hunter seems to know him."

"She does."

Duke looked through the photographs a second time. "You figure the two NFL linemen with him are his personal trainer and his personal stylist?"

"Absolutely," said Thumps.

Duke stood and extended his hand. "Welcome to the team, Deputy Dog."

"Piss off," said Thumps.

13

Thumps dumped the manila envelope on the passenger seat. Already this was feeling like a big mistake. A badge, a gun—what was he thinking? A cellphone? Really? Next thing he knew, his house would be rigged for internet, and he'd be watching cable.

Now that he was a deputy sheriff, he remembered the thing he liked best about photography, and landscape photography in particular.

The solitude.

When he was in the darkroom, he was there alone, in the dark, in the quiet. When he was in the field, he was alone with only the wind for conversation. Or he was in his car, driving out to the mountains or driving home.

Alone, alone, alone.

And now that he was a deputy sheriff, he remembered what he didn't like about law enforcement. The dealing with people in all stages of distress and anger. The interaction with other cops, with attorneys, with medical staff, with judges, with criminals, with victims.

And the guns.

Thumps had never liked guns. He knew the argument for keeping a gun as self-protection, and he also knew that it was mostly a myth. Sure, if someone came into your house, and if you had enough time to retrieve your weapon, and if you could shoot straight in a moment of panic and high drama, and if you didn't shoot yourself or a member of your family . . .

He had seen more than his fair share of guns when he was a cop on the Northern California coast. One guy he arrested had a rocket launcher in his garage and a 105-millimetre howitzer in his backyard. Another had a .950 JDJ that he kept in the house as a deterrent in case the Russian 49th Army showed up on his doorstep.

How much time had he spent on the range practising his marksmanship. Sure, he could probably still hit centre mass at twenty-five feet with a pistol. After that, all bets were off.

The last time Thumps had looked at the statistics, they suggested that no more than a quarter of all serving police personnel had ever fired their weapons while on duty. That seemed excessive, but then you'd expect that cops would find themselves in more situations where guns were a factor. What were the statistics for civilians?

Thumps sat in the car and tried to remember just how he had come to this.

Oh yeah, friendship. Another reason to be alone.

Except you never were alone. Thumps did not consider himself a gregarious person, and yet he had accumulated a good many people in his life. Claire and Ivory, Moses and Cooley, Al, Archie, Rawat and Stas, Beth Mooney, Ora Mae Foreman, Wutty Youngbeaver and the gang, Lynn and Lilly Langfield. Even Roxanne Heavy Runner.

And of course, Sheriff Benjamin "Duke" Hockney.

The complications of life. Thank goodness the first part of the plan for the evening was simple. Go home, feed the cats, get a change of clothes, drive back up to the resort.

Which brought him to the second and more complicated part.

Check on Claire.

Melton and his fiancée had taken Ivory back to Alberta with them. It made sense that Melton would want to spend time with his niece, would want her to meet the extended family. Maybe it was nothing more than that.

Maybe a cigar was just a cigar.

Claire would know soon enough. Should he ask? Or should he wait until she told him?

He could always go to the evening soiree with the coin dealers, sit around with the folks, get to know them, swap stories.

Or not.

If the junta was up to no good, they certainly weren't going to discuss their plans in front of a cop. Then there was the arrival of Boris No Last Name with Zarina Benoit and Cisco Cruz hard on his heels. Archie was prone to hyperbole, but it didn't mean that he was wrong in thinking that there was something nefarious afoot.

So, what was it that had brought everyone here?

Evidently, not the coin show and certainly not the amenities. Sure, there were a couple of places to eat in the area, but Buffalo Mountain wasn't one of them. Sure, there were things to do, if your idea of fun was hiking and gambling. But there was no theatre, no shopping, no beaches to lie on. Nothing to please or stimulate the sophisticated taste buds of city folk.

So, what was it that had brought everyone here?

WHEN THUMPS GOT home, the lights were on, and Cruz was sitting in the living room, watching television, Freeway and Cookie curled up beside him.

"Good. You got my message."

"*Cabrón*," said Cisco, "how can you not have cable?"

"We need to talk."

"I hear the sheriff made you a deputy," said Cruz. "Congratulations."

"Who's Boris?"

Cruz shook his head. "Man, you almost screwed the pooch on that one. Zee told me you did your best to blow her cover."

"I don't like being lied to."

"Nobody's lying." Cruz gave Freeway a rub. She promptly turned over, so he could get at her belly. "We're just not sharing."

"How about you tell me what you're not sharing?"

"And no internet?" Cruz shook his head. "Is that even legal?"

"Let's start with Boris," said Thumps. "The sheriff will have run his picture by now."

"So, ask Duke."

"I'm asking you."

Cruz yawned. "No secret. Dude is Boris Lukin. Big-time coin dealer out of Miami. His old man was Russian mob."

"Was?"

"Cancer. Couple of years back."

"And the son?"

"Mostly legit."

"And yet he has you and the FBI on his tail."

"Who says we're on his tail?"

"Right," said Thumps. "I forgot. You and your so-called fiancée are on vacation. A romantic getaway. With guns."

"Okay." Cruz held up his hands. "Hypothetically, let's say that the FBI is interested in some of the Lukin family's activities. And let's say that Lukin never leaves his compound in Florida."

"And then suddenly, he packs up and comes here."

"Hypothetically."

"Which would mean coming here is important."

"Hypothetically."

"Okay," said Thumps. "That explains Benoit. What about you? Are you FBI?"

"Hypothetically, maybe Zee needed a cover. You know, the happy couple on vacation. Maybe we know each other, and I'm tagging along. As a favour to a friend. Sort of like you and Duke."

"Hypothetically."

"Exactly," said Cruz.

"So, what happens now?"

Cruz stood and brushed himself off. "I go back to the resort."

"Not what I meant."

"Did you know the casino has a dance floor?" Cruz did a quick turn on his way to the door. "Zee's crazy for that shit."

THE DRIVE BACK to Buffalo Mountain was pleasant. The evening light settling in behind the mountains. The land quiet and at rest. Thumps left the radio off, enjoyed the peace of the moment. There would be little of that to be had, he suspected, in the days to come.

At least now he had a name. Boris Lukin. First there were five. Now there were six. Six whales. Six whales come to the same patch of ocean. The other dealers would know Lukin, and Lukin would know them, and if Thumps wanted to know more about the man with the stick pin, all he would have to do is ask.

There was no one at the front desk. No one to ask about the meeting. Just as well. He really needed to find Claire first, find out what was happening with Ivory. The coin dealers could wait.

"'Bout time you showed up."

Somehow Roxanne Heavy Runner had gotten in behind him when he wasn't looking.

"Bet you're looking for Claire."

"I am."

"Too late," said Roxanne. "She's already gone."

"Gone?"

"To Canada."

"This about Ivory?"

Roxanne held out her hand. "So, I'll need the key card."

"Key card?"

"To Claire's condo," said Roxanne. "You can't stay there tonight. Claire is letting Scoop use it."

"Okay."

"And when you come back here tomorrow, you can take my picture."

"For?"

"Have to have a reason?"

Most times, Roxanne had a voice like a tank crashing through a fortified position. Tonight, it was almost gentle, a soft pinging, as though she were only laying down small-calibre cover fire.

"No," said Thumps, "you don't have to have a reason."

"I don't much like pictures of me," said Roxanne. "You should know that from the jump."

"Head and shoulders?"

"Sure," said Roxanne. "Don't want to show too much too soon."

The question was out of his mouth before he could stop it. "This for a dating service?"

"You think I need a dating service." The cover fire was replaced with a full-out bombardment. "That what you're thinking?"

Thumps took a step back to escape the barrage. "There's a meeting I'm supposed to be at."

"That the one with all those big-shot coin guys?"

"Yes," said Thumps, "that's the one."

"Too late." Roxanne jerked her thumb in the opposite direction. "What's left of them headed up to your buddy's condo."

"Archie?"

"Photograph. Tomorrow," said Roxanne. "And maybe leave that smart tongue in your mouth."

14

Thumps had seen more of Archie than was good for his general well-being. The little Greek was safe enough in small doses. More than that and the man could be lethal.

Archie opened the door on the first knock.

"You're late."

Case in point.

"You were supposed to be at the meeting."

"No, I wasn't."

Archie grabbed Thumps's arm, dragged him into the room.

"You're the deputy sheriff now. You have to start taking the job seriously."

The dining room table was covered in books. Nicodemus Eliopoulos was sitting at the far end, his hair a wiry scramble, his glasses about to fall off the end of his nose.

"I told you it was a catastrophe," said Archie. "And what do you do about it?"

"This have anything to do with Boris Lukin?"

"See?" Nico pushed his glasses up. "Nothing to worry about. He's smarter than he looks."

"Boris Lukin. Yes, of course, Boris Lukin. Do you know who he is?"

"Big-time coin dealer out of Miami," said Thumps. "Old man was Russian mob."

"Big-time crook is what you mean," said Archie. "Makes his father look like small potatoes."

"Yes," said Nico, "Boris is not a nice man, not to be trusted."

"And he's here," said Archie. "Do you know what that means?"

Thumps helped himself to a chair at the table. "So, tell me about Boris Lukin."

"Gold Coast Currency," said Nico. "Boris's father, Arkady Lukin, started the company."

"The small-potatoes crook."

"Not in the coin business," said Nico. "In the coin business, Arkady was a major player. Honourable. His coins were good. His prices were fair. His assessments were always accurate."

"Which is more than we can say for the son."

"Yes," said Nico. "Boris is a crook in everything. Do you know how gold coins are valuated?"

Thumps took a stab at it. "By weight?"

"You're guessing," said Archie.

"First, you need to understand that there are two kinds of gold coins," said Nico. "Bullion coins and numismatic coins. Bullion coins are produced in large quantities. Krugerrands, sovereigns, Maple Leafs, Britannias. Their value is tied to the value of gold."

"Numismatic coins are different," said Archie. "These are coins that were in circulation, were common currency, coins with history, and their value depends on rarity and condition."

"Okay," said Thumps, "so, the value of bullion coins is more or less fixed by the price of gold."

"Exactly," said Nico, "whereas the value of numismatic coins can vary a great deal."

"Bullion coins aren't much fun," said Archie. "You might as well buy hog futures."

"But something like the 1879 double eagle . . ." Nico took off his glasses and wiped them. "Well, that's what we all live for."

"And that's worth?"

"Archie," said Nico, "you remember what the last one sold for at auction?"

"A million eight?" Archie scratched at the side of his head. "Give or take a couple hundred thousand."

"But there's no coin of that calibre in the exhibition?"

Nico smiled. "Nothing even close. Though it is a nice collection."

"Of course it's a nice collection," said Archie. "I organized it myself."

"Boris Lukin." Thumps let the name hang in the air. "Who invited Boris?"

"Knowing Boris," said Archie, "he invited himself."

Nico yawned, pushed out of his chair. "I must get to bed," he said. "It has been a long day, and I am no longer young. Tomorrow the exhibition opens, and I want to be at my best."

"And if you didn't invite him to your little get-together," said Thumps, "why is he here?"

THUMPS WAITED WHILE Archie cleared the table and brought out fresh coffee.

"No doughnuts, I'm afraid," said the little Greek. "There are a couple of chocolate chip cookies, but they're quite stale."

"I'm thinking you might be right," said Thumps. "There is something going on."

Archie nodded. "I asked Nico point-blank."

"And?"

"And he lied to me. I could see it in his eyes, could hear it in his jolly-jolly-everything's-okay Cretan voice."

"Cretan voice?"

Archie sniffed. "He's from Crete."

"Okay," said Thumps, "regional prejudices aside, there's something we're missing."

"And I can't figure out what it is." Archie sat back down at the table. "There's no way Nico would be involved in a robbery. The exhibition isn't worth his time or effort."

"What if one of them had a really rare coin they wanted to sell?"

"They'd put it up for public auction," said Archie. "Generate a ton of publicity. Get as many bidders as possible."

"What if the coin was stolen?"

"Sure," said Archie, "but why do it here? With everybody watching. Something like that you want to do on the quiet. Discreet and invisible."

"I imagine Poe and Souto and Hunter et al already have clients for that sort of transaction on their Rolodex."

"Cellphone," said Archie. "No one uses a Rolodex anymore."

Thumps took a sip of the coffee. "Just how stale are those cookies?"

THE COOKIES WERE very stale. The chocolate chips had turned a soft grey, and the cookie itself had hardened into a floor tile. None of which bothered Archie. He dipped the cookies in the coffee and held court with fantastic stories of gold coins. The Saddle Ridge Hoard, the Baltimore Find, the Wells Fargo Hoard.

Just before midnight, Thumps called time.

"Don't you want to know about the Granite Lady?"

"I want to go to bed," said Thumps, "and in order to do that, I have to drive home."

"You're not staying here?" Archie looked concerned. "With Claire and Ivory?"

"Claire's had to go to Canada."

"Canada?" said Archie. "That can't be good."

"Scoop Macleod is staying at her place here at the resort."

Archie spread his hands. "You could stay here with me. I have an extra bedroom. Have you heard the story about the 1933 double eagle?"

"No," said Thumps, "and no. I have my own bed and two cats who need me."

"Cats don't need people."

"That's an unsubstantiated rumour," said Thumps. "Started by dogs."

Archie helped himself to the last of the cookies. "Tomorrow," he said. "The exhibition starts tomorrow."

15

When Thumps got home, the first thing he did was call Claire. He debated waiting until morning. After all, it was late. But he decided that an inconsiderate call from a concerned lover was better than a tardy call from a reasonable one.

After all, they were lovers, weren't they? More or less. A couple for sure. Most of the time. Still, Claire hadn't bothered to call him, to let him know what was happening, or let him know where she was going.

Or why.

As Thumps listened to the phone ring, he was reminded once again that Claire lived her life on her own terms, and that he wasn't necessarily one of them.

THUMPS HADN'T EXPECTED that Freeway and Cookie would rush to his side the moment he stepped through the door.

And they didn't.

He found them curled up on the bed. If Thumps drew diagonal lines from corner to corner, he was sure he'd discover that the cats were in the exact centre.

"My bed," he told the cats.

He might as well have been talking to the ceiling.

"You two have your own bed."

Freeway yawned and stretched. Cookie rolled over on his back, so Thumps could rub his tummy.

"Not happening."

There were people who believed that cats could understand what you said, and there were other people who figured that even if cats could, the majority of them didn't care what you had to say.

"Okay," he said, "we'll have to do this the hard way."

Thumps picked up Freeway, carried her to the cat basket in the living room. With any luck, Cookie would come trundling along behind, not wanting to be out of sight of his mother.

But that was not to be. He was carrying the kitten to the basket when Freeway passed him on her way back to the bed.

"Great."

Thumps took off his jeans and shirt, crawled into bed, made a point of lifting the covers with his legs higher than necessary. The cats were unceremoniously tumbled to the far side of the mattress. There was the complaining, the turning around in circles, the licking of body parts, and then silence.

As he drifted to sleep, he consoled himself with the awareness that cats lived their lives on their own terms as well, and that he shouldn't read anything more into it than that.

He was at Al's early the next morning. A quiet, leisurely breakfast. Drive up to Buffalo Mountain. Attend the opening of the coin exhibition. Try to find out why Claire went to Canada.

An orderly and doable list of tasks for the day.

Until he pushed in through the door of the café. And then, it was too late.

"There he is," said Archie. "I told you he'd show up."

Eliopoulos looked at his watch. "An hour ago, you said he'd show up."

"And he showed up."

Thumps pushed past the two men to his favourite stool. Al set a cup on the counter and filled it.

"Thank god," she said. "If I had to listen to those two much longer, I would sell the place and move to Orlando."

"Where's Wutty and the gang?"

"Went to Helena. I didn't think I'd ever miss them."

"Breakfast," said Thumps. "The usual."

"One Archie is more than I can handle," said Al. "Do you know anything about the Stoics and the Skeptics?"

"Breakfast?"

"Or why I should care about perceptual relativism?"

Thumps put his forearms and head on the counter.

Al tapped him with the pot. "Don't be going to sleep on me."

"Not my problem."

Al clumped her way back to the grill. "It is if you want breakfast."

Thumps didn't have to look up. He could hear Archie on the move.

"Wake up."

"Aren't you supposed to be at Buffalo Mountain?"

"That's later," said Archie. "Right now, we need your help."

Thumps buried his head deeper in his arms, kept his eyes closed, tried to pretend he was alone in the world.

Archie took the stool on one side of Thumps. Eliopoulos took the other.

"I think he's ignoring you," said Nico. "Not that I blame him."

"He's just playing hard to get," said Archie. "He's done this before."

Thumps pushed himself to an upright position. "How about I meet you at the resort in a couple of hours. We can talk then."

"We're here now," said Archie.

"He wants to eat his breakfast in peace," said Nico. "We can wait."

"If we let him out of our sight," said Archie, "he might run off with his cameras, and we won't see him for a week."

"He'll come." Nico stood, tucked in his shirt. "You can see that he's an honourable man."

Archie followed Eliopoulos to the door. "Tell Al I'll bring her a copy of *The Republic*."

Al didn't reappear right away.

"Are they gone?"

"They are."

"I'm going to have nightmares about this for a while."

"Archie said he'd bring you a copy of Plato's *Republic*."

Al filled Thumps's cup. "How worried should I be?"

"Breakfast?"

"Don't you want to know why Wutty went to Helena?"

"He's moving?"

"No such luck," said Al. "He and Jimmy and Russell went to the big city to pick up Wutty's newest enthusiasm."

Thumps had lost track of Wutty's enthusiasms.

"You know how some things run on land and some things run on water?"

"Cars and boats?"

"Wutty's got one that does both."

"An amphibian?"

"Wutty calls it his *Little Otter*," said Al. "Personally, I don't see it. Cars are great on the road. Boats are great on the water. Why buy something that does both things poorly?"

"Variety?" said Thumps. "Supposed to be the spice of life."

"If you ask me," said Al, "it's salt."

Thumps looked at the grill. "Is there any chance I'm going to get breakfast?"

"That's why you came in."

"Yes. It was."

"And we got sidetracked by Archie and his buddy. And by Wutty and *Little Otter*."

"We did."

"So, now I'll make you breakfast," said Al. "And you can try to figure out why Wutty is getting a fish with wheels."

"I don't care why Wutty is getting a fish with wheels."

"Have you ever read this *Republic*?"

"Breakfast?"

"Don't tell me who did it."

"Nobody did it."

"It's not a mystery?"

"Only if you try to read it in the original Greek."

The eggs were perfect. The sausages hot and juicy. Even the toast was warm, the butter melted into the bread. The first few bites wiped out the memory of the buffet at Buffalo Mountain.

"So, Wutty figures the amphibian will add value to his tour business," said Al. "Figures to set up at Red Tail Lake. Drive people around the lake and then boat them across, all in the same rig."

"Makes sense."

"That's what worries me," said Al. "Lately, a lot of Wutty's ideas have been making sense."

"Knock on wood."

"If you discount the tipi."

"Wutty has a tipi?"

"Bought if off Eugene Big Bull," said Al. "Was going to set it on the shield where the river cuts a big curve around that grove of cottonwoods."

"Okay."

"Authentic Indigenous experience. Three nights in the wild. Cook your food over an open fire. A little drumming. Yada, yada, yada."

"Probably get some takers."

"Wutty figured it was going to be a real money-maker." Al began smiling. "Might have worked out if any of the lads knew how to set up a tipi."

"Ah."

"Stas went out there last week." Al filled Thumps's cup. "Said the poles are in one pile, canvas in another."

"Eugene didn't show them how to do it?"

"Eugene's over in Browning, visiting relatives."

"What about Moses or Cooley."

"I'm guessing he's too embarrassed to ask them."

"When's Eugene coming back?"

"Not too soon, I hope." Al leaned against the counter. "Listening to those three bicker is more entertaining than talk radio. At one point, they considered renting a cherry picker."

"A little overkill."

"Could have worked," said Al. "If any of those chuckleheads knew how to run one."

"So, they don't know how to put up a tipi, and they don't know how to run a cherry picker. They have any other good ideas?"

"Week's young," said Al. "Makes you wonder why we bothered to climb out of the trees."

Thumps chased the remains of the eggs with a piece of toast.

Al set the coffee pot on the counter. "Which brings us to you and Claire and Ivory."

"Al..."

"The adoption thingy looks to be a real mess," said Al. "Don't see how they can take Ivory away from Claire. She's the only mother that little girl has ever known."

"How do you know..."

"Hear you haven't been a lot of help."

"I only found out yesterday."

Al shook her head. "Eat your food. Don't apologize to me."

THERE WAS A box of doughnuts on the sheriff's desk. Duke was nowhere to be seen. Thumps checked the selection. There were two unglazed old-fashioneds. He broke one of them into quarters.

"You know the best way to catch a cop?" Duke walked out of the back. "Leave a dozen assorted unattended."

"How's Macy?"

"You ever talk to three doctors at the same time?"

"Not if I can help it."

"It's progressive," said Duke. "That was the only thing the three of them could agree on."

"That's it?"

"They talked about the side effects of various medications and procedures," said Duke. "Made me want to give up Aspirin."

Thumps went back to the box and grabbed another quarter. There might be, he imagined, a correlation between how much doughnut he ate and the interval between the eatings. For instance, if he ate a whole doughnut all at once, what would be the effect on his blood sugars and how long would it last? As opposed to his eating a quarter of a doughnut, waiting fifteen minutes, and then eating another quarter.

"They know something's wrong," said Duke. "They just don't know what it is or what to do about it."

Thumps considered asking Beth about his theory on doughnut-eating intervals the next time he saw her, but then she would know that he was eating doughnuts.

"Sort of like being a sheriff," said Duke. "I know a whole bunch about crime. I just don't know when it's going to happen or what I can do to prevent it."

Or maybe he should pursue the theory on his own, do his own research. Shouldn't take more than a few years.

Duke helped himself to a chocolate-coated doughnut. "How goes the gold-coin caper?"

"Not much of a caper yet," said Thumps. "You run that photo I gave you?"

"I did," said Duke.

"Did it come back as one Boris Lukin?"

Duke took a bite of the doughnut. "If you knew who he was, why did you have me run the photo?"

"Didn't know at the time."

"But now you know he's a big-time coin dealer out of Miami."

"Yes."

"And that his father, Arkady Lukin, was connected."

"As in criminal enterprise."

"As in."

Thumps put the doughnut to one side. Wait fifteen minutes. See how he felt.

"All of which tells us . . . ?"

"Got an old pal. Worked homicide in Helena. Retired, moved to Miami. Get away from the cold."

"Makes sense."

"Until he found out what summers in Florida were like." Duke examined the backs of his hands. "He'd move back today, but the housing market collapsed and he's stuck with a condo that's worth less than the mortgage."

"And he knows Lukin."

"Evidently, every cop in Miami knows Lukin. According to Sid, Boris Lukin is one of those M&M criminals, squeaky clean on the outside, dirty as hell in the middle." Duke rubbed his eyes. "Went to Harvard. Took over the coin business and everything else when Arkady died. Sid was real impressed that Boris has turned up on our patch. Seems the man never leaves his compound."

"Compound?"

"It's like a small country with water views, a celebrity chef, and its own air force."

"He has a private plane?"

"A fancy Gulfstream," said Duke. "According to Sid."

"'Let me tell you about the very rich,'" said Thumps. "'They are different from you and me.'"

"That some famous quote?"

"It is."

"Sid's going to ask around," said Duke. "Try to find out why Mr. Boris would leave the comfort of his private paradise to attend a Podunk coin show."

"Podunk?"

"Sid is a polyglot."

Thumps crossed his right leg over his left. And then he crossed his left leg over his right. "Benoit was waiting for Lukin when he arrived."

"So, the FBI knew Boris was coming here."

"Only explanation is they were watching him in Miami, and when he moved, they moved."

"Easy enough to do. Lukin's jet would have had to file a flight plan," said Duke. "As soon as they see where he's going, they call the field office in Minneapolis or Denver or Seattle and put an agent in place before Boris lands."

"Zarina Benoit."

"The stretch limo is out of Helena," said Duke. "Seems the two very large gentlemen came with it."

"Lukin flies out of Miami, lands in Helena, is picked up by Hulk One and Hulk Two, who drive him to Buffalo Mountain and a coin show that's not worth his time."

"Sounds about right," said Duke.

"But we still don't know why he came or why the FBI is on his tail."

"Details, details," said Duke. "Confidence is high, 'cause I have Deputy Dog on the case."

"You know, calling people names is a form of passive-aggressive behaviour."

"Also a form of affection." Duke pushed the box toward Thumps. "Have some more doughnut."

16

Thumps and Duke sat in the sheriff's office and listened to the old percolator bubbling away, doing its impressive impersonation of a thermal mud bath.

"You think that Benoit and Cruz know why Lukin has come to town?"

"Nope," said Thumps. "I think they're watching and waiting."

"So, we're all in the dark." Duke took his cup to the coffee pot. "Maybe we should pay Mr. Boris a visit."

"Sure," said Thumps. "Man's probably never seen a cop before. Show him your badge, he'll piss his pants, confess on the spot."

Duke poured a cup. "You know, when your blood sugars get low, you get grumpy."

"I've had an entire doughnut," said Thumps. "My blood sugars aren't low."

"And you're going to blame me for that?"

Thumps opened the box and looked in. "I am."

"I think it's time you had a hard word with your buddy," said Duke. "I'd prefer it if we weren't blindsided by something embarrassing."

The phone going off in the quiet of the office startled both men. Thumps jerked his hand away from the box. Duke spilled the coffee.

"Jesus!"

The second ring was more insistent.

"Well, don't just sit there," said Duke. "Answer the damn thing."

"You're the sheriff. It's your office."

"You're the deputy sheriff," said Duke. "You're closer, and you don't have coffee on your shoes."

Thumps was on the phone for less than a minute.

"Let me guess," said Duke. "The duct-cleaning people. For the tenth time this week."

"Remember that embarrassing blindside you mentioned?"

Duke put his cup on top of the file cabinet. "Buffalo Mountain."

"Nope." Thumps stood up, put on his jacket. "We're wanted at the hospital."

IN THUMPS'S MIND, the only difference between a morgue and a hospital was that in a hospital, some of the people were still alive.

Duke ran all the way with lights and siren.

"Tell me again what he said?"

"Hospital," said Thumps. "Now."

Duke pulled into a "No Parking Zone" and got out. "We're going to have to get you a uniform shirt and a hat, so you look official."

"No hat," said Thumps, "no uniform shirt."

"At least wear the badge, so people won't think you're my prisoner."

Hospitals smelled. Medical smells, cleaning smells, fear and sadness. The lighting didn't help. Why insist on a cold arctic white when the warmer end of the spectrum was available? And the unnatural quiet with the little bells ringing in the distance.

Ding, ding, ding.

As Thumps walked through the reception area, he resolved to watch his diet and his sugar intake. With hospitals as the alternative, you couldn't be too careful.

"Where'd he say he'd be?"

"Emergency," said Thumps.

THE EMERGENCY ROOM was crowded. Thumps had read somewhere that emergency rooms all across North America were at a point of collapse. COVID had devastated doctors and nurses as well as support staff. Partly it was the exhaustion that came with a pandemic, but the larger and more troubling issue was the unwillingness of the large medical corporations to pay health professionals.

Duke went to the front wicket. "Morning, Deloris."

"Sheriff."

"Looking for Cisco Cruz."

"He said you'd be in."

"You know Thumps?"

"The photographer."

"Right now, he's my deputy."

Deloris smiled a weary smile. "Guess there's hope for me yet."

Duke coughed. "You want to be a cop?"

"Figure it's the same sort of work I do here," said Deloris, "except I'd have a big, honking gun and a reason to shoot some of the idiots I have to deal with."

"You know, we try *not* to shoot people."

"Work here for a month," said Deloris, "and then see how you feel about that."

"Cruz?"

"Down the hall," said Deloris. "Third room on the left."

CISCO CRUZ WAS sitting in a chair beside an empty bed.

"They took her for an MRI."

Duke took off his hat, set it on the foot of the bed. "What happened?"

"Not sure," said Cruz. "We were supposed to meet, but then she didn't show. So I went looking. Found her in the condo, on the floor unconscious. Had a bad gash on her head."

"Someone attacked her?"

Cruz shook his head. "Not sure. It looked as though she fell and hit her head on the coffee table."

"She just fell?"

"They're running a tox screen as well," said Cruz. "Heart rate was elevated."

"Drugs?"

"Too soon to know."

"So, what do we know?"

"She has a concussion," said Cruz. "Has been in and out. Mostly out."

Thumps leaned up against the wall. "How do we feel about coincidences?"

"We don't much like them." Duke turned to Cruz. "Maybe now you'll tell us what's going on."

Cruz folded his hands on his lap. "I need a favour first."

"This is not a negotiation," said Duke.

"I'd ask her myself," said Cruz, "but you two are friends. Harder to say no to friends."

BY THE TIME Beth Mooney arrived at the hospital, Zarina Benoit was back in the bed. Her head was bandaged. There was an IV in one hand and wires snaking out from under the hospital gown that were hooked up to several monitors.

Thumps had seen better-looking corpses.

Beth leaned against the radiator, considered each man in the manner of a hammer contemplating a nail.

"Ask me what I was doing when you called."

"It was Cruz's idea," said Duke.

"And yet, you made the phone call," said Beth.

"Police investigation," said Duke. "We need your expertise."

"Gabby and I had just sat down to a lovely stuffed sole at Pappous's, paired with a yummy Sauvignon Blanc."

"Yummy?"

"With those tiny dolmades for an appetizer."

"Thanks for coming," said Cruz.

Beth pushed off the radiator, stood by the edge of the bed. "Let me get this straight. You want me to do an autopsy."

"That's right," said Cruz.

"On a living person."

"More a forensic evaluation," said Cruz. "Pretend she's dead."

"Got to say," said Duke, "it's inventive."

Cruz handed Beth a folder. "Here's the blood work, crime scene photos. I've asked them to send up the MRI results as soon as they have them."

"That's fast work," said Duke.

"She's a federal officer," said Cruz. "Not going to apologize for pulling strings."

"Didn't expect you would."

Beth took each page in turn. Every so often she would make a noise as though she were talking to herself. When she finished, she handed the folder back to Cruz.

"Without cutting her open," said Beth, "which isn't my first option, I'd say we're looking at two separate events. Blood work indicates that she was drugged. My guess is flunitrazepam or gamma-hydroxybutyric acid."

Cruz nodded. "Rohypnol."

"The date-rape drug?"

"Easy to obtain," said Beth. "Odourless, tasteless, easy to put into drinks. Virtually undetectable to the victim. Some of the newer stuff turns blue in alcohol, but there's plenty of the clear generic stuff kicking around."

"And the head wound?"

"Flunitrazepam can make you dizzy and disoriented," said Beth. "If she was standing when the drug took effect, or if she tried to stand up, there's every chance she would have fallen over. I'm guessing when she fell, she hit her head. You can see the blood on the edge of the table in one of the photographs."

"So, you don't think she was attacked?"

"I'd have to examine her body for bruises, her clothes for damage. There were no indications of sexual assault . . . I'd say no, she wasn't attacked."

"Thanks."

"MRI will show any damage to the brain tissue, but it's useless for concussion. We won't know about that until the drugs wear off, and she's conscious."

"Which brings us back to the matter of coincidences," said Thumps.

"Which none of us believe in," said Duke.

"And this is where you boys take over," said Beth, "and I go back to my lukewarm-heading-to-cold meal."

"I'll pay for the meal," said Cruz.

"No need," said Beth. "This was actually stimulating. We should do it more often."

THE MRI CAME back negative.

"You guys can go," said Cruz. "I'll stay here for a while in case she wakes up."

Duke turned his hat around in his hand. "You think Boris Lukin had something to do with this?"

"Let's see," said Cruz. "The FBI has been watching Lukin for the last year. Lukin knows he's being watched. He stays home, doesn't go out all that much, doesn't make any missteps. Then, out of the blue, he jumps in his jet and comes out to a coin show with nothing in it to interest a dealer at his level? So why is he here?"

"This is where you tell us," said Duke.

"FBI doesn't know. Lukin's leaving Florida caught them off guard. Zee was in Seattle working another case."

"So they had her drop whatever she was doing and fly here posthaste."

"She was supposed to watch Lukin and report back."

"We thinking that Lukin made her?" said Duke.

Cruz looked at Thumps. "Yeah, I'm guessing Lukin made her."

"All of which explains Benoit," said Duke. "But it doesn't explain you."

"I was in Seattle at the time."

"With Benoit?"

"Girlfriend," said Thumps. "Supposedly."

Cruz took a deep breath. "Ex-wife, actually. I was out visiting my son when she got the call."

"Benoit is your ex-wife?" Thumps tried to keep the shock out of his voice. "You have a son?"

"Head of the Seattle field office is an idiot. One of those political appointees. Daddy is a bigwig in DC. He gets all excited when the call comes in about Lukin."

Cruz sat on the edge of the bed, reached out and put his hand on Benoit's. "So, he sends her in with no HUMINT and no backup. Improvise, he tells her."

"Don't imagine she was too happy, you tagging along."

"Didn't tag," said Cruz. "I insisted. Figured her chances were better if we looked like a couple. In the end, she agreed."

"And if she hadn't," said Thumps, "you threatened to blow the operation."

Cruz shrugged. "Something like that. Not about to let my son's mother get killed because some suit can't find his ass with a fly swatter."

Duke put his hat on his head. "Okay, you stay here with your wife."

"Ex-wife."

"Thumps and I will figure out what's going on. Looks like someone wanted Agent Benoit out of commission for a while. Maybe we can find out why."

"Soon as she's out of danger," said Cruz, "I may have to have a little chat with Mr. Lukin."

"Not a good idea," said Duke. "As I recall, your chatting skills leave a little to be desired."

Thumps was at the doorway to the room when he stopped and turned back. "Your son," he said. "What's his name?"

"Duncan," said Cruz.

"As in Duncan Renaldo? The movie star?"

Cruz managed a small smile. "Duncan Renaldo Cruz. *The Cisco Kid*. My mother's favourite TV show. We did it to make her happy."

"I'll bet it did."

"Don't know," said Cruz. "Mom died a month before Duncan was born."

17

The sheriff dropped Thumps off at his house.

"Another doctor-go-round day. Blood tests. Scans and shit. I'll get up there as soon as I can."

"No rush," said Thumps. "Look after Macy."

Duke leaned on the wheel. "Maybe keep Archie from having a stroke."

THUMPS HAD LEFT his keys with Cruz, in case the man from Pie Town needed a place to stay while he was waiting for Benoit to wake up. Not that Cruz needed a key to get into the house.

Most times he just broke in.

Beth had put a different spin on Benoit. If she was right, then Benoit had been drugged but not attacked, the head wound the result of a fall. Thumps tried turning the facts around, so he could see them from all directions, hoping that he'd find a pattern.

Benoit is shadowing Lukin. Lukin knows that she's watching. Killing her is a no-fly zone. He'd have the whole bureau on his ass. Whereas drugging her is simply stupid. But it does sideline her. Which would suggest that time is what he needs.

But for what?

Who else had a reason to want Benoit out of the way? So far as

Thumps could see, no one. Still, something about Lukin making such an obvious move didn't feel right. Everything Thumps knew about the man suggested that he was smarter than that.

Maybe he'd just ask him. Did you and your lads drug Agent Benoit? Stir the pot a bit. See what came to the top.

But first things first.

SCOOP ANSWERED THE door on the second knock.

"Oh, hi."

"Sorry," said Thumps. "I should have called."

"No, come on in. I have coffee, if you like."

Scoop was dressed in a heavy robe, a Buffalo Mountain Resort logo on the lapel. Thumps reminded himself that some people like to sleep in. With two cats, he hadn't had much experience with late risings.

"Claire hasn't come back yet." Scoop brought a cup of coffee to the table. "Haven't heard from her either. She call you?"

"No."

"I'm a little worried," said Scoop. "She was upset when she left."

Thumps imagined that Claire had left more than just upset.

"You really think the uncle is going to want Ivory back? After all this time?"

Thumps tried the coffee. It was the standard stuff hotels and resorts left in rooms to show they cared. It was better than hot water, but only just.

"When you see Claire, could you tell her I'll be at the coin show?" Thumps brushed his hand against his pocket, remembered the cellphone. "She can call me at this number."

Along with the coffee packets, the resort had left a notepad in each unit. Thumps wrote the number on the pad. Maybe having a cellphone wasn't a terrible idea.

"Tell her she can reach me any time."

"I'll make sure she gets it," said Scoop. "But I'm not going to be around much longer. Cooley is coming by. He's going to take me to the band office. We're going to set up in the cafeteria."

"Great."

"You know what they want me to do?" Scoop didn't wait for an answer. "They want me to talk about inherited characteristics, especially the physical ones. You know, ears, noses, foreheads, hair patterns, hands. Stuff like that. And the medical stuff as well. Ailments and conditions that can be passed from one generation to another."

"Sounds like fun."

"You know how you go to a large gathering somewhere, and you look across the room and see a guy with big ears, and you say, 'Hey, that's got to be a Small Horn.'"

"You can do that?"

"Not really," said Scoop. "Not with dead accuracy. But you'd be surprised how many physical characteristics are inherited."

"And you're going to collect DNA samples."

"Hope to," said Scoop. "Moses is going to be there. Said he'd lend a hand."

Thumps smiled.

"People don't know what to make of me yet," said Scoop. "But they trust Moses."

Roxanne was waiting for him as he got off the elevator.

"You hear from Claire?"

"Haven't."

"She hasn't called me either," said Roxanne, "so you know it's serious."

Thumps tried to look around Roxanne to see if there was anyone in the dining room who might rescue him.

"Hope you brought your camera."

Thumps took the Fuji out of his pocket. "Right here."

"That's kind of small."

"It is."

"That thing get all of me?"

"It will."

"Okay," said Roxanne. "Where do you want me?"

Thumps had Roxanne stand by one of the windows, so the light caught one side of her face and gave her an air of mystery.

"Mystery's good," said Roxanne. "Lure 'em in close before you pounce."

Thumps shuddered slightly. "How about this one?"

Roxanne looked at the back of the camera. "That'll have to do."

"Great."

"Can you send it to my phone?"

Thumps wasn't sure how Roxanne had been able to formulate that question. He certainly didn't have an answer.

"You want me to send this photo from this camera to your phone?"

"You got a problem with that?"

Roxanne's voice had shifted into a lower register. In the distance, Thumps could hear bombs dropping and the faint whine of mortar rounds falling to earth.

"Not sure how to do that," said Thumps, "but I'll find out."

"My eight-year-old niece can do that."

Not mortars. Howitzers. Definitely howitzers.

"By the end of day," said Thumps. "You'll have it by end of day."

Roxanne nodded, rubbed her hands together. "And if you hear from Claire, I better be the first number you dial."

THUMPS WAS ON his way to the dining room when he was suddenly caught between a rock and a hard place.

"Mr. Lukin would like a word," said the rock.

The two bodyguards. Much larger close up.

"He'd like a word now," said the hard place.

"Sure."

"We're going to take you to his suite."

"I'm Thumps," said Thumps. "Thumps DreadfulWater."

"We know," said the rock.
"Kinda funny name," said the hard place.
"And you are?"
"I'm Jeremy," said the rock. "He's William."
Thumps nodded. "They call you Bill?"
"No," said William.
"Okay," said Thumps. "All good."

THUMPS WASN'T SURPRISED that Boris Lukin had reserved the penthouse. The view was priceless. He wanted to ask Lukin what the place cost a night.

"More than you can afford," said Lukin, reading his mind.

Boris Lukin was also larger up close. Dark-complected with thick black hair and black eyes. Thick chest. His arms hung at his sides as though they were too heavy to lift.

"Would you like some coffee?"

Thumps held up a hand.

"It's not the shit the hotel leaves in the room." Lukin lifted a finger. "William, get the man a proper cup."

"Yes, Mr. Lukin."

Lukin sat down on the sofa, motioned for Thumps to do the same.

"So, I know a bit about you, and you probably know a bit about me," said Lukin, "and knowing a bit about someone is generally dangerous."

"You want cream and sugar?" said William.

"Black," said Thumps.

"You see," said Lukin. "Now I know more. You take your coffee black. That tells me a great deal. I take my coffee black as well. So we have that in common."

"Pals?"

"No," said Lukin. "You think that I am a criminal. That was my father, and I am his son, and the reputation of the one is often passed on to the other. Do you understand what I'm saying?"

"Nope."

Lukin smiled. "Mr. DreadfulWater is a humorist."

Thumps tried the coffee. It was surprisingly good.

"You have questions you would like to ask me," said Lukin. "So, ask."

Thumps took another sip of the coffee. It wasn't just good, it was great.

"You know the FBI is following you."

There was a postcard on the table next to a book. The image on the postcard was of a bald eagle in flight.

"Of course," said Lukin. "Special Agent Zarina Benoit. Rather young, rather new in the field. Normally, they send more senior agents at me."

"Did you drug her?"

"I heard about that. Most unfortunate."

"Not an answer."

"Do I look like a stupid man?" said Lukin. "The FBI is watching me, and I'm going to go after one of their agents? Why would I bother?"

Thumps leaned over to get a better look at the bird on the card.

"To get her out of the way."

"Out of the way of what? I'm here for the coin show. And to see old friends. Nothing more."

"You don't mind if I don't believe you."

"Certainly not," said Lukin. "It's a free country. You can believe what you like."

Lukin picked up the postcard, slipped it into the book. "Do you know Fuljenz's work on double-eagle gold coins?"

"Nope."

"Published in 2002. This one is on the Type II coins, 1866 to 1876," said Lukin. "He also has one on the Type IIIs and one on Indian gold coins of the twentieth century. That one might interest you."

"Because I'm Indian."

"More coffee?"

Thumps couldn't help but enjoy the coffee and the view. He was tempted to ask if there were any doughnuts nearby.

"I had nothing to do with Agent Benoit. You have my word on that."

"Mr. Lukin's word is good," said William. "You don't get better."

"Will you be at the opening?"

"Yes," said Thumps, "I suspect I will."

Lukin rose off the sofa and went to the sliding doors. "Then I suspect I will see you there."

WILLIAM AND JEREMY rode with Thumps on the elevator. The doors opened. Thumps got out. The two men stayed where they were.

"Mr. Lukin likes his privacy," said William.

"That's our job," said Jeremy.

"I imagine you're good at it," said Thumps.

"Yes," said William. "I imagine we are."

18

Thumps stood by the bank of elevators and took stock of his situation.

For starters, he now had a gun that he didn't want to carry, a badge he didn't want to wear, and a cellphone he didn't want to use.

Along with an anxious Archie Kousoulas, an injured FBI agent, a friend whose wife was slipping into dementia, and a lover who was in danger of losing her child.

The good news—if there was any—was that he had little control over the people part. Archie was always anxious. Benoit was in the hospital. Cruz would make sure she got the best of care. Duke would do the best he could for Macy. And Claire was doing what Claire always did. Pull back into herself and lock everyone else out.

That left the coin dealers. *Ready or not*, Thumps thought to himself, *here I come*.

THERE WAS A sign near the reception desk that gave the time and place of the exhibition.

Six o'clock. The Crowfoot Room.

But in the meantime, where would one find a gaggle of nefarious coin dealers prior to a show? Thumps came up with at least three possibilities. They could be in their rooms, relaxing. They could be in the

Crowfoot Room, helping Archie with the final preparations. Or they could be in the bar, swapping stories.

In the bar, swapping stories was the correct answer.

Atticus Poe spotted him as soon as he came in, waved him over. Katheryn Souto and Emily Hunter were sitting next to each other. Otto Myers and Nicodemus Eliopoulos were holding down the other side of the table.

"Sit," said Poe. "You're just in time."

"Otto was telling us about the new store he's opening in Dallas," said Souto.

"Risky, risky," said Hunter. "Everything's internet today."

"Only high end," said Myers. "Very exclusive. People with money like to sit in comfort and look at the coins."

"And you'll do house calls?"

"Of course," said Myers. "Full service for the serious coin collector."

"Otto is tired of Salt Lake City," said Nico. "He should come to Athens. Greece is quite exciting these days."

"There's money to be made in Salt Lake," said Myers, "but the serious collectors are in Texas."

"What he means," said Souto, "is the folks in Utah don't want to pay his prices."

"My prices are fair."

Poe tapped a spoon on the table. "I don't think Mr. DreadfulWater is much interested in shop talk."

"I'm interested in the FBI following Boris Lukin," said Hunter.

"Is it true?" asked Myers. "Is the FBI following Boris?"

Thumps tried playing dumb. "Where did you hear that?"

Hunter smiled. "Boris told me."

"Couldn't happen to a nicer man," said Souto.

"I also heard that the FBI agent who was watching Boris was attacked," said Hunter. "Is that true?"

So much for dumb.

"You'd have to talk to the sheriff."

"'I shot the sheriff,'" sang Hunter, "'but—'"

"Once was funny," said Souto.

"Did Boris attack this FBI person?" asked Nico.

"A woman," said Hunter. "The FBI has women agents."

"The coin business has women dealers," said Poe.

"And is the better for it," said Souto.

"Please, we mustn't fight." Nico turned to Thumps. "Tell us more about this FBI agent and Boris."

"The deputy here thinks that Boris is responsible," said Hunter.

"You certainly seem to know a great deal about Lukin's business," said Souto.

"Meaning?"

"Nothing," said Souto. "Just an observation."

"Let us go back to Boris," said Nico. "Do you think Boris would do such a thing?"

"Why not," said Poe. "We've all dealt with the man."

"This is true," said Nico.

It was an opening that Thumps couldn't pass up. "What's true?"

"That the man is a crook," said Souto. "His father was a crook. The son is a crook."

"Another word for successful," said Hunter.

"Surely you're not having an affair with him," said Souto.

"Are we jealous?"

"We are not."

Poe tapped his spoon on the table, loudly this time. "Interesting as all this is, I think Mr. DreadfulWater is asking what we know about Boris Lukin."

Hunter sat back, her arms folded against her chest. "And it's his business because?"

Thumps fumbled in his pocket, came up with the badge, lay it on the table.

"I thought you were a photographer."

"That was yesterday," said Nico. "Today our photographer has become a policeman."

Hunter tilted her head. "How do we even know that thing is real?"

"Do you have a gun?" asked Myers.

"In my car," said Thumps. "And I have handcuffs in the trunk."

"Well," said Poe. "This certainly beats Otto and his new store."

Thumps looked around the table. "Lukin isn't here with you?"

"Boris?" Poe chuckled. "Boris wouldn't be caught dead with any of us."

"Except perhaps Emily," said Souto.

"Oh, piss off," said Hunter.

"I think what Mr. DreadfulWater is asking," said Nico, "is what we can tell him about Mr. Lukin."

"Would appreciate that," said Thumps. "Always good to know who everyone is."

"You still think we're obfuscating," said Poe. "Don't you."

"No," said Hunter, "he thinks we're lying."

Thumps smiled and waited.

"I will start," said Nico. "I am the oldest, and I have known Boris the longest."

"Boris is a crook," said Hunter. "Blah, blah, blah."

"Is much more complicated than that," said Nico.

NICO BEGAN THE conversation, but he was quickly joined by the rest of the dealers. For the next hour, Thumps sat back and listened to a running recitation of Lukin's life, business and personal, that had more turns and twists than the indoor waterslide in Billings.

Thumps tried to stay awake, but it was difficult.

"Boris and his father had one thing in common," said Poe. "They both lived life large. You know how kids like to use their phones to take photos of everything. Food, activities, friends."

"Nudies," said Hunter. "Bowel movements. Cock shots."

"That's the Lukin family before cellphones," said Poe. "Everything they did was on public display. Newspapers started calling Boris 'Limelight Lukin.'"

"Very different from Barca," said Nico.

Thumps blinked away the lethargy. "Barca?"

"Hannibal Barca," said Nico. "Arkady Lukin's elusive twin."

"Elusive, yes," said Souto. "Hardly a twin."

"Katheryn is right," said Nico. "Barca was nothing like Arkady or his son. Very reserved. Very private. You can find thousands of photographs of Arkady and Boris at galas and political rallies and celebrity parties. Only a handful of Barca, and most of those taken when he was a younger man."

"He was a coin dealer?"

"One of the best," said Poe. "The Lukins got all the press, but if you wanted a hard-to-find coin in mint condition and you wanted to buy it for a fair price, you went to Hannibal Barca."

"The two knew each other."

"They were in competition with each other," said Otto. "There are only so many high-grade gold coins in the world and only so many buyers with deep pockets."

"Cut to the chase," said Hunter. "Lukin Sr. killed Barca."

"We don't know that," said Myers. "Barca just disappeared."

"Disappeared," said Hunter, "as in dead."

"One of the unsolved mysteries of the coin world," said Poe. "One day Hannibal Barca was there, and the next day he wasn't."

"Barca was never a public figure," said Nico. "Not like Arkady and Boris. No one even knew where he lived. Some said Paris. Others London. He was rumoured to be in Montevideo, Moscow, Rome, and Madrid."

Poe took out his cellphone, swiped his finger across the screen. "This is him at the Paradiso in Barcelona."

The photograph showed a slender, austere man with a strong chin and deep-set eyes. He was standing at the bar, looking directly into the camera, as though he could see past the lens to something in the far distance.

"I met him once," said Souto. "In Istanbul. When my husband was alive. He was quiet. He was polite."

"And he then disappeared," said Nico. "And that was that."

Thumps stared at the photograph. There was something about the man that seemed vaguely familiar.

"Did he have any family? A wife? Children?"

"No," said Poe. "He was alone."

"I heard that he had a child," said Nico. "A daughter. His personal life was Barca's great secret."

"Or it was a rumour like so many of the rumours about Barca," said Myers. "You could fill a large room with the rumours about the man."

"Just before he vanished, he and Lukin were supposed to be brokering a deal for an extremely rare gold coin," said Poe.

"And?"

Poe turned his hands palm up. "Supposedly the deal went sideways."

Thumps turned to Hunter. "You said that Arkady Lukin killed Barca."

"Did I?"

"I heard it was Boris," said Nico. "To impress his father. But much of what you hear is not to be believed."

Thumps handed the cell back to Poe. "Which is why Boris isn't joining you?"

"That and he's an arrogant asshole," said Souto.

"And you're Mother Teresa," said Hunter.

"Do you know Dante?" said Nico. "The 'Inferno'? The circles of hell?"

"Violence, fraud, and treachery." Poe smiled. "What Nico is trying to say is that we don't run in the same circles as Boris."

"Doesn't want to be seen with the likes of us," said Myers.

"He's no better or worse than the rest of us," said Hunter. "He's just richer."

"And Hannibal Barca," said Thumps. "No one knows what happened to him?"

Thumps felt a rush come up behind him, as though he was about to be passed by a large transport truck.

"There you are."

Archie Kousoulas. The little Greek was quivering with anxiety.

"Why are you here?"

"We are drinking," said Nico.

"And sharing stories with Deputy DreadfulWater," said Hunter.

"Do that later." Archie grabbed Nico by the elbow and helped him out of the chair. "It's time for the photograph."

"Groan-fuck-groan," said Hunter.

"It's a nice idea," said Souto. "We don't get together that often."

"It's for the newsletter," said Archie. "We need a photo for the newsletter."

Thumps stayed seated while the rest of the dealers got to their feet and followed Archie out of the bar. Poe held back for a moment.

"Just to finish the story," said Poe. "All that was twenty years ago. So, if Arkady Lukin had anything to do with Barca's disappearance, the answer died with the old man."

19

It was only when he stood to leave and caught a glimpse of his reflection in the mirror behind the bar that Thumps realized he wasn't dressed for the upcoming social event.

Jeans. Work shirt. Runners. Windbreaker.

If he showed up to the opening of the exhibition dressed like this, Archie would never let him hear the end of it.

Two hours to go. Okay. Plenty of time to go home, catch a quick shower, change into something more appropriate. Maybe Claire would be back with good news, and they could take up where they had left off.

LATE AFTERNOON ON the high plains is all slants and angles. In the heat of the day, with the sun overhead, all the contours of the land are flattened, the colours bleached out like old bone. But then the light drops down like a pitcher throwing sidearm, and the features spring up and come to life. The shadows deepen, stretch out across the bunchgrass steppes, and the tops of the yellow willow, and the chokecherries burst into flame.

The panorama should have cheered him. On other days, Thumps would have pulled over, stopped to enjoy the light and the land and the sky. But today, he kept his eyes on the road, his hands on the wheel, his foot on the gas.

CRUZ'S MUSCLE CAR was parked at the curb. The ninja assassin was in the living room, on his cellphone. Freeway and Cookie were curled up on the sofa beside him.

"I'm on hold."

Thumps made a *who* with his mouth.

"Hospital," said Cruz. "Zee's awake."

Thumps wandered into the bedroom, thumbed through the possibilities in the closet. Not a lot to choose from. Which should have made the choosing easy. Instead, it reminded him of his truncated life.

When was the last time he had been to a party or some big to-do? In the last year, how many times had he taken Claire out to dinner? Three. That he knew the answer to that question was disheartening enough. That it was only three was downright depressing. What was he doing with his life?

The sports coat would have to do. The pale green shirt looked to have been ironed recently, and the colour went with most everything, didn't it? Charcoal slacks and his only pair of leather shoes. He would have liked for them to have been black.

The European look. Somewhere, someone had told him that Europeans wore brown shoes with dark slacks.

CRUZ WAS STILL on the phone when Thumps returned to the living room.

"Anything she needs," he was saying. "And under no circumstances are you to allow her to leave the hospital."

Whoever was on the other end of the line wasn't being co-operative.

"Don't give a shit about patient's rights. Put her back in a coma if you have to."

Cruz smacked the phone on the table.

"You believe it?"

"So, she's going to be okay?"

"Still groggy and disoriented," said Cruz. "They want to keep her until all the shit is out of her system."

"Probably smart."

"Evidently, she has other ideas."

"You wouldn't stay in the hospital."

Cruz rubbed Cookie and the big kitten began purring. "Do these two do anything other than eat and sleep?"

"Not much."

"You been to Zee's room?"

"Not yet."

"I've got it locked down," said Cruz. "Going to go back up there tonight. See if I can figure out what happened."

"What about the FBI?"

"They're sending a forensics team from Seattle. Should be here tomorrow morning."

"Shouldn't you wait for them?"

"Absolutely," said Cruz. "That's exactly what the agent in charge told me to do."

"I have to go to the gala opening of the coin show."

"How long do we need?" said Cruz. "It's a one-bedroom condo."

"I have to go to the gala opening of the coin show."

"And you will," said Cruz, "just as soon as we do her room."

Thumps held his arms out. "How do I look?"

"Great, so long as the party is in 1956." Cruz got off the sofa. "I have to stop at the hospital, maybe handcuff Zee to the bed. I'll meet you back at Buffalo Mountain."

"Tossing the room before the forensics team gets here is a bad idea."

"It's called taking the initiative," said Cruz. "The green shirt is a bad idea."

BY THE TIME Thumps changed, Cruz was gone. Freeway and Cookie were turning circles in the kitchen in a two-cat demonstration to show that their bowls were empty.

"The bowls are empty," Thumps told the cats, "because you ate all the food I just gave you."

The cats kept up the chanting, raised their placards on high, vowed to keep the protest going until there was a change of regime.

Thumps was unmoved. "You see me get a doughnut every time I want one?"

It was a poor analogy, but Thumps didn't care. And neither did the cats.

THE FIRST PART of the plan was to drive back to the resort and wait in the parking lot until Cruz arrived. Except when he got there, Cruz was standing by his car, looking annoyed.

"Where you been?"

"I had to feed the cats."

"*Pendejo*," said Cruz, "I fed them."

"What happened with Benoit?"

"She was gone."

"What?"

"I knew I should have handcuffed her to the bed."

"Where is she?"

BENOIT WAS WAITING for them in the condo. She was stretched out on the sofa, looking very much the worse for wear.

"What took you two so long?"

"You look like shit," said Cruz. "You're supposed to be in the hospital."

There was a movie on the flat screen that Thumps recognized immediately. *Avatar*. One of the worst movies ever made.

"Why is the sound off?"

"It's a really stupid movie," said Thumps. "White guy saves the natives once again."

"Is that on pay-per-view? The FBI paying for entertainment?"

Benoit gave Cruz the finger. "It got good reviews. How was I to know?"

Thumps smiled. Given the FBI's shaky relationship with Native people, the thought of the bureau paying for a shitty movie about colonialization was a small pleasure, but a pleasure nonetheless.

Benoit reached out with her foot and touched the bottle of wine on the coffee table, next to a large fruit basket.

"I'm guessing that's our culprit."

Thumps picked up the card that had come with the fruit. "Compliments of the management."

"I checked with the front desk, and management did not send up either item."

Cruz picked up the bottle. "They say how this got here?"

"Hey," said Benoit. "Crime scene. Use gloves."

"Let me guess," said Cruz. "Someone left the basket and the bottle at the front desk, asked that it be delivered to your room."

"Lucky guess."

"They say who?"

"All by internet and Visa," said Benoit. "We'll run the address and the card, but I'm guessing it will be a dead end."

"So, we know how," said Thumps. "We just don't know the why or the who."

"Pretty easy," said Benoit. "I'm watching Lukin. He doesn't like it, so he tries to put me out of commission."

"Why?"

"Maybe he just likes drugging FBI agents."

"Thumps is right," said Cruz. "Lukin is no fool. Why would he want that kind of heat? He does his best to stay off your radar."

Benoit closed her eyes. "You have a better explanation?"

"Not yet," said Cruz.

"Then you two can go and let me get some rest."

There were apples and grapes and bananas in the basket, along with some individually wrapped cheeses, a box of crackers, and a chocolate bar. All of which reminded Thumps that he hadn't had dinner.

"Does the name Hannibal Barca mean anything to you?"

"Sounds made up," said Cruz.

"Who is he?" said Benoit.

"Do a search. See what you can find." Thumps checked his watch. "I have to get to a coin show."

"Take Cruz with you," said Benoit. "I got one mother. I don't need another."

The Crowfoot Room was easy enough to find. All Thumps had to do was follow the people, the noise, and the smell of food in hot trays.

Cruz stopped Thumps just before he got to the double doors. "So, who's Hannibal Barca?"

"A name that came up," said Thumps. "Maybe something. Probably nothing."

"You asked Zee to run it."

"The feds have better resources than the sheriff," said Thumps. "And she needs something to do."

"And what are we going to do?"

Thumps took a deep breath. The food for the gala opening was from Archie's restaurant. He could smell the dolmades and the lamb keftedes.

"I don't know about you," said Thumps, "but I'm going to eat."

20

Thumps had been to any number of social events during his time as a cop and a photographer. Benefits for social causes, art openings, political rallies, celebrations of one sort or another. For a number of years before COVID, Archie had hosted readings by writers who were passing through on their way to somewhere else.

All of these occasions had a common look and feel. Ordinary people dressed up for the moment, milling around a large room with a glass of wine in their hand, chatting with one another and then moving on, a sort of musical chairs where there were no chairs to begin with and where no one was encouraged to sit.

And food. Not a full meal. Bits and pieces of food, small, delicate offerings that were more for show than sustenance.

Thumps made it to the food table before Archie caught him.

"About time you got here."

"I was sheriffing," said Thumps.

"That's not a verb," said Archie. "You sound like those talking heads on the sports channel who have decided that 'to football' is a proper infinitive."

"The dolmades are terrific."

"And this is why you have eight of them on your plate?"

"I'm hungry."

"And six keftedes?"

"They're small."

"They're small for a reason."

"Okay."

"They have to last all evening."

"I'm diabetic," said Thumps. "My blood sugars are low."

"Then stay away from the flourless chocolate torte."

Thumps helped himself to the cheese squares. "There's flourless chocolate torte?"

The mayor was here, along with most of the council. Beth Mooney and Gabby Santucci were in a corner, talking with a large man Thumps didn't recognize. Ora Mae Foreman was working a circuit through the assembled guests, handing out business cards as though they were door prizes.

"Looks like it's a success."

"Of course it's a success," said Archie.

"And there aren't any problems." Thumps speared a keftede with a toothpick. "So, you worried for nothing."

"What about Agent Benoit?"

"She's out of the hospital."

"Not what I meant," said Archie. "No one tries to poison a federal agent for shits and giggles."

"Cruz has it under control."

"He shoot someone?"

"I'm going to look at the coins," said Thumps. "If that's okay."

"Just stay away from the food."

ATTICUS POE WAS standing at one of the displays.

"A very nice uncirculated 1876 Liberty Head twenty-dollar gold piece," said Poe. "Minted one hundred years after the country was formed."

"Uncirculated?" said Thumps.

"Are you interested in how coins are graded?"

"Not really."

"Very wise," said Poe. "And here is an 1854 Indian Princess Head three-dollar gold. Quite rare."

"Expensive?"

"Not really," said Poe. "This one has wear."

"And everyone wants a perfect coin."

Poe touched the side of his nose. "Wouldn't you?"

Thumps looked at the coins in the case. "I can't tell the difference."

"Most people can't," said Poe. "Even the people who collect. That's why there are companies that grade coins and tell us what they're worth."

"You're kidding."

"Not at all," said Poe. "Why do you think one bottle of good wine costs a hundred dollars and another bottle of good wine costs a thousand?"

"So, it's all arbitrary?"

"Certainly not," said Poe. "There are a myriad of factors at work that give an object value. With coins, it's most often rarity and condition. And then there is desire."

"Two people wanting the same thing."

"You see," said Poe, "you already understand the Tao of collecting. Imagine two or more people with unlimited resources wanting the same item. And now imagine that there is only one such item in the entire world."

"The value goes up."

"The *perceived* value goes up." Poe straightened his jacket. "*Perceived* value and *real* value are myths. And yet both exist. If only for a moment or a year or a generation, sometimes a millennium. Coins, paintings, cars, yachts, watches, diamonds, action figures, non-fungible tokens, a single gram of antimatter. We like to imagine that value is constant and ever increasing, but in fact value is like the weather. Sunshine followed by storms followed by calm followed by a flooded basement and trees crashing through your roof."

Thumps leaned over the case, found himself wondering what the

Indian Princess three-dollar gold piece would cost him should he want to own it.

"In 1994, Bill Gates bought Leonardo da Vinci's *Codex Leicester* for thirty-one million dollars. Three years later, the document was scanned so now anyone can read it. Is it less valuable or is it more valuable?"

"I'm not sure I care."

"Let's not be truculent," said Poe. "We assign value to most everything in life. And if someone is willing to pay the price, then that becomes the thing's worth."

Thumps wondered if he could make another run at the food table.

"How much do you charge for one of your photographs?"

Maybe another dolmade. Or two.

"Are you familiar with Andreas Gursky's *Rhein II*?" Poe took a glass of wine off a passing tray, tipped it as though he was about to make a toast. "Look it up."

THUMPS MADE HIS way through the show, looked at the coins, then found a comfortable corner to settle in. Emily Hunter was wearing a tight black dress that reminded Thumps of a sock.

But in a good way.

Otto Myers was uncomfortable in a suit that was half a size too small, though perhaps it was not the fault of the suit. Katheryn Souto was in business attire, a dark grey pantsuit, smartly tailored.

He imagined that she had reached an age where cleavage and calves were no longer the currency they had once been and was relieved to be out of debt.

Nico Eliopoulos was predictable in a dark suit, a white shirt open at the neck, and a heavy gold chain. He was starting to bald, but the man had a full chest of hair that sprang out of his shirt like prairie grass after a spring rain.

Rawat and Stas were nowhere to be seen. Neither was Al. Or Wutty and the gang. He had expected that they would show. Who else wasn't here? The room was full, but it felt like a puzzle with a piece missing.

"Pretend you don't know me."

Thumps had never seen Cruz dressed up before, but here he was. Suit, soft grey shirt, tie. He had slicked his hair back, had found a pair of glasses that made him look like a waiter at a restaurant that only hired struggling actors.

"You got eyes on Lukin?"

And there it was. The missing piece.

"Cruz?" Archie popped out of the crowd, a glass of wine in one hand. "What are you doing here?"

Cruz backed up a step. "Pretend you don't know me."

"What?"

"He told me the same thing," said Thumps. "He's trying to be incognito."

"You look like a struggling actor."

"If Lukin comes in and sees the three of us together," said Cruz, "he'll be able to do the math."

"Nico says Lukin wouldn't be caught dead at a show like this," said Archie. "Man likes to be the centre of attention. Likes the spot on him. And there's not enough wattage in this room to run a flashlight."

"Where is he?"

"Probably up in his suite," said Archie. "Room service, pay-per-view TV, watch the river in the dark."

The dealers were all standing together in a semicircle. Hunter, Souto, Myers, Eliopoulos, and Poe. As though they had gathered together for a singalong.

Thumps watched them for a moment. "You sure he's still here?"

"Hasn't checked out," said Archie, "if that's what you mean."

"He didn't come for the coin show. He didn't come for the company."

"He's waiting," said Cruz.

"For what?"

"Something to happen," said Cruz. "That's what they're all waiting for."

"Soon as you two figure out what that something is," said Archie, "you let me know. In the meantime, stay away from the food. That's for the paying guests."

CRUZ RETURNED WITH a plate of food. "He can be an annoying little shit."

"You have no idea," said Thumps.

"But he can cook."

"Is some of that for me?"

"Get your own," said Cruz.

"You going to check up on Lukin?"

"I'd rather know where he is than not know."

"You could call his room."

"I could."

"Or you could let yourself in and snoop around."

"Which would be illegal, not to mention foolish." Cruz ate a keftede whole. "If he is in his room, he won't be amused."

"Not to mention Hulk One and Hulk Two."

"The casino." Cruz handed Thumps his empty plate. "If he's not in his room, he'll be in the casino."

Thumps stayed where he was. From here he could watch the people flow back and forth amidst the gold coins glowing in the display cabinets. Maybe he'd buy a gold coin. One of the small ones with an Indian head on the front and a buffalo on the back. Like the old silver nickels. A coin that had no value other than its weight in gold. Just to have one. No better reason than that.

He had just dismissed this fancy and decided to make his way back to the food table when he realized that Souto and Myers, Hunter and Eliopoulos, along with Mr. Atticus Poe, had vanished.

21

The dealers had been standing in a knot, looking like a small herd of ungulates on the graze, and now they were gone. As though they had all moved at the same time in search of greener pastures. Thumps made his way through the people, certain he would find the gang somewhere in the room. They couldn't have gotten far. And yet they weren't here.

Perhaps Cruz was right. Perhaps the casino was the answer. The dealers dealt in money. The casino dealt in money. It seemed a perfect match, so long as you ignored the obvious.

That collecting coins and losing your shirt had little in common.

Thumps was in the hallway, heading for the lobby, when the sheriff appeared in front of him.

"DreadfulWater."

"You run into the dealers?"

"The coin guys?" Duke tried to find the right word. "And coin . . . women."

"They all disappeared at the same time."

"Abducted by aliens," said Duke. "I've read about this."

"Lukin seems to be among the missing as well."

"The gala still going?" said Duke.

"Just left it."

"Is there any food?"

THUMPS STOOD NEXT to the food table and watched Duke help himself to everything.

"The meatballs are my favourite," said the sheriff.

"Keftedes."

"And the things in grape leaves are pretty good too."

"Dolmades."

"That's the nice thing about good food," said Duke, "it doesn't matter what you call it."

Thumps could stay with Duke and watch him eat or he could go to the casino and try to find Cruz.

"Is food all you two think about?"

Archie pushed his way between Duke and the table.

Duke licked his fingers. "Food from your restaurant?"

"Of course the food's from my restaurant. Why would it be from another restaurant?"

"Well, it's really good."

"That's because it's free," said Archie. "Stolen food always tastes better."

Duke looked around the room. "Good turnout."

"Don't change the subject."

"And nothing's happened."

"Yet. Nothing has happened yet." Archie searched the room. "Where's Nico? Where are Myers and Souto and Hunter and Poe?"

Duke devoured another keftede. "Abducted by aliens."

"That would get you off the hook," said Archie. "Wouldn't it?"

"Cruz thinks Lukin may be in the casino," said Thumps. "Could be the other dealers are there as well."

Archie took Duke's empty plate. "Then why don't you two go over there and help him. It's a big place. Three sets of eyes are better than one."

"I'm hungry."

"So, eat at the casino."

"If I eat at the casino," said the sheriff, "I'll have to pay for it myself."

"Exactly," said Archie.

When he was a cop, Thumps had been to a great many of the casinos that the small rancherias in California had set up as an economic base for the tribes in the area. Lucky 7 and Elk Valley near the Oregon border. Hidden Oaks, Rolling Hills, Colusa and Red Hawk farther south, along with Cache Creek and Thunder Valley.

The most distinctive thing about such casinos was that there was nothing distinctive. They were all exactly the same. Thumps suspected you could be dropped into a casino almost anywhere in the world and you would have no way of knowing where you were.

Casinos didn't have windows. They didn't have clocks. Everything was in dim shadows so you could pretend that no one could see you or what you were doing. Half-dressed women wandered through the slot machines and the blackjack tables taking orders for free drinks that rarely came.

No music. Just the sound of the machines and the shouts of joy and despair. And the stale smell of something that had been locked up and left in the dark far too long.

Duke hitched his pants. "Vernon Rockland has been trying to get a casino up at Shadow Ranch ever since he built the place."

"You see Cruz?"

"Hell," said Duke, "I can barely see you."

Thumps and the sheriff stood to one side, waited for their eyes to adjust to the dimness.

"They turn up the lights," said Duke, "would make our job easier."

"But they're not going to do that."

"Don't expect they will."

"If they did," said Thumps, "people might see that they're in hell and leave."

"Purgatory," said Duke. "Not hot enough for hell."

Somewhere in the depths of the casino, there were bells ringing and people shouting.

Duke pinched his nose. "And what the blazes is that smell?"

Thumps took the left side. Duke took the right.

"Work the floor," said the sheriff. "Meet in the middle."

"And if we find them? What's that going to tell us?"

"Tell us the aliens didn't get them after all."

THUMPS WORKED HIS way past the roulette wheel and the keno desk. He stopped to watch the action at the craps table, watched a man set a stack of chips on the green felt, watched as the croupier dragged the bet off the table with a long stick, watched as the man pushed out another stack, as though he were in a trance.

Thumps wasn't sure how much each chip was worth. And he didn't realize how long he had been standing there watching the man lose money, until a young woman in a skimpy costume floated by, asked him if he wanted a free drink.

Boris Lukin was nowhere to be seen. Neither were any of the other dealers. In fact, Thumps didn't recognize anyone. Chinook wasn't that large. He didn't know everyone in town, but he would have expected to see one or two familiar faces.

Maybe aliens were the answer after all.

Duke didn't have any better luck. "Don't think our friends are here."

"Did you see Cruz?"

"Nope," said Duke. "No Cruz."

"What say we get out of this hell," said Thumps.

"How'd Dante do it?"

"He and Virgil climbed up Lucifer's leg."

"Up his leg? What'd they do when they got to his groin?"

"Poem skips over that."

"You know," said Duke, "something simple like 'straight ahead' or 'off to the left' would have done the trick."

ALONG WITH NO windows and no clocks and not enough light to see where you were going or what you were doing, casinos did not have exit signs. Thumps could see the reasoning. Once they had you trapped inside, they did not want you to leave.

"That was fun." Duke stood in the parking lot, the stars bright overhead. "Wasn't sure I'd ever see the sky again. Good thing I have the My Location app on my phone."

"Still can't believe that worked."

"Technology to the rescue."

"I'll go back to the resort," said Thumps, "see if the gang has materialized."

"Don't call me unless someone dies," said Duke. "I got to get back to Macy."

"How's that going?"

"Her sister is staying with us. Going to look after Macy while I'm working." Duke stared out into the dark. "What's happening with Claire and Ivory?"

Thumps shook his head. "No idea. Ivory's uncle and his fiancée have her for the weekend."

"Just the weekend?"

"That seems to be the issue."

"The hell you say."

THUMPS WENT BACK to the gala. It was winding down, fewer people in the room. No Boris Lukin. No Katheryn Souto or Otto Myers, Nico Eliopoulos or Emily Hunter. No Atticus Poe. He couldn't prove it, but Thumps imagined that wherever they were, they were all together.

So far as Thumps could figure, the only thing they had in common was each other.

Thumps thought about calling Claire's room, just in case she had returned, but he didn't want to wake Scoop with questions that couldn't be answered.

THUMPS WAS STANDING by his car when a Ford half-ton pulled up alongside.

"Hoping I'd catch you." Cooley Small Elk was behind the wheel.

"Just heading home."

"It's late," said Cooley, "but I figured you'd want to know."

Thumps waited.

"Moses is in the hospital. We had to get the ambulance."

"He all right?"

"Don't know yet," said Cooley. "He's tough, and he's old, but after a while tough may not be enough."

"Shit."

"Can't visit him until tomorrow. Thought you would like to know."

"I'll make sure to go see him."

"He'll like that," said Cooley. "Tell him a couple of his favourite jokes, cheer him up. Maybe bring him a peach, if you can find any good ones this time of year."

"How bad is he?"

"He got dizzy," said Cooley. "Then he fell."

"And?"

"So, now his hip hurts. Scoop's staying with him in his room. Told the nurse she was his granddaughter."

"And the nurse believed her?"

"Think she was happy for the help."

"You got a room number?"

"Remember," said Cooley, "his favourite jokes and a ripe peach."

22

Thumps got home just before midnight. Freeway and Cookie were nowhere to be found. This wasn't the first time he had come home to an empty house, but tonight the bungalow felt bleaker than usual.

No doubt the cats were having a sleepover at Dixie's place with Pops the giant Komondor. A kind of animal play date. Thumps checked the spare bedroom and the closet, just in case mother and son were playing hide and seek.

No cats.

And no Cruz. Cruz would be up at Buffalo Mountain, looking after Agent Benoit. Duke would be at home, trying to make sense of what was happening to his world. Moses was in the hospital with Scoop by his side. And Claire was wherever Claire was, doing whatever Claire did.

Maybe she'd tell him.

He didn't feel lonely. Not exactly. More like the kid not chosen and left on the playground with nowhere to go.

He brushed his teeth, hung his shirt and slacks on hangers, crawled into bed, put the cellphone on the nightstand. In case Claire called and asked him to ride to the rescue. He couldn't imagine it happening, but he wanted to be ready if a shield and sword were needed.

AL'S WAS BUSY. Wutty and Russell and Jimmy were back and in their usual places. Al was prowling the counter with her coffee pot at the ready.

Thumps had to wait for a stool to open up.

"How was the big gala?"

"Great," said Thumps. "Figured I'd see you there."

"That's what I figured as well."

Thumps could feel a story on its way.

"Remember that amphibious thingy Wutty was bringing back from Helena?"

"*Little Otter?*"

"Well," said Al, "he brought it back."

"Okay."

"You want breakfast?" said Al. "Or do you want to hear the story?"

"Is that a real choice?"

"Not if you want breakfast."

Wutty waved a fork in the air, shouted, "Not my fault. Could have happened to anybody."

Al poured Thumps a cup of coffee.

"Wutty takes it out to Red Tail Lake, talks us all into joining him on the maiden voyage."

"Us all?"

"Stas and Rawat," said Al. "Me and the three stooges."

"Wutty, Russell, and Jimmy?"

"You know what a transom drain plug is?"

"Not a clue."

"Neither did Wutty."

"Could have happened to anyone," Wutty shouted.

Al shook her head. "Evidently, you're supposed to put the plug in before you launch the land and sea bus."

"It sank?"

"Not right away," said Al. "It waited until we were out in the middle of the lake."

"You could have drowned."

"Not likely," said Al. "We had life preservers, and it's not all that deep in that part of the lake."

"So, the bus sank."

"Only transportation we had," said Al. "By the time we walked to the general store, we were wet and tired, and it was late. How was the party?"

"There was free food," said Thumps.

"Speaking of which," said Al, "you going to visit Moses at the hospital?"

"Right after I have breakfast."

"That a hint?"

"It is," said Thumps.

"I made a little something for him," said Al. "You can take it up."

"Don't think the doctors are going to want him eating sausages and eggs."

"Oatmeal with apple and dried apricot," said Al. "You should try it some time. Might lose a little weight."

Thumps settled in on the stool and imagined how his day might unfold. Visit Moses, see how he was doing. Go back to Buffalo Mountain, have coffee with Archie, sit through the post-mortem of the gala, maybe remind him that he had been paranoid for nothing.

But first, he needed to call Claire. Thumps fished the cell out of his pocket. He could see where having a phone you could carry with you at all times was convenient. Being able to call Claire while he waited for breakfast was on the plus side of the ledger.

Duke Hockney being able to call him was on the other.

Thumps punched in the number, listened as the phone rang its way to a recorded message that said the person at this address had not set up her mailbox.

Whatever the hell that meant.

"That a cell?"

Thumps quickly tucked the phone back into his pocket.

"Cellphones, digital cameras." Al waved the coffee pot at him. "Next thing you'll be signed up for Hulu."

"Hulu?"

"Don't ask. So, what's happening with Claire?"

"Not answering her phone."

"No news is good news." Al frowned. "Don't know what idiot said that. Most times, no news is generally bad news."

"Don't see my breakfast."

"Everyone is always excited to share good news. 'I got a raise.' 'My kid just got accepted to Stanford.' 'Just bought a new car.' 'Got the final on my divorce.'"

"Al..."

"Whereas we tend to sit on bad news. 'The test came back positive.' 'They're foreclosing on the house.' 'My husband left me.' 'They cancelled *Forensic Files*.'"

"Al..."

"Or her phone may have run out of charge. How's yours?"

"My what?"

"Your cellphone," said Al. "You have to charge them, you know."

"I know that."

"Let Mother see."

Thumps reluctantly took the phone out, set it on the counter.

Al looked at the screen. "Half," she said. "It might last the day, but I wouldn't count on it."

"Breakfast?"

"You know what I say?" Al slapped a hand on the counter. "I say no news is no news."

Thumps tried Claire's number again and got the same message. In the background, he could hear Wutty arguing with Russell and Jimmy about the transom drain plug and who was supposed to have put it in place.

"What we have to do is dive down and put in the plug," said Wutty.

"We meaning you," said Russell.

"I'm not the one who forgot."

"It's your boat," said Jimmy.

"It's not a boat," said Wutty. "It's a Terex ZZ3 Otter."

"Right now," said Russell, "it's a sunken wreck."

"Once the plug is in," said Wutty, "we can pump air into the hold and get it floating again."

Al arrived in the nick of time with breakfast. "This is better than a rerun of *Trauma: Life in the E.R.*"

"Kinda feel sorry for Wutty," said Thumps. "Seems to have more than his share of bad luck."

"That's because he has more than his share of bad ideas," said Al. "You reach Claire?"

Thumps shook his head.

Al set the plate on the counter, turned it so the sausages were facing him. "No news is no news. That's what I say."

Thumps put pepper on his eggs, mixed a little salsa into his hash browns. Had just picked up a piece of toast when he felt the shadow on his shoulder.

"Thumps, my man."

Wutty Youngbeaver was standing next to him, a big smile on his face.

"Today's your lucky day." Wutty spread his arms, as though he were trying to hug the world. "Save the Otter Alliance."

Thumps kept his head down. "Eating breakfast."

"Sure," said Wutty. "You eat, I'll fill you in."

"Like to eat in peace."

"I'm guessing you heard about the little mishap with my amphibian."

Thumps took a bite of the toast.

"Due to unanticipated negligence, no names, my Terex ZZ3 Otter sank in Red Tail."

Thumps tried the eggs. Perfect.

"It's a minor setback," said Wutty. "All we have to do is get her floating again, clean her up, and we're back in business. But first I have to raise a little capital in order to raise the Otter."

"As in Save the Otter Alliance."

"Two hundred and fifty dollars," said Wutty. "That's all it costs to join. And for that, you get two free adventures on the Otter anytime."

Thumps went back to the sausage, cut it into pieces.

"Except peak season, of course."

"I'll pass."

"You know when they say support small business and shop local, they're talking about guys like me?"

The eggs were beginning to get cold. Thumps turned to Wutty.

"Tell you what," said Thumps, "you get Archie Kousoulas and the sheriff to join the alliance, and I'll join."

Wutty's smile faded. "That's exactly what they said."

AL ARRIVED WITH a takeout container. "So, did you join the Save the Otter Club?"

"Is that the oatmeal?"

"It is," said Al. "Tell Moses I said hello."

"Will do."

"Any word from Claire?"

Thumps pushed off the stool, picked up the container.

"You know what I say," said Al. "No news is no news."

23

There were other places Thumps tried to avoid, but hospitals were high on the list. Morgues were at the top, Beth Mooney's morgue in particular. With amusement parks, rock concerts, and all-inclusive vacations firmly in third place.

Moses was on the fourth floor. Scoop was sitting in the chair next to the bed, a photo album on her lap. Cooley was leaning against the wall. There was a metal tray with a juice box, a small bowl of something that looked vaguely like mashed carrots, but probably wasn't, and a cup of green Jell-O.

Thumps hadn't been able to find a peach at the Cash and Carry, but they did have a special on plums from Chile.

"Something from Al's." Thumps put the container on the tray, set the plum next to it.

Moses rubbed his hands. "Is it her special oatmeal?"

"With apples and dried apricots," said Thumps.

"And a plum," said Moses. "This is my lucky day."

Thumps looked at the bowl. "Is that mashed carrots?"

"I was afraid to ask," said Moses.

Thumps took a step back. Another good reason to avoid hospitals.

"Cooley was going to eat the Jell-O," said Scoop, "but he thought you might like it."

Hospital lights tended to bleach the colour out of blood and the life out of skin. Moses looked grey, as though he had been washed too often. His eyes were watery, his lips dry and cracked. There was an IV in his arm.

"How you doing?"

"Pretty good," said Moses. "But I'm not sleeping well."

"Every hour or so," said Cooley, "they wake him up to make sure he's still alive."

"Sometimes they take my blood pressure," said Moses.

"They think it's his heart," said Cooley, "but they're doing other tests as well."

"They wanted to put a tube in me." Moses glanced at Scoop. "I can't tell you where."

"It was a catheter," said Scoop. "They also wanted to do a colonoscopy."

"You don't want to know about that one either," said Moses.

"But you're feeling better."

"The doctors want to keep him for more tests," said Cooley. "His electrolyte levels are kinda low."

"The doctors are worried that I might die," said Moses. "But I'd rather die at home than live here."

Thumps gestured to the album. "Those photos?"

"They are," said Scoop. "Moses and his parents and his siblings."

"My mom and dad," said Moses. "Brothers and sisters. Some of my aunties and uncles are there. Cousins too."

Scoop got up, put the album on the edge of the bed, so Thumps could see the photos.

"Remember I told you about physical characteristics that could be inherited?"

"Sure."

"So, look at these photos." Scoop pointed to several of the more formal portraits. "What do you see?"

"What am I looking at?"

"Earlobes," said Scoop. "See the earlobes on the men?"

"That's an inherited characteristic?"

"Unattached earlobes," said Scoop. "You have dimples. I'll bet your father had dimples."

"I always wanted dimples," said Moses.

"Me too," said Cooley. "All the girls think dimples are cute."

"So, you can tell these guys are all related because they have earlobes?"

"Unattached earlobes," said Scoot. "See mine? They're attached. Whereas Cooley's and Moses's earlobes are unattached."

"That's 'cause we're related," said Cooley.

"Lots of people are going to have unattached earlobes," said Thumps. "They won't all be related."

"Of course not," said Scoop. "You look for other factors as well. Physical traits aren't a science. But they can be some of the indicators to watch for."

"I've always wondered why my earlobes aren't attached," said Moses.

Scoop chuckled. "You didn't even know what they were until today."

"But now that I do know," said Moses, "I'm a little worried."

"I guess having your earlobes attached is a little safer," said Cooley.

Scoop turned to Thumps. "Does this dumb and dumber act fool anyone?"

"Politicians," said Cooley. "We can fool politicians and most lawyers."

"You need help, just let me know."

"Thanks," said Cooley. "But me and Scoop can manage him."

"No one manages me," said Moses. "I'm still tough and scrappy."

"If he gets too scrappy," said Scoop, "we'll just leave him here."

"Okay, you can manage me," said Moses. "I'm not really that tough."

BUFFALO MOUNTAIN WAS as Thumps had left it. He pulled into the parking lot, turned the engine off, and his cellphone rang.

He was thinking, *Claire*, as he answered it.

"Where are you?"

Okay, not Claire.

"Buffalo Mountain parking lot."

"Good," said Duke. "Stay right there and wait for me."

Thumps started to ask why when he realized that the sheriff had hung up. Or whatever you did to end a cellphone call.

Had the sheriff really meant for him to wait in the lot? Surely, he meant to meet him inside, where there was food and coffee. If the sheriff was coming from town, he wouldn't be here for a while, and a while was enough time to order something tasty.

He got as far as the reception desk.

"You're here."

Archie looked as though he had just broken the world record for the mile.

"Where's Duke?"

"You okay?"

"No, I'm not okay," said Archie. "Why would you ask me that?"

"How about backing up a little."

"What?"

"As in, why are you upset?"

Archie grabbed Thumps by the arm and dragged him to the elevators. "We'll start without Duke."

"We'll start *what* without Duke?"

"He can catch up."

It was a short ride to the fifth floor. Archie was out almost before the doors opened and was down the hall on the fly.

The door to unit 519 was open. And it wasn't empty. Katheryn Souto was standing off to one side, Emily Hunter next to her. Nico Eliopoulos and Atticus Poe were in front of the sofa. Otto Myers was standing by himself, still as a statue.

Boris Lukin was slumped in the chair, face down on the table. Even from the doorway, Thumps knew the man wasn't asleep.

"Everybody stay calm," said Archie. "Thumps is a deputy sheriff."

Thumps had seen any number of dead bodies. Normally, there wasn't an audience in attendance.

"Who found him?"

Hunter looked at Souto. "All of us."

"I know how that sounds," said Poe, "but Ms. Hunter is quite right. We all found him like this."

Thumps checked Lukin. Stone cold. The body still in rigor.

"You all came to this room at the same time?"

"Yes."

"When?"

"About twenty minutes ago," said Souto.

"Whose room is it?"

"We don't know," said Poe.

"Our suites are all on the sixth floor," said Myers. "You can check with the desk."

"And Boris had the penthouse," said Nico.

Thumps could feel a headache coming on.

"Why did you all come to this particular room?"

There was a long silence. Finally, Nico stepped forward. "We were invited."

"It's true," said Myers.

The condo was all in order. No signs of a struggle. No lamp knocked over, chair tipped on its side, broken bottle.

"Lukin?"

"Don't think so," said Nico. "He is not a man who would do that."

"So, who did?" said Thumps. "Invite you, that is."

"Actually," said Poe, "as strange as it might sound, we have no idea."

"Then why did you all come?" Duke appeared in the doorway, large and looming. Beth Mooney was on one shoulder, Deanna Heavy Runner was on the other.

"I told you something was going to happen," said Archie. "Didn't I tell you that."

Duke hooked his thumbs in his belt. "Right now, I want all of you to clear the room and follow Deputy Heavy Runner into the hallway."

"Do you suspect foul play?" asked Souto.

"Deputy Heavy Runner will take your names and suite numbers. Any questions?"

Nico Eliopoulos tentatively held up a hand.

"Yes?" said Duke.

"The crime scene," said Nico. "Would it be possible for us to watch?"

24

The sheriff stood in the middle of the room and shifted his weight from one leg to the other.

"You got your camera?"

"It's in the car."

"Got the cellphone I gave you?"

Thumps took the phone out of his pocket, held it up.

"Use it," said Duke.

"To do what?"

"Take pictures," said Duke.

Thumps turned the phone over in his hand. And then he turned it over again.

"You do know that cellphones can take pictures."

Knowing that cellphones took pictures was one thing. Knowing how to set the f-stop, how to focus, where to find the shutter, was another matter.

"That piece of junk is at least six years old," said Beth.

"Eight," said Duke. "And it still works."

"Here," said Beth. "Use mine. All you have to do is tap this icon, aim, and touch that button."

"That's not a button."

"It looks like a button," said Beth. "Don't be literal."

"What's this?"

"You can switch between lenses," said Beth. "There's a wide angle, a normal, and a telephoto."

"Show him how he can send all the photos he takes with your phone to my phone," said Duke.

"Baby steps," said Beth, "baby steps."

THUMPS PHOTOGRAPHED THE body. He took pictures of the messenger bag on a chair, pictures of the remains of a cigar in an ashtray, pictures of two wineglasses on the kitchen counter, and of a wad of something wrapped up in a Kleenex at the bottom of an otherwise empty garbage container.

"Give me a hand," said Beth.

Thumps and the sheriff eased Lukin to the floor, and Thumps took more photographs of the body laid out on the carpet.

Duke stepped back and gave a low grunt. "Nothing much to suggest a cause of death."

Thumps took a close-up of Lukin's face.

"Still in rigor." Beth squatted down beside the body. "No nasty bullet holes. No blunt-force trauma. No obvious signs of poisoning."

Thumps handed the phone back to Beth. "Natural causes?"

"So far, so good," said Beth. "I'll know more when I get him back to the shop."

"Let's go through the condo," said Duke. "Just in case."

Beth stood up. "Before you two start your 'hard-target search of every gas station, residence, warehouse, farmhouse, henhouse, outhouse, and dog house in the area,' how about helping me get Mr. Lukin into a body bag and into the back of my wagon."

"Yes, Marshal Gerard," said Duke.

"Right away, Marshal Gerard," said Thumps.

Duke and Thumps rolled Lukin into a body bag. Duke got the front desk to send up a couple of the security guys and a luggage cart to help Beth get the corpse down to her station wagon.

Thumps went as far as the elevators.

Beth held the doors for a moment. "How's late morning sound?"

"I may sleep in," said Thumps.

"Don't be like that. I just had the walls painted. Doesn't have that musty smell anymore."

"Good to know."

"And that good-looking messenger bag?" Beth held the doors for a moment. "It's a Louis Vuitton."

DUKE WAS WAITING for him. "You got gloves?"

"Nope."

Duke took a pair out of his pocket and held them out. "Not to worry. It's like riding a bike. You start with the bag."

"Beth says it's a Louie Britton."

"Louis Vuitton," said Duke. "Didn't they teach you fancy brands in cop school?"

Thumps opened the bag. "Okay," he said, "for starters, we have a gun."

"Glock G43X." Duke dropped the clip, cleared the chamber, held the gun to his nose. "Hasn't been fired in a while."

"And we have a big pouch thingy."

"Travel wallet," said Duke. "Saw one in a movie about French cops."

"Passport, driver's licence, credit cards, notepad, bunch of cash."

"Watch looked expensive." Duke walked the room, taking his time, stopping every so often. "What's wrong with this picture?"

"Besides our dead guy?"

"If we believe our little rascals, they were invited to this room by a person or persons unknown, and when they arrived, en masse, they found Boris Lukin dead."

"Okay," said Thumps. "Let's say we believe them."

"So, they see the body, and what do they do?"

"Call the front desk."

"And the front desk calls the authorities."

"Meaning you."

"Meaning me."

It took Thumps a moment to put all the pieces into place. "So why are there two wineglasses with lipstick on the rim, a chewed-up cigar in the ashtray, and what looks to be a wad of gum wrapped up in a Kleenex in the garbage?"

"Two different shades of lipstick from the look of it," said Duke. "You see the problem? They come in. They see the body. They call it in like the good citizens they are. And then what? They sit down and have a party?"

"They were in the room twice," said Thumps. "At different times."

"That's what I'm thinking," said Duke. "I just can't figure out why."

Deanna Heavy Runner reappeared, handed Duke a clipboard. "Names and room numbers."

"Any problems?"

"They were all co-operative," said Heavy Runner. "The Myers guy was twitchy as hell, but I suspect he's like that in real life."

"Any thoughts?"

"Nope," said Deanna. "They all seem to be well-adjusted narcissists. That a novel?"

Thumps picked up the book. "Coins."

"Too bad," said Deanna. "I'm almost done with the one I'm reading."

Thumps slid the postcard out of the book.

"I use a piece of leather for my bookmarks," said Deanna. "They're nice and flexible, feel good to the touch."

It was the same postcard Thumps had seen in Lukin's penthouse.

"Bald eagle," said Deanna. "I saw one carry off a lamb. Suckers are strong."

Thumps turned the card over, handed it to Duke. "You might want to look at this."

On the back of the postcard was a short inscription.

Life is about finding questions you can't answer. Barca's eagle. Coin show. Chinook, Montana.

Duke looked at the message, turned the card over, looked at the eagle, turned the card over a second time, looked at the message once more.

"Sometimes a postcard is a postcard," said Duke.

"And sometimes it's a cigar," said Thumps.

"In this case," said the sheriff, "it might well be both."

25

Duke explained his strategy to Thumps as they rode the elevator to the lobby.

"Generally speaking, you got two ways to handle suspects. If there's only one person of interest, you stick them in a small room with a hot light, smack them around a bit, no food, no water until they confess."

"You do know it's the twenty-first century," said Thumps.

"If there are several suspects, then you line them up and smack them around all at once until they confess."

"As a comedy routine, it needs a lot of work."

"But what we're going to do," said Duke, "is take them in pairs."

"Pairs?"

"Two pairs and a single, to be exact. Alphas and betas. Mix and match."

"Sketchy," said Thumps.

"How about Myers and Souto? Eliopoulos and Hunter? Atticus Poe as a single?"

"Don't see how this is going to work?"

"Play them against each other," said Duke. "Strong against the weak. First group against the second group. Both groups against the single. See what shakes out."

"What about Benoit and Cruz?"

"You're wondering if they know that Lukin is dead?" said Duke.

Thumps would have put his money on Cruz and Benoit knowing that Lukin was dead. Word would have already spread through the resort. Too many people in the know, too many moving parts to keep it a secret.

So, they knew.

"A little difficult to ask the right questions when we don't know what happened to Lukin."

"You mean, did he have a heart attack, all natural-like," said Duke. "Or did someone whack him?"

"Whack him?"

"Technical terminology for murder," said Duke. "Soon as you get cable, you'll be able to keep up."

"What about the dealers?" said Thumps. "We still don't know why they are here."

"You don't buy the vacation thing? Get together with friends? Swap stories?"

"Do you?"

DUKE SET UP shop in the main-floor dining room, at a large table away from the windows and the distraction of the view. He ordered coffee and a fruit and cheese plate.

Myers and Souto were up first.

Duke took his time, settled himself in the chair, helped himself to the coffee, looked through his notebook, as though the answers to his questions were there.

"Mr. Myers," he began. "Ms. Souto."

"Mrs. Souto," she corrected.

Myers was chewing on something. "I don't know anything."

"How about we start off easy," said Duke. "With the stuff you don't know."

"What?"

"You said you don't know who invited you to that room. Is that correct?"

"Sure," said Myers. "That's right."

"Do you think it could have been Lukin?"

Myers's leg began twitching. "I guess."

"It wasn't," said Souto. "If Boris was going to invite us anywhere, it would have been to the penthouse."

"So he could show off?"

"Exactly," said Souto.

Duke helped himself to a grape. "How exactly did you get the invite?"

"Text message," said Souto.

"And you don't know who sent it?"

"Hey, he died of a heart attack," said Myers. "What's the big deal?"

"Standard stuff," said Duke. "We get a dead body, we have to fill out a bunch of paperwork."

Souto took her phone out of her purse. "Here," she said, "see for yourself."

"But you went to the room anyway."

"I was intrigued," said Souto.

Duke turned to Myers. "And I suppose you were intrigued as well?"

"Sure," said Myers. "I was intrigued."

"You chew gum, Mr. Myers?"

"What the hell kind of a question is that?" Myers looked at Souto to see if she wanted to weigh in. "Are we done?"

"How are you enjoying the vacation so far?"

Myers looked stunned, as though someone had hit him with a hammer. "What?"

"The vacation," said Duke. "Chance to see old friends."

"Yeah," said Myers. "Great. Just great."

ELIOPOULOS AND HUNTER were next. Eliopoulos took out a cigar, played with it for a moment, put it away. Hunter did the crossing of the legs thing, but with less precision and less effect this time.

"How long have you known Mr. Lukin?"

"We've done business," said Hunter.

"Same here," said Nico.

"Just business?"

"Is there a euphemism in your insinuation?" said Hunter.

"He wants to know if you and Boris had an affair," said Nico.

"You mean were we fucking?"

"Yes, ma'am," said Duke. "That's what I'm asking."

"None of your business," said Hunter.

"He died of a heart attack," said Nico, "didn't he?"

"Coroner will figure that part out," said Duke. "Deputy DreadfulWater and I are just trying to tie up the loose ends."

"Such as?"

"Such as why you all went to the room."

"We told you," said Hunter. "We were invited."

Duke nodded. "Would that be the first invitation? Or the second?"

THE SHERIFF WAITED for Atticus to get comfortable before he took the postcard out of his pocket and placed it on the table.

"I'm going to assume that you have one of these," said Duke.

Poe said nothing, stared at his coffee. When he looked up, he was smiling.

"I'm betting a lot of people figure you for a country bumpkin."

"I am a country bumpkin," said Duke.

"Is that Lukin's postcard?"

"I'm more interested in yours."

Poe turned the card over. "As you have guessed, mine is the same."

"And the rest of the folks? Souto, Myers, Eliopoulos, Hunter? They all got the same card?"

"I would assume that they did," said Poe.

"And this card is the reason all of you are here."

"I would assume it is."

"It's a lovely day," said Duke. "I got nothing much to do. Why don't you tell me the story about Barca's eagle."

"It's a long story," said Poe. "How much of it do you want to hear?"

"How about the half-hour TV version," said Duke.

Poe smiled. "Like *Death in Paradise*?"

"That's an hour program," said the sheriff. "Macy liked the first detective. She was sorry when he quit the show."

"Hannibal Barca," said Thumps. "Let's start there."

Poe turned the coffee cup, so the handle faced away. "Hannibal Barca was a coin dealer. Major weight. Mostly gold coins. I met him at a coin show in New York. I was twenty, twenty-one, working a booth. We got into a conversation about the 1927 D Saint-Gaudens double eagle."

"Sure," said Duke. "Who wouldn't."

"I'm guessing it's a valuable coin," said Thumps.

"Original mintage was around 180,000 pieces. That was before Executive Order 6102."

"This is beginning to sound more like a full-length movie." Duke signalled the server. "Anybody want pie?"

Duke got the apple. Poe had the pumpkin. Thumps ordered toast.

"Toast? You're kidding."

"I'm diabetic."

"Pumpkin is a vegetable," said Poe. "You should try the pumpkin."

"I've never been to New York City," said Duke. "What's it like?"

"Can't tell you," said Poe. "I've lived there all my life. The city is . . . normal."

"So, here must be strange," said Duke.

"You have no idea," said Poe. "I've never seen so many trees."

"How's the pie?" said Thumps.

Poe pushed the plate off to one side. "Appears I was wrong about pumpkin."

"Ditto for the apple," said Duke. "Okay. Hannibal Barca."

"Sure," said Poe, "but you'll need some background."

Duke poked at his pie with a fork. "We live for background, don't we Deputy DreadfulWater?"

"I think we're going to need more coffee," said Thumps.

Poe took off his glasses, cleaned them with his napkin. "From 1879 until 1933, America was on a gold standard."

Duke stopped poking his pie. "What'd they use before that?"

"Silver," said Poe.

"Franklin Delano Roosevelt and the Great Depression," said Thumps.

"Full marks," said Poe. "FDR could see that sticking with the gold standard was crippling the American economy. You want the background on that?"

Duke beat Thumps to the answer, but only by a blink.

"I suppose you just want the summary."

"Please."

"All right," said Poe. "History, history, blah, blah, blah. So, in 1933 FDR came up with Executive Order 6102. This required that all gold coins, gold bullion, and gold certificates be turned in to the federal government."

"That must have been a crowd-pleaser," said Duke.

"It was somewhat contentious," said Poe.

"What happened to the coins?" said Thumps.

"They were exchanged for face value, collected, and melted down."

"And the 1927 thingy is valuable because most of them were melted?"

"Probably fewer than a dozen examples left."

"And Barca was in New York to buy one?"

"No. Barca already had one. Carried it around in his pocket. He showed it to me."

"In his pocket?"

"Well, in a case. To protect it. But yes, in his pocket. Said it made him feel good to have it close."

"How much is this coin worth?"

"In today's market?" Poe rapped a drum roll on the table. "Average circulated, about $270,000."

Duke looked at Thumps.

"Uncirculated, it's worth north of a million."

"For a coin?" Duke snorted. "And he just took it out of his pocket and said, 'Here, kid, have a look'?"

"Not at the booth," said Poe. "He took me to dinner. He showed it to me then."

"And you'd never met him before?"

"Never. It was a rush. He already had a reputation, and I was just a kid."

"Sounds a bit too good to be true," said Duke.

"What can I say. We hit it off. Hannibal didn't have a family. Maybe he saw me as a son. Personally, I think he just liked showing me the ropes." Poe stretched, leaned to one side and then the other. "Anyway, after that, we stayed in touch. Every time he came to town, we'd get together, talk coins, have dinner."

"And he started throwing business your way," said Thumps.

"Yes," said Poe, "he did. Quite a lot, actually. If I'm being honest, I owe my success in the business to him."

Poe stopped, as though he had arrived at a fork in the road and was unwilling to go any farther. Thumps waited, but he didn't wait long.

"But?"

Poe shrugged.

"Something happened," said Thumps. "I'm guessing it was Arkady Lukin, Boris's father."

"Hannibal made a mistake," said Poe.

"What?" Duke tried to look surprised. "He sort of wandered into crime? A part-time crook? Circumstances beyond his control?"

"The sarcasm isn't necessary," said Poe. "Hannibal had a code. His word was good."

"Certainly could use more crooks like that," said Duke.

Poe's face hardened. "You didn't know him."

"So, tell us about the Lukins."

"First, I have to go to the bathroom," said Poe. "Either of you care to join me?"

Duke tipped his hat back. "Thumps and I will sit here and contemplate the unbearable lightness of being."

Poe stopped in his tracks. "Then I'll take my time."

DUKE LEANED FORWARD, his elbows on the table. "So, where do you suppose they are?"

It took Thumps a moment. "Cruz and Benoit?"

"They were supposed to be watching Lukin," said Duke. "He's dead. Where are they?"

"Maybe Benoit went back to Seattle."

"And Cruz went back to Pie Town?"

"Doesn't wash."

"No," said Duke, "it doesn't."

POE RETURNED IN good order.

"Where were we?"

"The Lukins," said Duke.

"Arkady Lukin, Boris's father, was both a coin dealer," Poe began, "and a career criminal. Money laundering for various organizations, rackets, protection, prostitution, drugs. If it turned a dollar, Arkady had a piece of the action. The son didn't fall far from the tree."

"Sounds like a fun family."

"Except when it came to coins," said Poe. "When it came to coins, Arkady was scrupulous. This is how Hannibal and Arkady met. Over coins. Gold coins to be exact. It became somewhat of a competition between them. The way they kept score."

"And Arkady wanted Barca's 1927 D?"

"No," said Poe. "Old man Lukin had one already."

Duke touched the postcard. "Barca's eagle?"

"Barca's eagle isn't the 1927 D. It's the 1933 Saint-Gaudens double eagle, twenty-dollar gold piece."

Duke frowned. "This sounds like more history."

"Sorry," said Poe, "but you asked for the story."

"So, Barca had a . . ."

"1933 Saint-Gaudens double eagle."

"And this is rarer than the 1927?"

Poe smiled. "The 1933 double eagle isn't supposed to exist."

Thumps held up a hand. "That's the same year as the executive order that recalled all gold coins."

"And there you have the conundrum," said Poe. "At the same time that Roosevelt was putting the executive order together, the Philadelphia mint was doing what they did best."

"Making gold coins."

"Exactly," said Poe. "The order hadn't been signed yet, and the mint was stamping out double eagles by the bagful."

"Left hand, right hand," said Duke. "Sounds like the government, all right."

"So, there's FDR with his hand on the order, and at the same time, there's the mint churning out double eagles."

Thumps leaned back. "The coins never left the mint. They were never released for circulation."

Poe pushed the remains of his pie to Thumps. "First prize goes to the Indian chief."

"Not a chief."

"Nevertheless, you have discovered the paradox. In 1933 gold coins were made illegal, and in 1933 you had gold coins being produced. Technically, none of those coins ever got into circulation. Technically, all of the 1933 double eagles were held at the mint and melted down."

"Technically," said Duke. "As in, boys will be boys?"

"And here," said Poe, "the sarcasm is justified. That's exactly what happened. As soon as the 1933 run of double eagles was stopped, a handful of dealers, aided and abetted by certain mint officials, spirited a small number of the coins away. No one knows how many. We know of one coin that wound up in the collection of Farouk I of Egypt, and there was a second coin that was recovered in a sting operation in 1996, but since then . . ."

"Enter Hannibal Barca," said Thumps.

"So Barca had one?" said Duke.

"That was the rumour."

"Did he ever show it to you?"

"No," said Poe. "If he actually had one, I never saw it."

"And?"

"And one day, he disappeared."

Thumps softened his voice. "As in dead?"

"No one knows," said Poe. "He was in town for a coin show. Rumour had it he and Arkady Lukin were going to meet."

"The '33 double eagle?"

"Rumour again," said Poe.

"Lukin wanted it."

"Who wouldn't," said Poe. "It's one of the rarest coins in the world. But Arkady swore there were never any plans to meet. Swore that he hadn't talked to Hannibal in over a year."

"No one just disappears," said Duke.

"Jimmy Hoffa," said Poe. "Amelia Earhart, Michael Rockefeller, Ambrose Bierce, the lost colony of Roanoke . . ."

"Okay," said Duke. "Point made."

"Anyway, Hannibal had a room at the Park Plaza. I was supposed to meet him there for dinner, and he never showed. I called his room. No answer. I went up and knocked on the door."

"And no answer," said Thumps.

"I thought maybe he had checked out, but his clothes were in the closet, his toiletries in the bathroom."

"Wait," said Duke. "Back up. Just how did you get into his room?"

"Called the front desk. Told them I heard screaming in the room. An assault. A heart attack. When security entered the room to check, I went in behind. Said I was his business partner."

"Clever. And the 1933 double eagle?"

"No idea," said Poe. "I always figured that Hannibal was killed because of that coin. But maybe he gave it to his daughter."

Thumps held up a hand. "You said he didn't have a family."

Poe saluted Thumps with his coffee cup. "Nice to see someone was listening."

"So, Barca had a daughter."

"Could have been a son," said Poe. "But the one time he mentioned a child, it sounded as though it was a girl."

"So, you don't have a name."

"Hannibal was a secretive man. I think he spread all sorts of rumours about himself so he could stay invisible. Maybe he had a child. Maybe he didn't."

"So, no idea where this child might be?" said Thumps. "No idea if this child has the double eagle? No idea if the child even exists?"

Poe took the postcard out of his pocket, placed it on the table. "It's the message. 'Life is about finding questions you can't answer.' It was his favourite saying," said Poe. "He had a bunch of them, but this is the one he liked best."

"So, anyone who knew him would know the saying."

"Probably," said Poe.

"Which means anyone could have sent the postcards to the dealers."

"Probably."

"That's a lot of probabilities," said Duke.

"Best I can do," said Poe.

"Let's say Barca had the eagle," said Thumps. "And let's say he passed it on to a son or a daughter. And let's say that the coin on the postcard is the same coin. Why?"

"Why what?"

"Why go through this elaborate charade? Surely Barca's kid could sell the coin under the radar. Must be enough crazy billionaires in the world who would buy the coin, no questions asked. Why bring all the dealers into play? Why here? How long has Barca been missing?"

"Twenty years."

"So, why now?"

"Life." Poe got to his feet, picked at a spot on his jacket. "The question that can't be answered."

26

The sheriff walked Thumps to his car.

"So, what do you think?"

"Not even trying," said Thumps.

"No point in letting the paucity of hard facts deter you," said Duke.

"Do you even know what *paucity* means?"

"Detective on *Death in Paradise* used the word. Macy looked it up." Duke leaned against the hood of the car. "At least we now know why all the dealers are here."

"The 1933 double eagle."

"Which may not even exist," said Duke.

"We don't know how Lukin died," said Thumps. "Natural causes, whacked."

"Or why Benoit and Cruz are here."

"They came for Lukin," said Thumps. "We just don't know why."

"Paucity, paucity, paucity."

"I noticed you didn't ask any of them about being in the room on two separate occasions."

"I'm guessing they know we know," said Duke. "But it doesn't hurt to let things simmer a while. See what sticks to the bottom."

"Are we going to take a guess?"

"We'd be fools not to," said Duke.

Thumps leaned up against the car next to the sheriff. "I'd guess that someone sent postcards to all of the dealers suggesting that Hannibal Barca's 1933 double eagle was for sale."

"Which is an illegal coin," said Duke, "and most likely subject to confiscation."

"Which makes it all the more valuable."

"The room where we found Lukin was where they were supposed to see the coin," said Duke.

"Makes sense," said Thumps. "They all get to see it at the same time in a neutral location."

"That's the first visit," said Duke. "Is there an auction on the spot? Do they all go to a neutral corner and make their bids via text?"

"Paucity," said Thumps.

"And then they all come back to the room," said Duke. "And find Lukin's body."

"Which means that Lukin went back a second time, without the others."

"Which would suggest that Lukin had already made the winning bid and was there to pick up the coin, had a heart attack . . ."

"Or our mysterious someone invited Lukin back to the room in order to kill him."

"And then invited everyone back for a second visit to mess with the crime scene."

"If it's a crime at all."

"Beth's," said Duke. "Tomorrow. Late morning. All will be revealed."

"You don't need me for that."

"True." Duke pushed off the car. "But dragging you to the morgue in the morning always puts a smile on my face."

THUMPS HALF-EXPECTED TO find Cruz's car parked in front of his house, the ninja assassin inside doing his laundry. Instead, there was a utility van at the curb. Dixie was standing in his front yard, talking with a man Thumps didn't recognize.

"There he is," said Dixie. "The birthday boy."

The man looked at his tablet. "You must be Mr. DreadfulWater."

Thumps nodded. "But it's not my birthday."

"It's in April," said Dixie, "but with all the presents you just got, you're going to feel like it's your birthday."

"Christopher Reno," said the man. "Reno Systems."

Thumps knew the name, or at least he had heard it in the last little bit. He just couldn't place it.

"You're the new deputy sheriff, right?"

The computer guy. That's where he had heard the name. The computer guy Duke had mentioned.

"It took me a while," said Reno, "but I've got everything up and running. Wireless internet, cable, laptop, touch-tone phones, cellphone, alarm system. Course, I couldn't hook your old TV up to the internet provider, but I finished a job over in Glory. Couple had a new eighty-five-inch OLED installed. Didn't want the old one, so I took it away. Works fine. Threw it in as a thank you for the contract."

Thumps knew Reno was speaking English, even though most of what he was saying didn't make much sense.

"What was wrong with my TV?"

Dixie slapped Reno on the back. "I told you he has a great sense of humour."

"Spoiler alert," said Reno. "Your cats are already crazy about the animal videos on YouTube."

"My cats?"

"I've left all the instructions on the kitchen table. The remote and the new laptop are in the living room. I did leave the old rotary in place, but it's no longer hooked up."

"Not hooked up?"

"Makes a great conversational piece," said Reno. "You have any problems at all, you call me."

"Problems with . . . ?"

"And I signed you up for a complimentary three months of Amazon Prime Video and a two-month free trial with Netflix."

"I only have cable," said Dixie. "Maybe Pops and I could come over and watch a movie with you."

Thumps had never been hit by a bus, but he imagined that this was how it felt.

"You did something to my house?"

"You bet," said Reno. "We brought her into the twenty-first century."

"Maybe I should apply to be a deputy sheriff," said Dixie. "The perks are first-rate."

INSIDE, THE HOUSE looked more or less the same. There was a new phone in the kitchen next to the rotary.

Okay, so far so good.

The living room was another story. His old TV was gone, replaced with a giant flat screen. The thing was easily three times the size of the old set and took up much of the wall. The set was on. With the sound off. Freeway and Cookie were lying on the floor, their tails twitching, as they watched a dog sliding on ice.

He had never seen the cats smile, wasn't sure that cats could smile.

There was a remote on the coffee table, next to a laptop.

The sheriff had much to answer for.

Thumps sat on the sofa, leaned back, closed his eyes, and worked on controlling his breathing. Deep breaths in. Deep breaths out. Slowly brought his pulse back down, little by little. Hummed the opening lines of "I Shot the Sheriff" over and over until it became a soothing mantra.

THUMPS WOKE TO Peter Sellers telling his cabinet that they couldn't fight in the war room. The cats had disappeared, and someone had thrown a blanket over him.

And he was hungry.

"*Ese*, you're awake."

Cisco Cruz. Standing in the doorway to the kitchen.

"Zee is making us dinner," said Cruz. "Give us a chance to talk."

Thumps hadn't realized just how large the flat screen was. It was as though Sellers and George C. Scott were in the living room with him.

"Great movie," said Cruz. "Kubrick at the top of his game."

Thumps pushed the blanket to one side, sat up.

"Can't believe you got cable," said Cruz. "And internet. And that TV. Okay, it's a few years old, but what the hell."

The good news, Thumps told himself, was that he had found Cruz. Or more accurately, Cruz had found him. Not that it mattered. And maybe now he'd get some answers.

"Where have you been?"

"You mean ever since someone offed Lukin?"

"No evidence of that," said Thumps. "Looks like a heart attack."

"You know how many drugs can make a murder look like a heart attack?"

Offhand, Thumps couldn't think of any. He was sure that there were a few. And now that he had internet service, he could look them up. If he wanted to.

"Sodium pentothal, potassium chloride, fentanyl, thallium—"

"Okay, fine."

"Some of them are detectable if you do the right test and know what you're looking for. Others are tougher."

"So, you think Lukin was murdered?"

"Murdered is more interesting than natural causes," said Cruz. "Although if Lukin was murdered, then Zee's tail is in a wringer."

Thumps stood up, folded the blanket, padded his way to the kitchen. The oven wasn't on. There were no pans on the burners. Nothing laid out on the butcher block he used as a preparation table.

"I thought you said Benoit was making us dinner."

"She is," said Cruz. "In a manner of speaking."

Cruz quickly moved to the door, held it open, as Benoit breezed in with two large paper bags.

"Home is the hunter." She put the bags on the butcher block. "Home from the hill."

"Takeout?"

"Not just any takeout," said Benoit. "This is from Pappous's."

"I don't normally get sweaty for Greek cuisine," said Cruz, "but the little guy makes a mean lamb stew."

"I got a variety," said Benoit. "You each owe me forty dollars."

"Forty dollars?"

"Includes the bottle of wine and the tip."

Thumps got dishes down. Flatware, glasses, napkins. Benoit opened the containers, set them on the table.

"*Bon appétit.*"

"A toast," said Cruz. "To old friends."

"Who lie to you," said Thumps.

"Eat first," said Cruz. "Accusations later."

The food was delicious. Thumps was hungrier than he had imagined. The lamb stew was particularly good, and he had two helpings.

"Any coffee?" said Benoit. "There's nothing like coffee after a good meal."

"Maybe you'd like a cigar," said Thumps, "or a brandy?"

"Thumps is unhappy with you," said Cruz.

"Thumps is unhappy with the both of you," said Thumps. "There's a dead body in the morgue, and I'm willing to bet that you two had something to do with it."

"You think one of us killed him?" Benoit put her fork down. "My job was to keep him safe."

"And a great job you did," said Cruz.

"Go stick your head in a toilet. I almost got killed. What have you done? Eat doughnuts and pretend you're a secret agent?"

"I didn't lose the principal."

"Oh, is that how it's going to be." Benoit picked up a knife, pointed it at Cruz. "This is all my fault."

Thumps shook his head. "I can see why you two split up."

Benoit stopped pointing and turned on Thumps.

"What did you say?"

Thumps had liked it better when Benoit had the knife aimed at Cruz. "Why your marriage didn't work out."

"Marriage?" Benoit glared at Cruz. "Really?"

"We needed a cover story."

"So you told him we were married?"

"You weren't married?"

Benoit slammed the knife on the table. "What else did this flutter-brain tell you?"

Thumps felt as though he were up to his knees in mud. "About you . . . and him? The divorce? Duncan?"

Benoit frowned. "Duncan?"

"Your son?"

Cruz held up his hands. "Hey, it was a good cover."

Thumps stared at Cruz. "You don't have a son named Duncan?"

"If I did," said Cruz, "I probably wouldn't name him Duncan."

"And your dead mother?"

"Cover story," said Cruz. "Cover story."

Thumps got the coffee pot, brought it to the table. "Okay," he said. "Let's start at the beginning."

27

When Thumps was a cop in Eureka, he had taken Anna and Callie to a local theatre to watch a nature film where biologists pulled a five-hundred-pound, thirty-foot-long anaconda out of a flooded grassland in the Orinoco Basin. It took six full-grown men to drag the snake out of the water, and they were exhausted by the time they got the reptile onto land.

Pulling the story of Boris Lukin out of Cruz and Benoit was harder. And considerably more annoying.

"So, Lukin was a government informant?"

"Not an informant exactly," said Cruz. "From time to time, he would funnel certain information to certain government agencies."

"On?"

"You know," said Cruz.

"No," said Thumps, "I don't."

"Jesus, Cruz," said Benoit. "Loose lips."

"Hey," said Cruz. "He's a deputy sheriff. He's one of us."

"Loose lips is listening," said Thumps.

"Okay," said Cruz, "so Lukin was in bed with certain terrorist groups."

Thumps took a moment to put that piece in place. "Wouldn't that be more the business of the CIA and NSA?"

"Domestic terrorist groups," said Benoit.

"We got more than our fair share of them," said Cruz. "And they can be just as lethal as the international baddies."

"And these baddies would have an interest in Lukin being dead."

"If they knew about Lukin," said Cruz. "Which they didn't. The only reason I'm telling you any of this is because Lukin is . . ."

"Dead," said Thumps.

"Any word on how he died?" said Benoit.

"Autopsy is tomorrow morning," said Thumps. "If there's something to find, Beth will find it."

"What we haven't figured out," said Benoit, "is why Lukin came here in the first place."

Thumps smiled, topped up his cup. "You want the half-hour sitcom or the two-hour movie?"

AFTER THUMPS FINISHED the story, he picked up all the dishes and put them in the sink.

Cruz sat back, sighed. "All this because of a coin?"

"A 1933 double eagle," said Thumps.

"Son of a bitch," said Benoit. "He should have told us."

"The coin's illegal," said Thumps. "What would you have done? Arrest him? Break up the sale? Confiscate it?"

"All of the above," said Benoit, "although any shit to do with money is really Treasury's job."

"Which is why he didn't tell you."

"And you think it somehow got him killed?" said Cruz.

"We don't know that," said Thumps. "Beth first, then you can jump to conclusions."

"Let's hope that he died of natural causes," said Benoit. "If it's murder, my next posting will be in northern Alaska. Or west Texas."

"Won't matter whether he died of natural causes or was murdered," said Cruz. "It was on your watch. The asset's dead. Bureau's going to look for someone to flush down the toilet."

"We're both floating in the same bowl," said Benoit.

Thumps was always amazed how one thing could lead to another. "Did you two know each other before you got here?"

Benoit started to open her mouth. And then thought better of it.

"That's it. You flew out here from Seattle," said Thumps. "But Cruz flew in from somewhere else."

"Pancho . . ."

"Such as Miami," said Thumps. "You were Lukin's liaison. You were his handler."

Cruz snorted. "Not hardly."

"Liars don't get pie," said Thumps.

"There is no pie," said Cruz.

"Figure of speech," said Thumps.

"Be nice if you two shut up for once," said Benoit.

Thumps stretched his legs out under the table. "Benoit is drugged, and as soon as the two of you are out of the way, Lukin dies."

"Yeah," said Cruz. "The coincidence doesn't play well with us either."

"So, what are you going to do?"

Benoit looked over to the refrigerator. "You sure there's no pie?"

BENOIT AND CRUZ left just before midnight, with nothing settled. Thumps went back to the living room and watched the second half of a show on strip mining for gold in Alaska. Thumps couldn't believe the devastation that attended the process. Acres of forest ripped up and turned into ugly mud flats and stagnant holding ponds. Much of the show was taken up with bulldozers breaking down, wash plants breaking down, trucks breaking down.

The more the miners tore up the landscape, the more Thumps found himself rooting for more things to break down.

At the top of the hour, the show switched to a program on border security. One woman coming back from Canada was caught with a few flakes of marijuana in a baggie. Hardly worth the border guard's time, but he spent most of the show threatening to throw the woman into jail and hitting her with a large fine. Another portion was about two men who were stopped at the Canadian border with a trunk full of pistols and rifles. One of the guys gave the border guard a lecture on the right to bear arms and how the U.S. was protecting Canada from invasion by China and how border guards had no jurisdiction over sovereign citizens.

Thumps picked up the remote and after several tries managed to change the channel to women arguing over wedding dresses.

It took him another minute to find the power button.

He sat on the sofa for a while. He wasn't tired, didn't feel like going to bed. Was Alberta in the same time zone? The call to Claire went straight to voice mail and the mailbox that she still hadn't set up.

Thumps wasn't sure if she would even know that he had tried to reach her, if there would be a record of the attempt. In case there were any questions later about the level of his concern.

Something he could point to. Something he could show Roxanne.

And Moses. Had he gone home? Was he still in the hospital?

The main number for the hospital took him to an electronic answering service that cautioned him that only two people were permitted in a patient's room at a time and that masks needed to be worn. There was the option to dial a department by name, or to press nine if you knew the staff member you wanted to speak to, or to press five to speak with a patient.

Thumps pressed five and was asked to punch in the patient's security code on his touch-tone phone. There were no options if you didn't know the number. Thumps tried pressing zero, hoping it would take him to the main desk or admissions, and a robotic voice thanked him for calling and hung up.

Okay. Check with Roxanne tomorrow. If anyone would know where Claire was, it would be Heavy Runner. And call Cooley Small Elk. The big man wasn't going to let Moses out of his sight.

Sometimes being part of a close-knit community was stifling.

Sometimes it was a comfort. Whatever the pluses and minuses, it was better than gold mining in Alaska, border crossings, wedding dresses, and electronic voices that took you nowhere.

THE PLAN WAS to sleep in the next morning, get to Al's late. With any luck Thumps would be able to fortify himself with a hearty but quiet breakfast before he had to brave the calamity of Beth's house of horrors.

The plan worked. The café was mostly empty.

"You're late," said Al. "You missed everyone."

"Some days I get lucky."

"Wutty has his *Little Otter* floating again. Rawat and Stas are packing for their big fishing trip."

"Breakfast, please," said Thumps. "The usual."

"Moses is out of the hospital, and I hear tell you got internet and cable."

"And coffee."

"As well as a cellphone."

"Maybe you know who's trying to sell a 1933 gold double eagle?"

"I'm a gossip, not a psychic." Al wiped the counter down. "You want to talk about Claire?"

"You hear about Morris Dumbo and his new girlfriend?"

"You're changing the subject," said Al.

"Okay," said Thumps. "Let's talk about breakfast."

AL WAS AT the grill, working on a mound of hash browns, when Emily Hunter walked into the café. She stopped at the door, did a quick survey of the interior, and decided to stay.

"So, this is the place."

Hunter sat on the stool next to Thumps.

"Long way to come for a meal," said Thumps.

"Couldn't manage the buffet another morning."

Al brought the coffee pot. "This your new girlfriend?"

"What?" Thumps felt his face flush.

"That's right," said Hunter. "Thumps here is a real stud."

"I heard he was more a dud."

"Very funny," said Thumps.

"I like her," said Al.

"Fine," said Thumps. "Why don't you get me my breakfast, and then the two of you can go somewhere and trade insults."

"Grumpy," said Hunter.

"You have no idea," said Al.

"Breakfast?" said Thumps.

"You staying for breakfast, honey?"

"I am," said Hunter. "I'll have what he's having."

Hunter waited until Al had filled her cup and was back at the grill. She opened her purse, took out a postcard, pushed it to Thumps.

"Here's mine," said Hunter. "Guessing it's the same as everyone else's."

The postcard with the eagle on the front, the inscription on the back.

"I've only seen three of them," said Thumps, "but yeah, I imagine they're all the same."

Hunter nodded. "Don't you just love a good mystery?"

"Is that what this is?"

"Absolutely," said Hunter. "Someone must have told you the story of Barca's eagle by now?"

"Pieces."

"Hannibal Barca," said Hunter. "The mystery man of the coin world. My mother met him on two occasions. Said he was a proper gentleman. Very quiet. Didn't talk much about himself. Had some of the best gold coins my mother had ever seen."

"A 1933 double eagle."

"I don't think so," said Hunter. "If she had seen one of those, she would have told me."

"But Barca was rumoured to have had one."

"Rumours," said Hunter, "run through the coin business like blood."

"And Arkady Lukin?"

"Ah, yes," said Hunter, "Barca and Lukin. A most unlikely match. Lukin was flamboyant, loud. Loved to boast about his deals and his coin collection. Everything he did had to be large, large, and larger. Whatever the best was, he had to have it."

"Life of the party."

"Actually, he was a boor. Thought he could make panties melt with a smile."

"Must have been some smile."

"He came to Chicago to look at a particularly nice collection of Indian heads. Tried to hit on my mother." Hunter moved her knife away from her cup. "Then he tried to hit on me. I was eighteen at the time."

"Don't imagine your father was impressed."

"Dad was dead by then. It was just me and my mom and my sisters," said Hunter. "More than enough firepower to sink his battleship."

"And Boris?"

"Worse than the father."

Al brought the plates, steaming from the grill. "I gave you extra hash browns 'cause this is your first visit, so don't be expecting this on a regular basis."

"Everything looks lovely."

"And watch out that this one doesn't sneak a forkful," said Al. "He's got no control when it comes to food."

Thumps gave Hunter a chance to get into the meal.

"So, everyone's in town in the hopes of buying this 1933 double eagle. Even though it's not supposed to exist. Even though it's illegal."

"Not necessarily," said Hunter. "A few of us just want to see it."

"And have you?"

"Yes," said Hunter. "I have."

28

Hunter was a slow eater and a slow talker. She was halfway through the hash browns and her third cup of coffee before she got to the condo where Boris Lukin's body was found.

"We were there earlier."

"All of you?"

"Yes," said Hunter. "All of us. Eliopoulos, Souto, Poe, Myers, Lukin, and me."

"How did you know to go there?"

"Text message," said Hunter. "No idea who sent it. Just gave us a room number and a time."

"So you went."

"Of course we went." Hunter put more pepper on her eggs. "Who wouldn't."

"And?"

"And the place was pretty much as you saw it. Except for the laptop. There was a laptop open on the table the first time."

"Okay."

"So, we're all standing in the room when the laptop comes to life. And there's the double eagle. Or at least a video of the double eagle."

"Not the actual coin?"

"It was a sales pitch, really. The video showed the coin from all angles and up close, a copy of the local paper to give a timeline, and an enhanced voice that told us what we were to do if we were interested in owning the coin."

"Any of this strike you as a little unusual?"

Hunter smiled. "My family has been in this business for generations. This isn't the weirdest thing I've seen. It's not even in the top ten."

"Really?" said Thumps. "Bidding millions of dollars on a video?"

"Believe it or not."

"Sounds like a scam."

"We were to text our bids to a particular number. Winning bid gets invited back for a one-on-one with the coin. The rest of us go home."

"Did you bid?"

"I did," said Hunter. "I had a buyer who wanted the coin."

"But you didn't win?"

"I told him it wouldn't be enough," said Hunter. "He's a cheap billionaire."

"Can I ask you how much you bid?"

Hunter didn't break stride. "Ten million."

Thumps put his fork down.

"It sounds like a lot," said Hunter.

"It is a lot."

"Not to someone who brings in billions every year."

"I don't know anyone who brings in millions."

"Anyway, I didn't win the bid."

"So, one of the others bid more than ten million."

"My guess," said Hunter, "is they had buyers with deeper pockets or who wanted the coin more."

"Any idea who?"

"Dealer or the actual buyer?"

"Either," said Thumps. "Both."

"Not a clue," said Hunter. "You might want to ask them individually. They might tell you, they might not."

"Why'd you tell me?"

"What does it matter?"

"It might be the reason Lukin was killed."

"Good," said Hunter. "I'd hate to think that self-centred bastard died of natural causes."

Thumps glanced at his watch. Beth wouldn't mind starting without him. The sheriff could manage by himself. All in all, it was pleasant sitting in Al's talking with Hunter. And he was working on the case, wasn't he?

"You think someone killed him?"

"It's a delicious thought."

"Any thoughts as to why?"

Hunter pushed her plate to one side. "Boris was a crook. He was a cheat. There are any number of people in Miami who won't shed any tears."

"Montana isn't Miami."

"You should ask his two rent-a-bodyguards," said Hunter. "Maybe someone made them a better offer."

"There were no signs of foul play," said Thumps. "Those two don't look that subtle."

Hunter put her hand on Thumps's. "How about the FBI agent and her sidekick?"

Thumps waited. Kept his mouth shut.

"I know about them," said Hunter. "Boris told me. Wanted to show off. Demonstrate what an important man he was, dragging two feds in his wake."

"Why would they kill him?"

"Why not? Wouldn't be the first time the government stepped over that line."

Al arrived with the coffee pot. "You're not finishing your breakfast?"

"It was first-rate." Hunter stood, took a twenty out of her purse, stuck it under the pepper shaker. "Best breakfast I've had in a long time. But I never finish what's on my plate. Keeps me hungry."

Hunter took her time walking down the row of stools to the front door. Al watched her until she was on the street.

Al set the coffee pot on the counter. "Wouldn't mess with that one."

"She's a person of interest."

"Wouldn't let Claire hear you say that."

Al started to fill Thumps's cup, but Thumps stopped her.

"I have to be at the morgue."

"Lucky you," said Al. "This the dead guy from the resort?"

"It is."

"You still squeamish about Beth's morgue?"

"I'm not squeamish."

"Okay," said Al. "Terrified."

THE OLD LAND Titles office was a two-storey brick building. Beth and Gabby Santucci lived on the second floor. Beth's doctor's office was on the first floor. The basement was the county morgue.

There were three buttons on a keypad.

Normally, Thumps would start with button number one, the residence. Then he would press button number two, the doctor's office. He never pressed button three willingly, and if there was someone else with him—the sheriff, for example—he would let that person do the honours.

Today, there was no sense wasting time or karmic energy. He knew where Beth would be.

"Yes?"

"It's me."

"Welcome to my castle here in Transylvania." Beth and her creepy impersonation of Boris Karloff. "Please come down to the graveyard."

There was a buzz, and the door clicked open. Someone, Thumps thought, not for the first time, should put Dante's caution over the doorway.

"*Lasciate ogne speranza, voi ch'intrate.*"

The stairs down into the basement creaked and moaned, as though they were arthritic and didn't appreciate being stepped on. Beth was standing by a steel table in an apron that had seen better days and needed to be burned. The sheriff was at her side. Lukin was on the table, looking the worse for wear.

"The Karloff routine is getting pretty lame."

"Are you kidding?" said Beth. "I nailed it."

"It was pretty good," said Duke.

"What do you think?"

"He looks dead."

"No," said Beth, "the colour. Of the walls."

"I voted for California Hazy," said Duke, "but what do I know."

Beth waved a scalpel at the walls. "It's called Careless Whispers."

Thumps took a moment to consider the new colour. "Looks great."

Beth shook her head. "Why do I bother."

"Beth just gave me an initial assessment of Mr. Lukin."

"If you had been here," said Beth, "I wouldn't have to repeat myself."

"Maybe just cut to the chase."

"As in, did he die of natural causes or was he murdered?"

"We're still debating that," said Duke. "Seems our Mr. Lukin had a bad heart."

Beth held up a stainless-steel bowl. "I washed off the blood so you wouldn't pass out."

In the bowl was a metal disc with wire leads.

"I don't pass out," said Thumps.

"You get woozy," said Beth. "And I for one don't want to try to catch you."

"Is that a pacemaker?"

Beth shook the bowl. The pacemaker made a rattling sound.

"It is indeed."

"So, he died of a heart attack?"

"Yes," said Beth. "His heart stopped."

"So natural causes."

"Beth is still rooting around in Mr. Lukin, looking for anything unusual."

Thumps felt his stomach turn over.

"Such as?"

"Well," said Beth, "I think the blood work will rule out any poisons. We don't have any obvious signs of trauma. Gun shots, blunt force, that sort of thing."

"Which leaves?"

"Sudden cardiac arrest is not the same thing as a heart attack," said Beth. "A heart attack generally occurs when the blood flow to the heart is blocked. Sudden cardiac arrest is not normally due to a blockage. It's normally a result of irregular heart rhythm."

"Hence the pacemaker?" said Thumps.

"Hence," said Duke.

"There are all sorts of risk factors," said Beth. "Family history of coronary artery disease, smoking, high blood pressure, obesity."

"Diabetes," said Duke.

"Our Mr. Lukin was overweight, a smoker, had a pacemaker. From the look of him, he wasn't particularly active."

"Okay," said Thumps, "I have diabetes. But I don't smoke or drink. And I'm active."

"You eat doughnuts," said Beth.

"So, Mr. Lukin died of sudden cardiac arrest as opposed to a heart attack."

"It would appear," said Beth. "I have to send the pacemaker in for analysis and that will take some time."

"In the meantime," said Duke, "our charming coroner has made a curious discovery."

"I didn't catch it at first," said Beth. "Mr. Lukin, as you can see, is quite hairy, particularly his back."

Thumps looked at the wall. He couldn't really decide if the colour was an improvement over the old colour, but looking at the walls meant he didn't have to look at Lukin's body.

"What do you see?"

"Careless Whispers."

"The body," said Beth. "Take a look."

Beth had shaved a small patch on Lukin's back.

"Here and here," she said.

"Insect?"

"Possible. Going to have to dig a little deeper."

Thumps swallowed, took a deep breath.

"In the meantime," said Beth, "why don't you boys go run down a gang of rustlers or round up a bunch of doggies or whatever else you do while you're waiting for me to solve the case for you."

"Works for me," said Thumps.

"There was one other curiosity." Beth held up a plastic baggie. "I took these dark threads off Lukin's shirt. They don't match anything he was wearing. Have no idea where they came from."

"Good talk," said Thumps. "Time to go."

"I'm going to stay and watch," said Duke. "Beth's going to open his head and look at his brain."

The room did a quick spin. Thumps reached out and steadied himself on the stair railing.

"Now see what you did," said Beth.

"Graduated exposure therapy," said Duke. "Desensitizes the emotions."

"You made that up."

"Get out of here," said Beth. "Some of us have to work."

29

Thumps stood outside the old Land Titles building and said a little prayer for sunshine and fresh air. It would be nice if a stiff breeze came along to blow the smells of the morgue out of his clothes and hair.

Nature's smudge.

"Get in."

Fancy sports car at the curb. Cisco Cruz at the wheel. Zarina Benoit in the passenger seat. Thumps had read somewhere that if prey animals stood still, predators couldn't see them.

"Don't make me arrest you," said Benoit.

"Maybe I'll go back to the morgue."

"Don't worry," said Cruz. "He's bluffing."

The back seat of the Mustang was a design afterthought. Thumps had to sit sideways to have enough room for his legs, the seat belt wrapped around him at an awkward angle.

"I could have walked."

"Does he always complain like this?" said Benoit.

"Always," said Cruz.

"Coffee," said Benoit. "I need coffee."

"Dumbo's," said Thumps. "Take the next right."

"Isn't that the shop with the great doughnuts and the racist asshole?"

"New management," said Thumps. "Same doughnuts."

Thumps had to crawl out of the back seat on his hands and knees.

"He's just doing this for sympathy," said Cruz.

"It is a small back seat," said Benoit. "I wouldn't want to sit in it."

"I won't be getting in the back again," said Thumps.

"*Cabrón*, how can you say that?" said Cruz. "This is a beautiful car."

FANCY WAS AT the counter when Cruz and Benoit and Thumps came into the café.

"Sit wherever you like, yeah?"

Cruz took a moment to take in the interior. "Can't believe it's the same place. Remember it as dog-shit brown all over."

"It was Bustervated," said Thumps.

"Like the TV show?" said Benoit. "I love that show."

"Where's the asshole?"

"On a trip with his Puerto Rican girlfriend."

"You're kidding," said Cruz.

"Hard to believe, I know."

"Look," said Benoit, "they have Bavarian creams."

Thumps led everyone to a table at the far end of the café.

"Mr. DreadfulWater," said Fancy. "You brought friends."

"Not friends," said Thumps. "They're government assassins."

"Then I'm guessing they'll be wanting coffee."

"And doughnuts," said Benoit. "One of the Bavarians for me."

"Coffee and a couple of the apple spice for me," said Cruz.

"And an unglazed old-fashioned for the local law?"

"Remember," said Cruz, "you're diabetic."

Thumps had a flash image of Boris Lukin lying on Beth's table.

"Maybe just coffee."

Cruz waited until Fancy had vanished into the kitchen. "So, tell us."

"Tell you what?"

"The autopsy," said Benoit. "Was Lukin murdered?"

"You should ask the sheriff."

"How about we ask you?"

"We're all on the same side," said Cruz. "We should be sharing."

"Says the man who doesn't share," said Thumps.

"I share," said Cruz.

"'Benoit is my fiancée'?" Thumps held up one finger. "'We're thinking about settling down in Chinook'?"

"*Ese* . . ."

"'Benoit is my ex-wife'?" Thumps held up three fingers. "'We have a young son named Duncan'?"

"Enough with the fingers," said Cruz. "Sometimes I have to improvise."

Fancy came out of the kitchen with a tray. "Okay," she said. "Bavarian and two apple spice. With coffee on its way."

"Looks great," said Benoit.

Fancy came back with the coffee pot. "You two really government assassins?"

"That's us," said Cruz.

"As in Dag Hammarskjold, Salvador Allende, John Kennedy, Bobby Kennedy, Malcolm X, Martin Luther King?"

Benoit and Cruz froze in place.

"I'm just slagging you." Fancy filled the cups. "Land of the free, home of the brave, fair play, baseball, apple pie, and all that, yeah?"

"Yeah," said Benoit. "All that."

Thumps could see he was going to have to watch his step around Fancy Whelan.

"I hear there's a dead fellow up at the resort," said Fancy. "You get that sorted yet?"

"Not yet," said Thumps.

"Well, I'll leave that to you and your assassins," said Fancy. "You need another doughnut or more coffee, you just give me a shout."

Cruz finished his first doughnut, started in on the second. Benoit took her time with the Bavarian, used a knife and fork to eat the pastry.

"You know I can't show you the bureau's file on Lukin," said Benoit. "It's classified."

"So is the autopsy report," said Thumps, "until it's made public at the inquest. Ongoing investigation and all that. And the inquest can't happen until the blood work results come in, and the state lab is likely backed up. And then there's the data off the pacemaker, which will probably require a subpoena."

"You know," said Benoit, "you're not as funny as you think you are."

"He can be pretty funny," said Cruz.

Thumps put his cup down. "Your laptop able to connect to the bureau's database?"

"If I want it to," said Benoit.

"The name Hannibal Barca mean anything to you?"

Benoit looked at Cruz, who shook his head.

"Barca," said Thumps. "Look him up. See what you find."

"Why?"

"Quid pro quo," said Thumps. "I'll tell you what we know about Lukin."

"We can find that out on our own," said Benoit. "We can be persuasive."

"You want to go head-to-head with Beth and Duke?" Thumps wet his finger, picked pieces of doughnut off Cruz's plate. "I'm faster and easier."

"Barca spelled the way it sounds?" said Cruz.

FANCY BROUGHT MORE coffee and a second Bavarian.

Benoit worked her laptop. "Okay, I got one photograph and a bunch of nothing."

"Anything that links Barca to Lukin?"

"Barca was a coin dealer," said Benoit. "That's as close as they get."

"Your files say what happened to Barca?"

"Nothing," said Benoit.

"Okay," said Thumps. "Send what you have to Duke."

"Why don't I send it to you?" said Cruz. "You've got internet now. What's your email?"

Thumps could picture the sheet of paper Christopher Reno had left him. He just couldn't see what Reno had written on it.

"You don't know your email address?"

"I left it at home."

"Nobody leaves their email address at home," said Benoit.

"Give me your cellphone," said Cruz.

Thumps fished it out of his pocket.

"It's locked," said Cruz. "What's your password?"

"Let me guess," said Benoit. "It's at home with your email."

"Okay," said Cruz. "Let's try something simple. Boris Lukin."

"Quid pro quo," said Benoit. "You remember quid pro quo?"

"Beth is still working on it," said Thumps. "It could be natural causes. It could be something else."

"Okay, and until we know for sure," said Benoit, "we'd appreciate it if you didn't mention any of this to anyone."

"You mean about the FBI co-operating with the locals?"

"We're not co-operating," said Benoit. "The FBI doesn't co-operate."

"We're just having doughnuts and coffee with a pal," said Cruz.

Benoit looked at her watch. "But right now, we have to get back to the resort. The forensics team will be arriving shortly."

"You want me to drop you off at your house?"

"Would I have to ride in the back?"

"I've got shotgun," said Benoit. "So, yeah."

THUMPS STAYED BEHIND, sat at the table, picked up doughnut crumbs with his finger.

"Friends deserted you?" Fancy filled Thumps's cup.

"They did."

"Ready for that old-fashioned?"

"Better not," said Thumps.

"Diabetes is not much fun."

"Pain in the ass. Can I ask you a question?"

"Sure, yeah."

"You have an email address, right?"

"Couldn't live without it," said Fancy.

"Did it come with a password?"

Fancy's smile filled the café. "You think I could be a government assassin?"

"You want to be a government assassin?"

Fancy threw the dishtowel over one shoulder, picked up the coffee pot, grinned. "Don't want to be making doughnuts all my life, now do I."

30

Fancy was at the counter helping a customer when a phone began ringing. Neither the customer nor Fancy seemed concerned that a phone was going unanswered.

"Think that's your phone, yeah."

There was a virtual button on his phone that was lit up. He tried tapping it. Nothing. It kept ringing.

"You have to use your finger to swipe it," Fancy called out. "Left to right."

Not intuitive, Thumps thought to himself. Not intuitive at all.

The woman on the other end was pleasant. They were cleaning ducts in his neighbourhood, and a crew could stop in and do the job quickly and efficiently. What time tomorrow would be good?

He had gotten these calls before on his rotary phone. They were scams. Annoying as hell. How they had gotten his cellphone number so quickly was troubling.

"Important?" asked Fancy.

"Duct cleaning," said Thumps.

"I like the ones that tell me I'm about to get hit by a fine from the tax people if I don't call the number they give me," said Fancy. "Or the one about the Amazon purchase for a couple thousand dollars that has been charged to my Visa."

"How come I can get calls without using my password, but I can't call out?"

"Did you forget your password?"

"Didn't even know I had one," said Thumps. "The new guy in town set me up with internet and phone."

"Christopher Reno," said Fancy. "Yeah, he likes my sour cream glazed. Probably did a temporary password. Figures you'll change it later. Try one, two, three, four."

Thumps tapped the numbers. The screen came to life. "It worked."

"So, now," said Fancy, "you'll have to change that password to one that you'll remember."

"I can remember one, two, three, four," said Thumps.

"So can everyone else," said Fancy.

At least now he could try Claire. The call went right to voice mail and the mailbox that still wasn't set up. Claire not answering her phone was not good news, no matter what Al said.

Thumps was debating a refill and the doughnut he wasn't supposed to have. Maybe it was time to put his theory of doughnut-eating intervals to the test.

He had just convinced himself to proceed with the experiment when his phone rang again.

"This time," said Fancy, "they're calling about the big prize you've won."

"You feeling lucky?" Ora Mae's voice sounded close, as though she were standing outside in the parking lot.

"Ora Mae?"

"Well, it's not Rihanna."

"How did you get this number?"

"Duh. Where are you?"

"Dumbo's."

"Get your ass over here," said Ora Mae. "And, while you're at it, grab me a couple of the maple glazed."

"I'm not the doughnut taxi."

"And put on your 'let's make a deal' shirt."

Thumps put the phone back in his pocket. The damn thing was beginning to be annoying. Who didn't have his cell number?

"Who was that?"

"Ora Mae Foreman."

"The real estate lady," said Fancy. "Bet she wants a couple of maple glazed."

"She does."

Fancy put the doughnuts into a small white box with a red ribbon tied around it. "Sheriff say anything about the black licorice and the sweet corn and blueberry doughnuts?"

Thumps waited a beat too long. "He said they were . . . formidable."

"He did, did he?"

"His exact words," said Thumps. "Verbatim."

"Not much for fabrications and forgeries," said Fancy, "but I do like a man that has posh words."

Thumps was in Dumbo's parking lot before he remembered that his car was at home. He felt a little silly walking down the street, holding the box level, so the doughnuts wouldn't slip together, as though he were bringing a corsage to a prom date.

The house was deserted and quiet. No cats. Wherever they were, they would make their way home. Or they wouldn't. No Cruz, no Benoit, no sheriff, no Archie. A perfect moment. The temptation to crawl into bed and let the day pass him in the fast lane was overwhelming.

The instruction sheet was on the counter. Reno was clear and succinct. Password for the internet, password for the cellphone, password for the streaming services. Spending just a couple of minutes with the ins and outs of the new reality was enough to send Thumps to the rotary to call Reno and tell him to take everything out and put things back the way they had been.

Except the rotary no longer worked.

At least now he knew the password for the cellphone, and he'd be damned if he was going to change it. Even if he knew how. Oh, yes, at the bottom of the page. Instructions for that as well.

Thumps folded the sheet, slipped it into his back pocket. Next time he was near a copier, he'd make a dozen copies and strategically place them around the house. He'd put one in his car, have another reduced to the size of a credit card and laminated, so he could carry it in his wallet.

No fool him.

Ora Mae Foreman was in her chair, a bottle of champagne on her desk.

"You know what this is?"

"Champagne?"

"Carbonated success."

"You sold a house?"

"Sold three," said Ora Mae. "And if I can kick the lead out of your ass, I can sell four."

"You sold my house?"

"No, of course I haven't sold it. That would be illegal. But I can sell it with one phone call."

Thumps looked around the office. "Where are the demon spawn?"

"At the resort," said Ora Mae. "They wanted to see the gold-coin show. Don't change the subject."

"The coin show?"

"What can I say?" said Ora Mae. "They like money. They want to see what it looks like."

Thumps couldn't imagine two twenty-somethings having any interest in a bunch of coins in glass cases, even gold ones. What had interested him when he was twenty?

Oh, right. That.

"The way I see it," said Ora Mae, "you sell your house now, you'll get top dollar. And you wouldn't have to buy back into the market right away. You could go out to Claire's place, live with her. Couple of years of fresh air and communing with nature and a six-year-old who will then be seven or eight, the market cools off, maybe even drops, and the three of you can get a nice place in town, and Bob's your uncle."

"I actually have an uncle named Bob."

Ora Mae didn't break stride. "Or, you can buy in right away. Spend a little extra to get a really great house. Claire sees you do that, she can't help but be impressed with that kind of commitment and foresight."

Ora Mae stopped to take a breath.

"You know how birds do it, don't you?"

"Birds?"

"The boy birds make a nest, and they give open-house tours for the girl birds, and if the ladies like the look of the place, they move in."

Thumps was tempted to tell Ora Mae about Ivory and the possibility that her uncle was going to try to take her back, but there was nothing to be gained by sharing such information.

"Where is Claire anyway? I called her a couple of times."

"Think she went up to Standoff to visit friends."

"Standoff? That's in Alberta."

"I guess."

"Don't be guessing." Ora Mae narrowed her eyes. "There something I should know?"

Thumps shook his head. "Maybe I should look at some of these houses before they disappear."

"Now that's what I'm talking about," said Ora Mae. "Initiative. Make a new man of you."

Ora Mae handed him several sheets of paper.

"Here's the listings for four properties that you should consider. The last one on the list is my favourite. Little over an acre. Backs onto the national forest. Take your time. Walk by them, check out the neighbourhood, see what's there."

"Okay."

"Just don't take too long," said Ora Mae. "If I were you, I'd start looking right now."

Thumps heard the phone ringing. It was only after the fifth ring that he realized it was his phone. Claire. At last.

"DreadfulWater."

Okay, not Claire.

"Where are you?"

"In town."

"What the hell are you doing there?" said Archie. "We need you here."

Thumps didn't want to ask the little Greek why he was needed.

"There's been a development."

"Have you seen Claire?"

"Claire?" said Archie. "This isn't about Claire."

"Archie . . ."

"And Duke said you should stop by Dumbo's and pick up more doughnuts."

"I'm not stopping by Dumbo's."

"A dozen assorted," said Archie. "You know how Duke gets when he's annoyed."

31

Driving alone in the sanctuary of his car was where Thumps had some of his best ideas. And some of his worst. Today, the trip across the prairies and up into the mountains produced a little of both.

The problem was, many times he couldn't tell which was which.

Selling his house and moving onto the reservation with Claire and Ivory was tempting. Likewise, selling his house and buying a larger house in town with enough room for three people seemed a reasonable idea as well. It was the selling of his bungalow that bothered him. There was nothing to say that Claire would be interested in living together. They had talked about it, had even moved to the edge of a decision. But something always caused them to step back.

If Thumps sold his house, he would be cutting a tether. And if the relationship didn't work out, what was there to keep him in Chinook? Friends, sure, but the house was his anchor. Without it, he could well drift away.

After all, he hadn't chosen Chinook.

He had been on his way east with no destination in mind, had been stranded in town with a broken fuel pump. That he stayed was a combination of circumstance, fatigue, sorrow, and the realization that there was no place in the world he wanted to be.

You had to die somewhere, and at the time, Chinook looked to be as good a place as any.

Good ideas, bad ideas, sad ideas. Maybe the car wasn't the sanctuary he thought it was. Maybe he should get out and walk more.

Archie hadn't said just what the "development" was, and Thumps didn't feel any sense of urgency. The little Greek had sounded more bemused than angry. Whatever it was, it wasn't in the same category as a homicide or the destruction of a historic building.

Deanna Heavy Runner was waiting for him in the lobby.

"Penthouse."

"You want to give me a hint?"

"I could." Deanna pressed PH on the pad. "But where's the fun in that?"

Duke and Archie were in the suite. Otto Myers was handcuffed to a chair. His cheek and nose were red and swollen.

"A lawsuit," Myers was shouting. "Can you spell *lawsuit*?"

Duke bent over, put his face next to Myers's. "Now I'm going to ask you politely one more time to keep your voice down so you don't frighten the horses."

"Lawsuit!" bellowed Myers. "I will own your damn town."

Duke straightened up. "Officer Heavy Runner, would you kindly take Mr. Myers down to the cruiser, drive him to the jail, put him in the holding cell until we can get him arraigned."

"Judge Blankenship is out at Red Tail Lake for the fishing derby," said Deanna. "Probably have to keep the prisoner over the weekend."

"What?"

"One of the inconveniences of our great judicial system."

"You can't put me in jail."

"Sure, I can," said Duke. "Breaking and entering. Impeding an investigation. Assault on an officer . . ."

"She attacked me," said Myers. "Look at my face."

"At which point, Officer Heavy Runner had to defend herself and subdue the suspect."

"Look at my face."

Duke turned to Thumps. "I don't see a doughnut box."

"That's because there are no doughnuts."

Duke shook his head. "You're almost as annoying as Myers here."

"Tell Thumps what happened," said Archie.

"You already know what happened," said Duke.

"Sure," said Archie, "but good stories are hard to find."

"That's not what happened," says Myers. "It was all a misunderstanding."

"You're going to love it," said Archie. "You're going to love it."

THUMPS SAT DOWN on the sofa. Duke leaned on the counter. Deanna stood next to Myers to make sure the man didn't pick up the chair and try to make a break for it.

The story was simple enough and not all that dramatic. Lukin's body was discovered on the fifth floor. But he was staying in the penthouse. So, Duke had locked down both units, and Deanna had dutifully put an X of crime-scene tape across each doorway, had sealed the units with a large warning sticker that said "Crime Scene. Do Not Cross" in yellow and black.

The idea was that Deanna would process each unit, starting with the one in which Lukin's body had been discovered. She had done that, had moved on to the penthouse, where she discovered the seal on the door had been broken.

"Myers was hiding in the closet," said Duke.

"Attacked Deanna," said Archie. "Tried to escape."

"I didn't attack her," yelled Myers. "I didn't try to escape."

At this point in the storytelling, Duke began to smile. "Assaulting one of my deputies will always put me in a sideways mood, but part of me feels sorry for any man stupid enough to take on a Heavy Runner woman."

"Roxanne hears about this," said Archie, "he may not get out of here alive."

"That's not what happened," said Myers. "It was all a misunderstanding."

"Anyway," Duke continued, "Deanna tried to stop him. Myers took a swing at her. And things got western pretty quick."

"You believe it," said Archie. "He took a swing at a Heavy Runner."

"We were just in the process of chatting with Mr. Myers when you showed up," said Duke. "Maybe you want to do the honours."

Thumps leaned in to Myers. "You really took on a Heavy Runner?"

Deanna took Myers down to the cruiser. Thumps felt some sympathy for the man. He was no match for Deanna, but assaulting a police officer was not something that Duke was going to let slide.

"So," said the sheriff, "what do you figure?"

"Myers was searching Lukin's quarters," said Archie. "That's pretty obvious."

"He was looking for Barca's eagle," said Thumps. "Myers is frightened of his own shadow. But he just couldn't help himself."

"We don't even know if the coin exists," said Archie.

"Doesn't matter," said Thumps, "so long as everyone believes it does."

"So," said Duke, "what do we know, what do we suspect, why didn't you bring doughnuts?"

Archie nodded. "Six major coin dealers come to a regional coin show."

"Because someone sent them each a postcard with the promise of a 1933 double eagle."

"With the ninja assassin and an FBI agent along for the ride," said Archie.

"Cruz and Benoit are another issue," said Thumps.

"Which is?" said Archie.

"Police stuff," said Duke. "Nothing to do with the coin show."

"You're going to stonewall me?" said Archie. "After I've almost solved Boris Lukin's murder all by myself?"

"We don't even know if it was murder," said Thumps.

Duke pushed off the counter. "Oh, about that. Appears Boris Lukin was indeed murdered."

"How?"

"Those marks on his back?" said Duke. "Beth is pretty sure it was a stun gun."

"Stun guns don't kill," said Archie.

"Man had a bad heart," said Thumps. "Maybe the killer didn't know that."

Duke put his hat on. "Well, this is certainly another fine mess you've gotten me into, Deputy DreadfulWater."

"We should round up the suspects in one room," said Archie. "Grill them until somebody makes a mistake."

"That's what they do on *Death in Paradise*," said Duke. "Always seems to work for the gang on Saint Marie."

"Sure," said Thumps. "What could possibly go wrong?"

32

The one room "with all the suspects in it" was the Antelope Room. It was down the hall from the Blackfoot Room. Thumps momentarily considered naming the rooms in his house—the Freeway Room, the Cookie Room, the Pops Room—and gave it up immediately.

Duke and Deanna and Archie took care of the roundup. By the time Thumps got to the room, everyone was there, including Otto Myers, who was now handcuffed to another chair and not looking any happier.

"Could someone take these fucking handcuffs off me?"

"You're a flight risk," said Duke. "Quit squirming. You're going to chafe your wrist."

Souto gave Myers a motherly smile. "You really broke into Lukin's penthouse?"

"I didn't break in. I had a key."

"That you took off the cleaning crew's cart," said Deanna. "That's theft."

"I borrowed it. I was going to give it back," said Myers. "Until you jumped me."

"How about we all settle down," said Duke. "There have been a few new developments."

The room went silent.

"It appears that Boris Lukin was murdered." Duke let the word hang in the air. "So, what was simply a fluster-duck is now a homicide."

"You sure he was murdered?" said Poe.

"Very sure," said Duke.

"Holy shit," said Hunter. "That is so cool."

"Yes, ma'am," said the sheriff.

"Then I'm a suspect."

"Actually," said Duke, "you're all suspects."

EVERYONE ARRANGED THEMSELVES at the long table. A very corporate look. If Thumps didn't know any better, he might have thought he was about to address the board of directors for a multinational.

Nico Eliopoulos began rubbing his head. "Mr. Lukin was murdered."

"Don't sound surprised, Nico," said Souto. "He was an obnoxious man."

"Sure," said Nico. "But to be murdered."

"I'm sure no one wants to speak ill of the dead," said Duke. "Then again, strikes me as the perfect time to do just that."

"How was it done?" asked Poe.

"So," said Duke, "who wants to be first?"

"Sure as hell not going to railroad me," said Myers.

"Why is Otto handcuffed to the chair?" asked Hunter.

"How about you, Mr. Poe," said Duke. "What was your relationship with Boris Lukin?"

"We didn't have one," said Poe. "And yes, why is Otto handcuffed to the chair?"

"Is he under arrest for killing Boris?" said Souto.

"Not yet," said Duke. "Can we get back to speaking ill of the dead?"

"Maybe we should start at the beginning," said Thumps. "Work our way forward."

"The 1933 double eagle," said Nico.

"Ah," said Poe. "*C'est l'essentiel. La raison d'être.*"

Hunter made a popping sound with her mouth. "Show-off."

"In particular," Thumps continued, "a 1933 double eagle that Hannibal Barca is supposed to have had in his possession."

"You really do mean the beginning," said Hunter.

"That old saw," said Myers. "Never much believed it."

"Let's pretend that it's true," said Thumps. "Nineteen years ago, Hannibal Barca went to Manhattan for a coin show."

"Twenty," said Poe. "Twenty years to be exact."

"The day of the show, Mr. Barca was supposed to have a meeting with Arkady Lukin."

"That's right," said Poe.

"And dinner with you in the evening."

Poe nodded. "But he never showed."

"How long did you wait until you reported him missing?"

"The following evening," said Poe. "Hannibal hadn't checked out of his room, he hadn't tried to call me. He had just vanished."

"And you told the authorities about the meeting with Lukin?"

"I did," said Poe. "The police questioned Arkady. Turns out he was in Miami at the time. His alibi was solid. And he swore that there had been no arrangements for such a meeting."

"Is this going somewhere?" said Souto. "This is a very old story, and it's been beaten to death."

"You think you could speed things up?" said Duke. "I'd like to get home in time for the game."

"And I'd like someone to take off these damn handcuffs," said Myers. "This is illegal confinement. You're all witnesses."

"Oh, put a sock in it," said Hunter.

"Fast forward to the present," said Thumps.

"Thank you," said Duke.

"Out of the blue, each of you receives a postcard with a picture of an eagle on the front and a cryptic message on the back suggesting that the double eagle Hannibal Barca was rumoured to have had is available for sale, that it would be sold here at the coin exhibition."

"Which is the reason all of you came out here in the first place," said Archie. "To mess with my exhibition."

"I've always wanted to see the American West," said Nico. "But, yes, I came to see the eagle."

"Which brings us to the first part of the puzzle," said Thumps. "Let's imagine that twenty years ago, Hannibal Barca *did* have a 1933 double eagle. What happened to it? If Barca was killed when he went to New York, it stands to reason that the eagle was stolen at that time, and now the person who stole the eagle and killed Barca is trying to sell it."

"Well, that's not Arkady Lukin," said Souto. "Even if he did kill Barca and steal the eagle, he's dead."

"He had an alibi," said Hunter, "but he could have hired someone to kill Barca and steal the coin."

"And he would have passed the coin on to his son," said Nico. "This is what fathers do."

"Possible," said Thumps. "But then why did Boris Lukin come out here with the rest of you?"

"You're babbling," said Myers. "Would someone please take these handcuffs off me?"

"If Arkady Lukin did, in fact, have Barca killed and stole the coin, then, as you say, it stands to reason that Boris would have inherited the coin from his father. And that would mean that Boris sent the postcards."

"Which makes no sense," said Archie.

"No, it doesn't," said Thumps. "If he had the coin and wanted to sell it, why do it like this? He could have just called up any number of billionaires with limited scruples."

"Meaning most billionaires," said Archie.

"He didn't need to put it up for auction in the middle of nowhere."

"I see your point," said Duke. "I resent the insinuation."

"We are in the middle of nowhere," said Archie, "and that's the way I like it."

"So, you're saying that Boris didn't have the coin?" said Hunter.

"I think Boris *wanted* the coin," said Thumps. "I'm guessing that his father wanted the coin and never got it, and when the postcard arrived, the son saw a chance to own something the father couldn't have."

"Freud?" said Souto. "Really?"

"Which means someone else has the eagle," said Nico.

"Yes," said Thumps. "I think someone else has the eagle."

"Any idea who that might be?" said Poe.

"Not a clue."

Myers smacked the table with his free hand. "So why are we all sitting here? Why am I in handcuffs?"

"Here's what I think," said Thumps. "I think you all came out here in the hopes of buying a very rare coin."

"One of the rarest," said Hunter.

"Also illegal," said Nico.

"Making it even more valuable," said Poe.

Thumps nodded. "What's it worth? Ten, twenty million?"

"Somewhere in between," said Poe. "Be my guess."

"You could name your own price," said Souto.

"So, after you all received your postcards, I'm guessing you contacted your very best buyers and arranged for a maximum figure to bid on the coin. After you saw the video of the coin, you placed your bids via text message? Is that correct?"

"Hypothetically," said Souto.

"Highest bidder would then get to see the coin in person, examine it, complete the transaction."

"Hypothetically," said Myers. "I want it noted that all this is hypothetical."

"Noted," said Thumps. "So, here's what I want to know. After you saw the video of the coin, how many of you believed it to be real?"

"It's a trick," said Myers.

"God," said Hunter, "grow up, Otto."

"Why does this matter?" said Souto. "There's no way any of us could tell unless we saw the coin in person."

"Show of hands," said Thumps. "How many of you think the coin was real?"

The hands went up slowly. Everyone except Myers.

"I'm not sticking my hand in the air until you take off these cuffs."

"Are you suggesting that one of us killed Boris to keep him from bidding?"

"Wouldn't be any way the killer knew who was going to bid what," said Archie. "No way to control the winning bid."

"And with Lukin's death," said Duke, "the long arm of the law gets involved. Can't imagine that's something that our killer would particularly want."

"So, the second piece of the puzzle," said Thumps. "Why was Lukin killed?"

"You have a theory?" said Poe.

"More a vague idea," said Thumps.

"You want to share with the rest of the children?" said Hunter.

Thumps looked around the table. "Not just yet," he said. "May be wrong. Don't want to look foolish."

"A murder? A rare coin that isn't supposed to exist? Handcuffing Otto to a chair?" Hunter waved her finger in a circle. "I think we've moved past foolish."

"There is one question that I keep coming back to," said Thumps. "What if there was no winning bid?"

"You mean, if there was a reserve price that no one met?"

"No," said Thumps. "What if all the bids, high and low, were rejected?"

"Why would our mystery seller do that?"

"Like I said," said Thumps. "Don't want to look foolish."

Poe got to his feet. "I sense this meeting is over. Are we free to go?"

"You are," said Duke. "But I'd appreciate it if you could all stick around for a bit."

"Until the end of the show," said Souto. "Then I'm out of here."

"I'm too curious to leave," said Hunter.

"I'll stay," said Poe. "I still have to see the sights."

"The mountain air is quite refreshing," said Eliopoulos.

"You mean cold as hell," said Souto.

DUKE WAITED UNTIL all the dealers had left the room. "Well, that was a whole lot of nothing."

"And what was that nonsense about all the bids being rejected?" said Archie.

Thumps leaned on the table. "What if I told you I know who killed Boris Lukin and why?"

"You know who killed Lukin?" Duke's eyes went hard. "You know why?"

"No," said Thumps, "but I'm hoping that the killer thinks I do."

33

Thumps and the sheriff walked to their cars.

"You happen to notice that we're spending a good deal of time standing in parking lots?"

"Stars are nice."

Duke stopped at his cruiser and looked up. "Fall sky. Can't beat it."

"Resort is a bit bright."

"Light pollution," said Duke. "Think about those poor bastards in Los Angeles. They can't see shit, *and* they can't breathe."

"Benoit sent you the FBI file on Hannibal Barca," said Thumps. "Maybe you could print it off. We could take a look at it tomorrow."

"What's wrong with all that nifty equipment Chris installed at your place?"

"Don't think he put in a printer."

"What you mean is you haven't found it yet and don't know how to make it work."

"Beth say anything else about Lukin?"

"Such as?"

"Did she really say that Lukin was murdered or were you just shaking the tree?"

"Why do you ask?"

"You let Myers slide. That's not like you."

"Myers is an idiot. Deanna could have put him in the hospital. Figure the black eye and the bruises are time served."

"So. A stun gun."

"Beth's going to send the body over to Helena for confirmation," said Duke. "You know your constellations?"

"You mean like Orion and the Big Dipper?"

"Yeah."

"Can't say I do."

"According to Macy, they're up there somewhere." Duke sat back on the hood of the car. "You ever think about that?"

"Constellations?"

"Stars," said Duke. "They've been floating around up there from before we were born, and they'll be there long after we're dead."

"Okay."

"I'm not sure if that's comforting or sad."

The night air had turned cold. Thumps was going to have to start wearing a warmer jacket.

"Didn't you want to get home in time for the game?"

"Couple of years back, Macy and I drove up the Beartooth Highway. You ever been?"

"Nope."

"Nice view of the Milky Way from the top. Sometimes you can catch the northern lights. You and Claire should go sometime."

"Sure."

"That was my segue," said Duke, "into your personal life."

"There's a reason they call it 'personal.'"

"My job is to make sure all my deputies are of sound mind and body."

"Claire and I are fine."

"She and Ivory back from Alberta yet?"

"Personal."

Duke leaned back. "Only get so many nights like this," he said. "Seems a shame to waste even one."

"I'm going home."

"Oh, look." Duke shaded his eyes. "A shooting star. We should make a wish."

"World peace," said Thumps.

Duke straightened his hat, opened the car door. "Yeah, that was my thought as well."

THUMPS DROVE OUT of the mountains, followed the stars home. He could have been more generous. Duke had wanted to talk, something the man didn't do that often, and Thumps had cut him off. He was willing to listen to the sheriff, he just wasn't willing to share, in part because he didn't have anything to bring to the conversation.

He knew why Claire had gone to Alberta, but he had no idea what had happened. She hadn't asked him to go with her. She hadn't called. She hadn't answered his attempts to reach her.

There was a pattern to this. Every time she got upset, she closed herself off from the world. From Thumps. Came out only when she was good and ready, didn't let anyone else share that dark, lonely space.

What was he supposed to do with that? How was he to explain it to someone else?

CRUZ'S CAR WAS at the curb. As Thumps pulled up behind it, he could see the ninja assassin sitting on the front porch. Pops the dog was at his feet. Freeway and Cookie were on the windowsill.

"Thank god you got home before this monster dog loved me to death."

"I'm tired. I'm grumpy. I want to go to bed."

"Look at this." Cruz lifted a leg. "You know what dog slobber does to good shoes?"

"What are you doing here?"

"Don't you want to know about Zee?"

"No."

"She got recalled to Seattle," said Cruz. "She's going to take the hit for Lukin."

Thumps opened the door. "And you're concerned because? She's your fiancée? Your ex-wife? The mother of your child?"

"You are grumpy."

"None of the above?"

"You should take friendly lessons from the dog."

"The dog that just slobbered on your shoes?"

"There's that."

Thumps went into the kitchen, opened the refrigerator. Cruz followed.

"Why are you here?"

"What do you mean?"

"Boris Lukin is dead. Benoit has been recalled to Seattle. Why are you still here?"

"Loose ends," said Cruz. "I don't like loose ends."

Thumps helped himself to a handful of grapes. "Is this your way of asking for an update on the case?"

"Nope," said Cruz. "I know Lukin was murdered. I know how."

"You talk to Beth?"

"Sort of."

"You tapped her phone? You broke into her office?"

"Let's just say I'm up to date. What neither of us knows is the why and the who."

"So?"

"So, let's be a team," said Cruz. "You and me. Solve the case. Save the damsel. Slay the dragon."

"No."

"No? How can you say no?"

"I'll leave the spy stuff to you."

"*Cabrón*, you wouldn't be the spy. I'm the spy. You'd be like my sidekick."

"I'm going to bed," said Thumps. "Let yourself out."

"Small problem," said Cruz. "When the agency pulled Zee, they also checked us out of the resort."

Thumps could feel his shoulder creeping up his neck. "And you have no place to stay?"

"I was thinking I could stay with you," said Cruz. "That way, we could compare notes."

"There are no notes to compare."

Cruz made himself comfortable at the kitchen table. "What about that coin? The 1933 double eagle? It's rare. It's valuable. It's illegal."

"All of the above," said Thumps.

"You talked to Lukin, didn't you?" Cruz stretched. "Before he died."

"Hard to do after."

Cruz didn't smile. He didn't move.

"More like he talked to me," said Thumps.

"About?"

"He knew about you and Benoit."

"He mention anything else?"

Thumps searched Cruz's face, came up empty. "Such as?"

Cruz sat up straight, put both hands on the table. "Just before Lukin left Miami, he gave us a name. Black Ice."

"And this is a name for . . . ?"

"We don't know," said Cruz. "Could be an individual. Could be an organization. Could be an operation."

"Could be Lukin screwing with you," said Thumps. "Dangle a mysterious something in your face, keep you interested."

"Could," said Cruz.

"You think this Black Ice, whatever it is, got him killed?"

"No, I don't," said Cruz. "Like you say, everything points to the coin."

"K.I.S.S.," said Thumps. "We know that all the dealers, including Lukin, were in that unit together. We know that they all watched a video that supposedly showed the coin. We know they were encouraged to bid on the coin via text message."

"High bid gets to see the coin in person," said Cruz.

"Right," said Thumps. "So we have to assume that Lukin was high bid, that he went back to the room to see the coin in person."

"And you think he bought it?"

"You said the FBI has been sitting on Lukin for more than a year. You must know where all his money is buried."

"Trust me, I'm not FBI."

"Ex-wife? Son?"

"But I can say with some authority that there have been no large money transfers."

"Then if Lukin didn't buy the coin, why was he in that room?"

"Maybe he was high bid, but then he reneged. Killer got pissed. Killed him."

"With five other dealers waiting in the wings to buy the coin?"

"You're not a lot of help," said Cruz.

Thumps got out of his chair. "Guest bedroom," he said. "Sheets and towels are in the closet."

"What about the cats? I don't sleep with cats."

THUMPS TOOK THE cellphone with him into the bedroom. If Claire tried to reach him, he didn't want to miss the call. He sat on the edge of the bed and looked out the window. The stars weren't as bright as they had been in the mountains, but they were still there, bright sparks in a black sky, comforting and sad.

34

Thumps was up early the next morning, but Cruz was already gone. The fancy sports car that had been parked outside the house the night before was in the wind.

Just as well. Cruz was a big boy. He could find trouble on his own. Between the sheriff and Claire and a murder that was a dead end, Thumps had plenty already, thank you very much.

AL'S WAS CROWDED, his usual stool taken, and Thumps had to sit next to Chintak Rawat and Stas Black Weasel.

"Mr. Thumps," said Rawat, "you are here early."

"He cannot sleep in," said Stas. "He is long arm of law now and no longer lazy photographer."

"I'm still a lazy photographer."

"Yes," said Stas, "but now is hobby."

Rawat warmed his hands on the cup. "Have you found a house?"

"Yes," said Stas, "tell us exciting news."

"I would recommend a bungalow," said Rawat. "Stairs are fine for young people, but as we get older, it is best to do all our living on one floor."

"But with children," said Stas, "distance is good."

"Who told you I was looking for a house?"

Thumps knew the answer to the question before it was out of his mouth.

"Something with a garage," said Rawat. "As we age, scraping ice off the windshield is no longer enjoyable."

Thumps couldn't remember a time when scraping ice off a windshield had been enjoyable.

"Home ownership," said Rawat. "Such a good investment. Over the years, your equity will increase, and you will be able to leave it to your children."

"Also, money pit," said Stas. "Repair this, repair that. New stove. New dishwasher. New furnace, air conditioner. Very expensive."

Al came down the counter with the coffee pot.

"Well, if it isn't the country squire."

"Coffee, please."

"I vote you get a place in the country. Couple of acres. Raise chickens. Maybe get a horse for Ivory. Commune with nature."

"Breakfast," said Thumps. "The usual."

"Course, if you wanted country, you could always move in with Claire," said Al. "But in my experience, when two people get together, it's always better to start fresh."

"Don't think I'm buying a house," said Thumps. "Don't think Claire and I are getting together."

Al pointed the coffee pot at Rawat and Stas. "I told you he'd get cold feet."

"Yes," said Rawat, "it is difficult giving up the glory of bachelorhood."

"Living alone is lonely," said Stas, "but can leave dishes in the sink. Can leave toilet seat up."

"But the companionship of someone who loves you is not to be underestimated," said Rawat.

"Can always get dog," said Stas.

"So," said Thumps, "what's Wutty up to today?"

"Told you he'd try to change the subject," said Al.

"You did indeed," said Rawat.

"This isn't about Wutty," said Al. "It's about you. We don't want you to make a mistake."

"Mr. Stas and I are ready to assist you with the search."

"I will help with mechanical. Make sure pipes are strong, roof is tight, electricity is correct."

"And I can counsel you on the floor plan and the aesthetics of colour and space."

"Right now," said Thumps, "I just want to be fed."

"That's my job," said Al. "Got to keep your strength up for the job ahead."

RAWAT AND STAS started in on the difference between vocation and avocation. Thumps was able to lean on his elbows with his thumbs in his ears and reduce the discussion to a dull drone.

By the time Al brought Thumps his breakfast, both men had headed out to their respective jobs. Rawat at his pharmacy. Stas at his garage.

"Hard to find better friends than those two," said Al.

Thumps had just peppered his eggs when the phone in his pocket began vibrating and ringing.

"I heard you got a new cellphone," said Al. "I just didn't believe it."

"Hello."

"Thumps?"

"Cooley?"

"Hey, wow, it's really you."

"It's me."

"You busy?"

Over the years, Thumps had learned that there was no good answer to this question.

"Depends."

"You at Al's?"

"How did you know that?"

"I can hear the grill in the background," said Cooley. "You eating breakfast?"

"I am."

"When you finish, you might want to come out to Moses's place."

"He okay?"

"You just about finished?"

"Not really."

"You might want to eat a little faster," said Cooley. "See you soon."

Thumps was trying to think of what to say next when he realized that the phone was dead.

"That Claire?" said Al.

"No," said Thumps. "It was Cooley."

"Don't care for them myself," said Al, "but I can see where cellphones could be handy."

"Sort of like credit cards?"

"No need to be abusive," said Al.

"Think I can get some salsa?"

"Long as you keep your mouth shut about credit cards."

Thumps didn't like to eat fast. It upset his stomach. Normally, he would take breaks at certain points in the eating to enjoy the coffee and just drift. Today, he dispensed with the drifting and finished up in good order.

Al came by with the coffee pot, just as Thumps was leaving money on the counter.

"What's the rush?"

"Moses."

"The old man okay?"

"Don't know," said Thumps. "Cooley called."

"So, no news?"

"Nope."

"Well, you know what I say," said Al. "No news is no news."

THE SUN WAS bright. The day was warm. If Thumps didn't know better, he might think that he was driving through an early summer landscape. Most of the fields were yellow, the harvest in, but there were patches of green here and there, as though time might reverse itself and hold winter at bay.

It was an illusion, of course, a moment in time for which the high plains were famous. Lull you into a false sense of comfort one day, freeze your ass off the next.

There were several cars parked around Moses's house, as though the old man had decided to host a garden party. One of them was Claire's. Thumps had just opened his door and swung his legs out when he heard a shriek.

"Dog!"

Thumps had barely cleared the car when a spinning dervish came flying around the corner of the house and crashed into his groin with a thud.

"Dog!"

Thumps managed to stay on his feet. Ivory unwrapped herself from around his waist.

"Did I hurt you?"

Thumps suppressed a moan, forced a smile. "No, honey, you didn't hurt me."

"Then you can chase me," she shouted, and was off on the run.

"That is also what love looks like." Claire was standing at the side of the house. "Are you going to live?"

Thumps stayed bent over at the waist, took a few deep breaths. "Eventually," he said.

"Then you might as well come inside." Claire took his arm. "There's coffee and fruit."

Thumps could see Ivory racing through the stand of cottonwoods. "Shouldn't someone be watching her?"

"Spoken like a parent," said Claire. "I like that."

"And?"

"Watch and learn." Claire cupped her hands to her mouth. "Ice cream!"

Ivory stopped in her tracks, turned, and raced back to the house. "Ice cream, ice cream, ice cream."

Thumps straightened up. "I think I read somewhere that you're not supposed to bribe children."

"Really."

"You went to Alberta."

"I did."

Ivory came sliding to a stop. "Where's the ice cream?"

"Inside, Ms. Monster."

"I'm not Ms. Monster." Ivory bolted into the house. "It better be chocolate!"

Thumps waited for the last waves of nausea to come ashore. "You going to tell me about it?"

Claire held the door open. "Yes," she said. "I am."

35

Moses was sitting in his chair, a blanket over his lap. Scoop was at the stove. Cooley was setting the table.

"Ho," said Moses. "There you are."

"Here I am," said Thumps. "How are you feeling?"

"Pretty good," said Moses. "That Scoop has been feeding me magic soup."

"Chicken broth," said Scoop.

"With rice," said Moses. "Who would have thought to do that?"

"The old man doesn't eat right."

"She thinks she's my wife," said Moses. "I play along."

"You like the attention," said Cooley.

"But I'm too old," said Moses. "So I told her she should marry Cooley."

Scoop turned scarlet. "Be quiet, old man. No one wants to listen to your nonsense."

"I'm a beloved elder," said Moses.

"You're an old man with a wonky heart," said Scoop.

"I have the heart of a bear," said Moses, "the strength of a moose."

"The brain of a chicken," said Scoop.

"In a few days," said Moses, "I'll be good enough to draw water and chop wood."

"We don't draw water anymore," said Cooley. "We have indoor plumbing."

"I knew that."

"And if any wood needs chopping," said Cooley, "I'll be doing it."

Thumps sat down next to Moses. "What'd the doctors say?"

"You know," said Moses, "that was my first time staying in a hospital."

"You've gone to the hospital before," said Cooley. "To visit friends."

"All things considered," said Moses, "I'd rather stay in a hotel."

"Wouldn't we all," said Claire.

"I don't think I have much blood left," said Moses. "Every time I went to sleep, they woke me up. They took pictures of all parts of my body. It was embarrassing."

"The gowns they give you in the hospital are pretty revealing," said Cooley. "The front is okay, but the back keeps coming open."

"It was embarrassing."

"Then take care of yourself, old man," said Scoop, "and you won't have to go back."

"Where is the old man going?" Ivory came out of the back room. "Can I go too?"

"See what a bad influence you are on the young," said Moses.

Claire stopped Ivory with a look. "Did you wash your hands?"

"Yes." Ivory twisted around on one foot.

"Did you wash your hands?"

"Sort of."

"Then go back and wash them again."

LUNCH WAS CHICKEN soup with rice, salad, and warm bread with butter.

"I voted for chili," said Moses, "but the women are hard of hearing."

"Nothing wrong with our hearing," said Claire.

"When you say something intelligent," said Scoop, "we'll listen."

"You see what I have to put up with," said Moses.

Ivory trotted over and put her arms around Moses. "I listen to you, old man."

Moses sighed. "I suppose there is still hope."

"We have to watch him like a hawk," said Scoop. "Make sure he doesn't wear himself out."

"Make sure he stays hydrated," said Claire. "Watch the salt intake."

"This is what the doctors did," said Moses. "They talked to each other as though I wasn't in the room. A couple of times I had to remind them that I wasn't dead yet."

Claire looked at Thumps. "You're not eating."

"Had breakfast at Al's. Didn't know there would be lunch."

"If Dog doesn't eat lunch," said Ivory, "I won't eat lunch."

"No lunch," said Claire, "no ice cream."

"That's not fair."

"Why don't I take you outside," said Scoop. "So the adults can talk."

"I'm an adult," said Ivory. "I like to talk."

"Maybe Cooley will come with us," said Scoop.

"Sure," said Cooley. "You can hide, and I'll try to find you."

Ivory banged through the door on the fly. "Can't find me."

Cooley lumbered after her. "Yes, I can."

THUMPS HELPED CLAIRE clear the table. Moses stayed in his chair with his eyes closed.

"I'll just sit here while you talk," he said. "I'll try not to listen."

"You can listen if you want to," said Claire.

"I'm senile," he said, "so I'll probably fall asleep. On occasion, I may rouse myself to offer sage advice."

"Alberta?"

Claire left the dishes to drain. "You remember what happened?"

"Melton and his fiancée were supposed to spend the weekend at the resort with Ivory," said Thumps. "But then they took her back to Alberta."

"To visit relatives at Standoff," said Claire. "That's what they said."

"So, you went to Standoff?"

"Lethbridge, actually," said Claire. "It's just off the reserve."

"Okay."

"I stayed at the Lethbridge Lodge. Right on the edge of the coulees. It's not as nice as Buffalo Mountain," said Claire. "But it has a nice panorama of the coulees."

"You were worried that Melton and Ona were going to keep Ivory."

"I was," said Claire.

"But?"

"Ivory can be a little shit." Claire smiled. "According to Melton, she decided that she wasn't going to eat. Then she hid under the bed. Then she started crying. Then she started throwing up. They didn't know what to do."

"So, they called you, and you told them you just happened to be in Lethbridge."

"Something like that."

"'The Ransom of Red Chief,'" said Moses in a soft voice. "That's a pretty good story."

"She wanted to know where her mother was." Claire's eyes were moist. "She wanted to know where Dog was."

Thumps waited.

"I had to explain that we didn't have a dog."

"Child-rearing, up close and personal."

"I felt sorry for them," said Claire. "Melton and Ona. They wanted to do the right thing. Ona wanted Melton to know that she was happy to take Ivory on, and Melton wanted her to know that he was a responsible sort of guy."

"They hadn't talked the Ivory question out ahead of time?"

"Evidently not," said Claire. "So, the three of us sat down and did just that."

"Where was Ivory?"

"Asleep on my lap." Claire smiled. "She'd worn herself out."

"And now you're back. She's back."

"Yes," said Claire, "she's back. Melton and Ona decided that they need to work on their relationship before they take on children."

"Smart."

"It was."

"So, she's all yours."

Claire took Thumps's hand, held it for a moment. "She's always been mine."

Moses stirred under the blanket. "Did they pay you to take her back?"

Claire turned in her chair. "What are you talking about?"

"In the O. Henry story," said Moses, "the guys who took the boy had to pay the father to take his son back."

"Go to sleep."

"I'm trying," said Moses, "but this is all very interesting."

Claire turned back. "I hear you've been busy, Deputy DreadfulWater."

"Giving Duke a hand with a case."

"The dead guy at the resort."

"Dead end."

"And that you've been looking at houses."

Thumps could feel the room getting smaller. "Ora Mae's idea."

"I hear she gave you some listings," said Claire.

"She did."

"Anything nice?"

"Haven't looked."

"When the dust settles, maybe we should." Claire stood, went to the door. "I'm going to stay here. Cooley and I are going to look after Moses for a while. Can you give Scoop a ride back to the resort?"

"Sure."

"She's going to put her project on hold for a while, move out here full-time, look after Moses."

"How does he feel about that?"

"Who asked him?" Claire opened the door and shouted, "Ice cream!"

There was a long squeal and the sound of a tornado ripping across the prairies.

"What about it, Dog?" said Claire. "You want ice cream as well?"

36

Thumps waited until the road flattened out and began the long climb into the mountains.

"Claire says you're going to look after Moses."

"Someone has to," said Scoop. "He's pretty weak."

"Cooley's out there a lot of the time."

"Cooley's great," said Scoop. "But he has a job. I can work anywhere."

"You staying in the house?"

"In one of the trailers," said Scoop. "I'll set up my office there. People come out to visit Moses, I'll ask them if they'll give me a DNA sample."

"That should work," said Thumps. "Everyone on the reservation knows Moses."

"And they'll feel more comfortable at his place than in some conference room at a resort or the band office cafeteria," said Scoop.

"A win-win."

"But I'm going to need to find a car," said Scoop. "Something cheap. Something I can afford. Have to be able to get to the store or the hospital."

"I think Moses will really enjoy the company."

"People who live alone generally like to stay living alone," said Scoop. "I'll just hang around in case he needs me."

"You may find him out in the yard chopping wood."

"I expect I will."

"And?"

Scoop shrugged. "No interest in suffering fools. He wants to chop wood, he can chop wood."

They were off the flat now and into the trees. Soon they would pick up the river and follow it up to the resort.

"The dead guy," said Scoop. "You ever figure out what happened?"

"Boris Lukin."

"Was that his name? Was it a heart attack?"

"Not sure," said Thumps. "The sheriff is still looking into it."

"I heard it might have been murder," said Scoop. "I could never figure out how one person could kill another, but I guess it isn't that hard."

"No," said Thumps. "It's not."

"But you'd have to have a reason."

"In most cases."

"Have you ever killed anyone?"

THUMPS PARKED AGAINST the trees.

"I can take you back once you get all your stuff together."

"It's okay," said Scoop. "Cooley's going to pick me up."

"He's a great guy," said Thumps, "once you get to know him."

"Yes, he is."

"He looks tough and dangerous, but he's really gentle."

Scoop kept her eyes on the road. "Yes," she said, "I know."

THUMPS WASN'T SURE where he'd find the sheriff, but he was pretty sure that Archie would be in the Crowfoot Room with the coin exhibition.

He was at the entrance when his phone rang.

"Hello?"

Thumps could see the little Greek across the room, standing with Souto, Hunter, Eliopoulos, and Poe, could see where cellphones could get pretty silly.

"Where have you been?"

"Archie," said Thumps, "turn around."

"There you are."

"Archie," said Thumps, "we can hang up now."

"Mr. DreadfulWater," said Poe. "Good to see you again."

"You and the sheriff solve the case yet?" said Hunter.

"Not yet."

"I leave tomorrow," said Souto. "Do drop me a postcard if you ever figure it out."

"Something with an eagle on the front?" said Thumps.

"An eagle," said Eliopoulos. "Yes, that is quite clever."

"It's no joke," said Archie.

"*Au contraire*," said Souto. "The coin world will be talking about this for years."

"Where's Myers?"

"Man has a serious gambling habit," said Archie. "You can hardly blast him out of the casino."

"Do you think that the 1933 double eagle is a hoax?" asked Souto.

"No idea," said Thumps. "You all saw the coin."

"We saw a video of the coin," said Hunter. "Looked real enough."

"We're asking," said Eliopoulos, "because there's been no contact."

"Contact?"

"What Nico is saying," said Archie, "is that they expected that they would be contacted again about the coin."

Thumps let that play in his head for a moment.

"Someone went to a great deal of trouble to get us all here," said Souto. "Supposedly to sell the coin."

"Lukin could have had the coin," said Thumps. "Someone could have killed him and taken it."

Hunter made a face. "You're smarter than that. If Boris had had the coin, he would have just sold it quietly, probably in Europe, China, Russia. That's where the big money is."

"So, if Boris didn't have the coin," said Souto, "it's still in play."

"Except," said Poe, "it isn't."

"None of you has been contacted?"

"Nope," said Hunter.

"Maybe the seller just contacted one of you."

"Don't mind Thumps," said Archie. "He doesn't know much about auctions."

"Evidently," said Souto, "he doesn't know squat."

"Maybe whoever has the coin has been put off by Lukin's death."

"They're coin dealers," said Archie. "They don't scare easy."

"Archie is hosting a dinner for all of us tonight at his restaurant," said Eliopoulos. "Perhaps he will invite you, and we can continue this conversation."

"He can come," said Archie, "so long as he stays away from the octopus."

THUMPS WAITED UNTIL he was in the lobby. Then he dialed Duke's number.

"DreadfulWater."

"How did you know it was me?"

"Pops up on my phone," said Duke. "How do you think?"

"I knew that."

"Sure you did. Where are you?"

"Buffalo Mountain," said Thumps. "Did you get the info that Cruz sent?"

"I did," said Duke, "and it ain't much."

"As in?"

"General background, conjecture, couple of photographs."

"You at the office?"

"I am."

"I'm coming in."

"You think this Barca guy has something to do with Lukin's death?"

"'When you have eliminated the impossible, whatever remains, no matter how improbable, must be the truth.'"

"You sound like a Chinese fortune cookie."

"It's Sherlock Holmes."

"It's Arthur Conan Doyle," said Duke, "and every idiot and their brother uses that quotation."

"I'll be there shortly."

"I was hoping to get out of here early. Literary event at the Tucker this evening. Macy wants to go."

"Ah," said Thumps. "A little culture."

"Terminal boredom," said Duke. "It's a bunch of poets."

THUMPS MADE IT to town in record time. He didn't have flashing lights and a siren, but he figured if he got stopped, it would probably be Deanna on patrol, and she'd understand.

Duke was banging the old percolator against the side of the filing cabinet.

"Easier ways to kill it," said Thumps.

"It's got calcium buildup," said Duke. "Every so often, I have to shake it loose."

"Or you could just throw it away and get something that was made in this century."

Duke gave the percolator a couple of extra shakes. "File's on the desk."

Thumps quickly scanned the pages. There were three photographs of Hannibal Barca. Two were from a distance, at a party of some sort. The third was Barca standing next to another man who looked vaguely familiar.

"Who's this guy?"

Duke pointed the percolator at the file. "On the back."

Two names. Hannibal Barca. Arkady Lukin. He turned the photo over again. The two men were smiling. Lukin had his hand on Barca's shoulder. They were both dressed in tuxedoes. Two friends at a party.

Duke came over to the desk. "Told you it was thin."

"Barca and Lukin Sr. knew each other."

"We already knew that." Duke put the coffee pot on the desk. "Oh, word to the wise. Avoid Beth for the next while."

"Why?"

"FBI."

"The FBI?"

"They took her body."

"Boris Lukin?"

"Said it was a matter of national security." Duke made a snorting sound.

"Imagine she's livid."

"Doesn't even come close," said Duke. "She called me, and I had to put the phone in the refrigerator to keep it from melting."

Thumps looked around. "Where is the phone?"

"I told you," said Duke. "In the fridge."

Thumps took the photo out of the file. "You got a magnifying glass?"

"This another Sherlock Holmes reference?"

"Damn it, Duke."

"Top drawer, Mr. Sensitive."

Thumps put the glass on the photograph, held it in place, just to be sure.

"You think Beth is still at her office?"

"You *want* to go to the morgue?"

Thumps put the photo back in the file. "I think I know why Boris Lukin was killed."

"The hell you say."

"Let's pay Beth a visit."

"I'll call Macy," said Duke.

"She mind if you're a little late?"

"With poetry, you won't be able to tell."

37

The arrangement of the floors in the old Land Titles building reminded Thumps of something from classic literature or from the bible or one of the epic poems about heaven, purgatory, and hell.

"Good news," said Duke. "You don't have to spend any time in the basement."

Thumps pressed the button for the second floor.

"Yes."

"Beth. It's Thumps and Duke. Can we come up?"

There was a long buzzer sound and the door clicked open.

"You go first," said Duke. "She likes you better."

"You're the sheriff," said Thumps. "You're more intimidating."

BETH WAS SITTING on the sofa looking very much like a gathering storm. Gabby Santucci, Beth's partner, was at the stove.

"You chaps want tea?"

"This chap is fine," said Duke.

"Same here," said Thumps.

"Tell her you like the colour of the walls," said Gabby, "or she's going to kill us all."

Thumps took his time looking. "I like it."

"Ditto," said Duke.

Beth's face darkened. "One of you want to tell me why the FBI swooped in and made off with my body?"

"National security?"

Thumps could hear the thunder in Beth's voice.

"*My* body. *My* case. I'm the coroner of record. I'm in the middle of *my* autopsy and the Fucking Big Idiots come along and help themselves to *my* work?"

"She's thinking about painting the walls again," said Gabby. "Whenever she gets really upset, she paints the walls."

"And then you two show up," said Beth. "A day late and a dollar short."

"We need your help," said Thumps.

"Not only did they take *my* body, but they took *my* case file as well."

"What about his personal effects?"

Gabby poured the hot water into the teapot. "You mean like his clothes."

"Clothes, shoes, watch, jewellery."

"They took everything."

"Shit. What about an inventory? Did you do an inventory?"

The storm on the sofa moved to category three. "Of course I did an inventory."

"You still have that?"

Beth took in a deep breath, let it out slowly. "Yes, I have a copy of the inventory."

"And the crime scene photos?"

"You have something, don't you?"

"Maybe," said Thumps.

"Yeah," said Beth. "The crime scene photos are on my phone."

Thumps and the sheriff spent the next while sitting at the table, going through the inventory and the photographs.

"I was at the resort when Boris Lukin first arrived. I had a camera with me. I took a couple of shots of him getting out of the limo."

"Why?"

"No good reason," said Thumps. "Just testing it out."

"You were practising being a spy," said Gabby. "That is so Gabriel Allon."

"She's a fan of Daniel Silva," said Beth.

Thumps took the photographs that Lynn Langfield had printed off for him out of his bag.

"Here's Boris arriving," said Thumps. "What do you see?"

"Dead man walking," said Duke.

Thumps turned Beth's phone around. "And here's Lukin dead on the floor. What do you see?"

"Dead man on the floor," said Duke.

"Now check the inventory."

"What am I looking for?" said the sheriff.

Gabby leaned over the first photograph. "What's that?"

"It's a stick pin," said Beth.

"But in the crime scene photo, even though it looks as though Lukin is wearing the same suit, there is no stick pin."

"And there is no stick pin in the inventory," said Beth.

"Maybe he took it off, stuck it in a pocket," said Duke. "Put it in a drawer."

"Then it should have turned up in his effects," said Beth. "And if it had, it would have been noted in my inventory."

"Well," said Gabby, "that should make you happy."

"Me?" said Beth.

"You know something the FBI does not."

The sun came out, the clouds parted. "I do, don't I."

"Maybe now," said Gabby, "you won't have to paint the walls."

THE LIGHT WAS dropping, but night was still off in the distance.

"You want to join Macy and me?" said the sheriff. "Immerse yourself in culture that rhymes."

"Could be free verse."

"Good god," said Duke, "I hadn't thought of that."

"I'll pass," said Thumps. "I have a dinner to go to."

"This the one that Archie is hosting for the dealers?"

"It is."

"Can I come?"

"You have to take Macy to the reading."

"I'd rather eat."

Thumps walked with Duke as far as the corner.

"I'm guessing you're thinking that Lukin's death had nothing to do with the coin."

"Not directly," said Thumps. "I think Lukin's death had everything to do with Lukin."

"Because of a missing stick pin."

"Only thing that makes sense."

"You can explain it all to me tomorrow," said Duke. "Over coffee. And doughnuts."

"And I'm supposed to bring the doughnuts?"

Duke touched the brim of his hat. "You are."

THE DINNER WASN'T until eight. With any luck, Thumps would be able to double-check his suspicions, shower, dress, and be at Pappous's on time.

Cruz's car was back in front of the house. Of course. Where else would the man from Pie Town go? The government was no longer paying per diem. Thumps's place was free. A no-brainer.

At least he would keep the cats entertained.

Cruz was in the living room at the new computer. Freeway and Cookie were perched on the arm of the sofa, watching the computer screen intensively.

"Hey, Pancho, this is one hell of a set-up. You even know how to use it?"

"Make yourself at home."

"Just stopped by to pick up my stuff," said Cruz. "And then I saw all the new stuff. Oh, and you're out of cheese."

Thumps pulled up a chair, sat down next to Cruz.

"Since you eat my food, sleep in my bed, maybe you can show me how to get online."

"Easy, *ese*. Nothing to it. What do you want to find?"

"Miami," said Thumps. "They must have big galas in Miami. Can you find pictures of the galas?"

"Little vague," said Cruz. "Can you narrow it down?"

"I'm looking for photos of Arkady and Boris Lukin at big galas."

"Timeline?"

"Last twenty years."

"Shit, Pancho, you don't want much."

"Can you do it?"

"Put on some coffee," said Cruz. "And watch the magic."

Thumps made coffee. Cruz hadn't found the box of cookies in the freezer, and Thumps cut up a couple of carrots into sticks.

"Okay," said Cruz, "here we go. Which ones do you want?"

"All of them."

Cruz worked the keyboard. "The state's got more galas than cockroaches."

Thumps brought out the coffee, poured a cup for Cruz.

"Here's old man Lukin at St. Jude Children's Research. And here he is at Women of Tomorrow. Arkady and Boris at the Miami City Ballet gala and, a couple years later, at the Florida Grand Opera event."

"Keep going."

"This is why I never want to be rich," said Cruz. "You imagine having to go to shit like this all the time?"

"Keep going."

"Okay," said Cruz. "Working our way up to the present, here they both are at the Zoo Miami gala and the Vizcaya Ball."

"When did Arkady die?"

"Couple of years back."

"Show me Boris after his father died."

"Are those carrot sticks?"

"They are."

"Carrot sticks," said Cruz. "Really?"

"There are also cookies."

"Who feeds their guests carrot sticks?"

"You're not a guest," said Thumps. "You're a pain in the ass."

"You know I could kill you with a carrot stick?"

"Boris Lukin," said Thumps. "Photos of him after his father died."

"Zee was more fun," said Cruz. "Okay, here's one of him at the Met Gala in New York. That's a biggie."

"Can you enlarge that photo?"

"Simple tap . . . and *voilà*."

Thumps picked up a carrot stick and took a bite.

"*Cabrón*," said Cruz, "you really going to eat that?"

38

Thumps watched as Cruz worked his way through more photos of Boris Lukin at various galas. The ninja assassin was right. Galas were the one percent's version of the backyard barbecue.

"How many of these do you want to see?" said Cruz. "Are there any more cookies?"

"All gone," said Thumps.

"Hey, maybe Dumbo's is still open."

"Focus."

Cruz sat back. "That's all there is. What do you want to do with it?"

"Can you put these photos into a file of some sort?"

"Electronic or printed copy?"

"I don't think I have a printer."

"Electronic it is."

Cruz decided to use Thumps's next request as a teaching moment.

"See this?" said Cruz. "That's the search box. You type in a subject, such as 'world's most expensive guns,' and hit enter."

"World's most expensive guns?"

"It's just an example."

"I don't want expensive guns. I want the number for Langfield's Camera."

Cruz took his fingers off the keyboard. "So, what do we do?"

"Type 'Langfield's Camera' into the explore thingy."

"Search bar." Cruz typed the name in. "Ta-da."

Thumps called the number. Lynn answered on the first ring.

"I need a favour."

"If I can."

Thumps took the next few minutes to explain what he needed.

"No problem," said Lynn. "But if you had a photo printer, you could do this yourself."

"I have a cellphone now," said Thumps, "so anything's possible."

"I close in an hour."

"I'll be there before that."

"And when you come in," said Lynn, "I have an idea to run past you."

Thumps ended the call. He hadn't noticed it before, but the off button on the cellphone was a red circle with a white icon of an old rotary phone in the middle.

The new era of phones with the old version at its heart. There was something prophetic about that. Something creepy, as well, as though the new technology had swallowed the old.

Which, in fact, it had.

"You want me to keep working for you," said Cruz, "there better be something more than cookies and carrot sticks."

"How about the free room?"

"I had to check into the Tucker," said Cruz. "On my own dollar."

"You don't like my place."

"*Cabrón*, your place is fine. But there's no decent food."

"There's no decent food at the Tucker."

Cruz got to his feet. "Yeah, but at the Tucker, I can get room service."

"Don't you want to know why Lukin was killed?"

"Does it have anything to do with Black Ice?"

"No," said Thumps. "It doesn't."

"Then I'll let the FBI clean up this mess. I've got other things on my plate."

"Such as . . . Black Ice?"

"Pancho, you're worse than the cats."

THE LIGHTS WERE still on at Langfield's. Lynn was standing by the printer.

"Almost done," he sang out over the noise of the machine.

Thumps walked the glass display. There was something elegant about cameras, even the new ones. The Fuji that he had just bought was a good example. It was new in every way, but it had the lines and the look of an older camera from another era. It was comfortable in the hand and almost completely silent.

"Okay," said Lynn. "Here you go."

Thumps spread the photographs out on the counter. "These are great."

"Here's an envelope," said Lynn. "You want to hear my idea?"

"Sure."

"Okay, so you've spent any number of years dragging your field camera over hill and dale. I'm guessing you know this country like the back of your hand."

"Some of it."

"You see much of the wildlife?"

"Sure."

"Antelope, buffalo, moose, deer?"

"All the time."

"Birds as well, I'd suppose," said Lynn. "Hawks, eagles, ducks. That sort of thing."

"What's your point?"

Lynn turned the monitor around so Thumps could see it.

"This is Doug Jensen. He's a videographer. Films all sorts of stuff. Corporate events, rocket launches, stock footage, wildlife. In fact, he has an instruction video on filming wildlife."

"Videography?"

"Guy is smart as hell and easy to understand."

"You think I should get into videography?"

"You might want to give it a try. That Fuji of yours will do video. It doesn't do a great job, but you could play with it. Bring the footage to me, and I can show you how to edit it. If you like chasing animals around, I can set you up with a professional rig. Good money to be made if you know what you're doing."

"Wildlife videos."

Lynn handed Thumps the envelope. "Think about it. Maybe watch some of Jensen's videos. I hear there are gyrfalcons in the Upper Clark Fork river valley. Pretty rare. They would be worth filming."

"How much would a video rig cost?"

Lynn started smiling. Thumps could hear him smiling as he walked all the way back to his car.

When Thumps returned to the house, Cruz was gone. The bed had been stripped, and the sheets were sloshing about in the washing machine. There was a note on the kitchen table. A list of groceries Thumps needed to pick up. Several items were marked as urgent.

The man from Pie Town had left the computer running. It was playing cat videos to the delight of Freeway and Cookie, who were sitting next to the monitor, batting at the screen.

Thumps sat on the sofa, put his head back, and went through what he knew and what he didn't. It felt as though there was one piece missing. He couldn't see where it fit or what it looked like. Just a nagging feeling at the back of his head.

He went to the computer, lifted the cats off the table. Freeway immediately jumped up onto the arm of the sofa and let out a yowl.

"Cat video time is over."

Another yowl.

Thumps ignored her, worked the mouse, typed "Atticus Poe" into the search box. Most of what came up, he already knew. Father: Isaac Poe. Mother: Naomi Alleyne. Father died when Atticus was three. Raised by his mother. High school, university, started in the coin business when he was still in his teens. Had his own store in Manhattan. Just a repeat of everything Archie had found.

He tried "Isaac Poe" and got dozens of hits, none of them the right Isaac Poe. It was as though Atticus's father hadn't lived long enough to do anything worth noting.

He checked his watch. If he hurried, he could get dressed and be at the dinner before Archie brought out the first course. He turned back to the computer and typed in "Naomi Alleyne." As with Isaac Poe, there were multiple entries.

Thumps clicked on each one in succession. One of the Naomis was a veterinarian in Denver. Another was a consultant in St. Paul, Minnesota. A third was a fitness instructor in Portland. The fourth entry was simply a photograph of a young, dark-skinned woman with a somewhat gentle, somewhat sad smile. She was standing in an open atrium. A banner at the far end said "JA New York."

Thumps put "JA New York" into the search bar. Amazing, he thought as he read through the entry. The internet was truly amazing.

He got off the chair, stretched his back and shoulder. Freeway began kneading the arm of the sofa. Cookie jumped onto the table, rubbed his cheek against the monitor.

"Not happening," he told the cats.

But they weren't deterred. They held their ground, twitched their tails expectantly, called out to him, desolate and heartbroken.

Thumps shook his head, moved the mouse into position. "Just this once," he said. "Just this once."

39

Pappous's was brightly lit, full of warmth and good cheer. Thumps was sorry he hadn't thought to ask Claire if she wanted to come, but then he wasn't here to enjoy himself.

This was work.

He might eat a little, but only if the opportunity presented itself.

"Thumps." Archie came rushing up. "Is that the only suit you have?"

"You gave me this suit."

"Yes," said the little Greek, "but you're allowed more than one."

The restaurant was crowded.

"We're running late," said Archie. "Waiting for the dealers to get here from the resort. I need my head examined."

"Something wrong?"

Archie rolled his eyes. "I let Wutty Youngbeaver talk me into providing the carriage service for driving the dealers down here from the resort."

"Let me guess," said Thumps. "*Little Otter*."

"It sounded like fun," said Archie. "He'd pick them up, take a detour to Red Tail Lake . . ."

"Float across the lake in the evening light, drive into town."

"Should I be worried?"

"The last time Wutty took *Little Otter* on the lake, it sank."

"What?"

"But he figured out what went wrong and fixed it," said Thumps, "so you should be okay."

The colour started to return to Archie's face. "Sure, sure, come to the Kousoulas coin show. We kill one and drown the others."

"I'm going to mingle."

"Stay away from the octopus," said Archie. "That's for the important guests."

Thumps had been under the impression that the dinner was going to be a small affair, just Archie and the dealers, but he should have known better. The coin show had been a big event, so dinner had to be equally notable.

Which meant inviting everyone.

THUMPS FOUND SCOOP and Cooley at the back of the room, in a corner.

"Hey, Thumps."

"Cooley," said Thumps. "Scoop."

"Scoop and I were just talking about similarities," said Cooley. "Did you realize that both Scoop and I have a double *o* in our first names?"

"I was telling Cooley about the physical characteristics he shares with Moses."

"My nose," said Cooley. "I had never really noticed. And the two of us have pretty much the same hairline."

"Course, they're related by blood," said Scoop, "so you'd expect some of that."

"Still," said Cooley, "it's so cool."

Thumps opened the envelope and took out the photographs. "I could use some of your expertise."

"If I can."

"Just looking at the physical characteristics," said Thumps, "do you see any relationship?"

"I recognize him," said Cooley. "That's the dead guy at the resort."

"Is this official?" asked Scoop.

"Sort of," said Thumps. "More curiosity."

Scoop went through the photos one by one. And then she went through them again.

"Don't hold me to it," she said, "but I'd certainly think that these two are related. The noses are quite distinctive, as are the lips."

"Arkady and Boris Lukin. Anything else?"

"And oddly enough, these two," said Scoop. "The eyes and the dimples. Dimples are definitely something you inherit."

Thumps slipped the photos back into the envelope. "Thank you."

"Was I helpful?"

"I think so."

"We're having a picnic tomorrow," said Scoop. "By the river."

"You should come," said Cooley.

"You could bring Claire and Ivory."

"Three's a crowd," said Thumps.

"Moses is already three," said Cooley. "Besides, friends aren't crowds."

The noise level in the room was building, and people were still coming in. When he had been a cop, he had had to take a course on fire safety. He tried to remember the factors that determined the number of people you could have in a room. Something about square footage, the height of a ceiling, the placement of exits.

"Not crowds like this though," said Scoop. "It's getting pretty noisy, and I don't know anyone."

"But the food is pretty good," said Cooley.

"Archie said we could take some back to Moses," said Scoop.

"Octopus," said Cooley. "I can't wait to see what Moses does with octopus."

THUMPS MADE ANOTHER circuit of the restaurant, bumping into people, dodging elbows and wineglasses. He was near the entrance when a shout went up and Wutty Youngbeaver came through the door, his arms over his head, as though he had just won the heavyweight championship of the world.

Followed by the coin dealers. Archie came forward to greet them, and the crowd followed.

Ora Mae Foreman pushed in at his elbow. "You don't look happy."

"It's noisy," said Thumps. "And crowded."

"It's called a party," shouted Ora Mae. "You have a chance to look at those listings I gave you?"

Thumps cupped his ears. "I can't hear you."

"Don't be like that."

Thumps held the envelope in his hand and looked at the tangle of people. So much for Plan A. Time to come up with a Plan B.

"Can you do me a favour?"

"If it has a down payment and a mortgage," said Ora Mae, "I'm all yours."

"The group that just came in," said Thumps. "I need you to give this to the individual in the leather jacket."

"Do I look like the postman?"

Thumps closed his eyes, tried to block out the clamour.

"Are any of the listings you gave me on open house?"

"As a matter of fact," said Ora Mae, "they are."

"You help me out, and I'll go to them."

"Take Claire with you?"

"Maybe."

"And Ivory?"

"Ora Mae . . ."

"The one on Birch has a really cute nursery."

"Ivory doesn't need a nursery."

"Who's talking about Ivory?"

The noise level, which had been unacceptable, was now beginning to draw blood. Thumps could feel his body start to seize up. Even free food couldn't hold him.

Thumps held the envelope out. "Please."

Ora Mae snatched it, gave it a shake. "Don't be thinking I'm going to carry your water whenever you come by with a bucket."

Thumps smiled a thank you.

"I'm doing this for Claire and Ivory," said Ora Mae. "So I better hear you made all the openings."

ARCHIE AND THE dealers had disappeared, swallowed up whole by the crowd. Thumps took one last look before he slipped out the door and into the night. He moved down the block to a safe distance, found a brick pillar to lean against.

With any luck, his hearing would return in due course.

"Deputy Dog."

Sheriff Duke Hockney was standing in the shadows of a storefront. Sports jacket. Dress shirt.

"You look nice."

"Macy didn't want me looking like a cop," said Duke. "Evidently, it scares the literary types. How's the party?"

"Very loud."

"Hard to miss that." Duke rolled his neck. "There's a noise ordinance, you know."

"How's the poetry reading?"

"Two women, one guy," said Duke. "One of the poets read a poem about the alphabet and animal noises. I left when she got to *j*."

"What was *j*?"

"Jaguar," said Duke. "Imagine that. Three poets in Chinook, all at the same time."

"You'd think there would be an ordinance."

Duke shoved his hands in his pockets. "You figure this mess out?"

"Boris Lukin?"

"We got another mess I don't know about?"

"Maybe," said Thumps. "Probably. More or less."

"Anything we can take to court?"

"Nope."

"Well," said Duke, "ain't that the shits."

Thumps pushed off the pillar. "Going to sleep in tomorrow."

"You always sleep in." Duke tugged at his jacket. "I better get back. Don't want to miss *v*. No telling what that'll be."

"Mr. DreadfulWater. Sheriff Hockney."

Atticus Poe came down the block, staying to the shadows and the half-light.

"Mr. Kousoulas is a fine host," said Poe. "I'm a poor guest."

"Too noisy for you?" said Duke.

"Very much," said Poe. "As it was for Mr. DreadfulWater, I expect."

"If you don't mind animal noises," said Duke, "there's a poetry reading just down the street."

Poe smiled. "Thank you, no. I was hoping we might have a conversation."

"Sure."

Poe held up the envelope. "A lovely woman gave me this. Said it was from you. Most intriguing. We should talk."

"We should."

"Not now," said Poe. "I'm tired. Might we meet tomorrow?"

"Sure."

"I'm told that there is a most excellent doughnut shop in town."

"Dumbo's," said the sheriff. "Best in the state."

"Shall we say near noon?" Poe turned, started back to the restaurant. "I look forward to it."

DUKE WAITED UNTIL Poe was out of hearing. "Okay, what was that about?"

"Doughnuts," said Thumps.

"You can be an asshole or you can be my deputy," said Duke, "but you can't be both."

"Boris Lukin."

"Hot damn," said Duke. "Doughnuts and homicide. Hell of a way to start a day."

"Don't you have to get back to the reading?"

"Absolutely." Duke buttoned his jacket, gave his shoulders a shake. "I wouldn't forgive myself if I missed *v*."

"Any idea what that's going to be?"

"My money's on a vulture," said Duke. "But then I thought *j* was going to be a jackass."

40

Al's was busy. All the regulars were there. Wutty and Russell and Jimmy were at the front, guarding the grill. Rawat and Stas were in their centre positions, deep in conversation. Al was patrolling the counter, coffee pot in hand, towel over one shoulder.

"Hey, Thumps." Wutty turned on his seat. "Just the man I want to see."

"How's *Little Otter*?"

"Fantastic and afloat," said Wutty. "Took those coin guys out on Red Tail Lake last evening. Major success."

"Except for the guy who puked all over the deck," said Russell.

"Man could hurl," said Jimmy.

"Someone got sick?"

Wutty dismissed it with a wave of the hand. "Not my fault if someone gets seasick."

"Who was it?"

"Short, chunky guy," said Russell. "From Salt Lake City."

"Otto Myers."

"Said he was going to sue Wutty for operating an unsafe craft."

"He was just upset," said Wutty. "He should have said something before he got in *Little Otter*."

"Smelled pretty bad," said Jimmy. "Almost made me want to hurl."

"You could have cleaned it up," said Russell.

"The Vomit Comet," said Jimmy.

"A little consideration," said Wutty. "We're eating."

"Headed in that direction myself," said Thumps.

Wutty blocked Thumps with a foot. "Business first. I was talking to Lynn over at the camera store, and he said you were branching out into video, and it just so happens, I'm looking for a video partner."

"You need to keep looking."

"Chance of a lifetime," said Wutty.

"You could get footage of people puking as they rock and roll across the lake," said Jimmy.

"Think about it." Wutty pulled his foot back. "Just think about it."

THUMPS FOUND HIS favourite seat and settled on it. Al came by with the coffee pot.

"So, Mr. DeMille," said Al, "are you ready for your screen test?"

"Breakfast," said Thumps. "The usual."

"You at Archie's last night?"

"For a bit."

"I was going to go," said Al, "but I figured it would be noisy and crowded."

"You have no idea."

"You and Duke ever find who killed that guy at the resort?"

"Nope."

"Not a good start to your deputy career."

"Breakfast."

"Hear you're looking at houses."

"Breakfast."

Al picked up the pot, headed back to the grill. "Go with a bungalow. Your legs will thank you when you're old and broken down."

Thumps held the cup in both hands, let the warmth fill his fingers and float up his arms. It was the magic of coffee. Hot as well as therapeutic. It also cleared the brain, helped put everything into perspective, allowed for the clarity needed to plan the day.

Breakfast. Grocery shopping. Meet up with Duke and Atticus Poe. With an afternoon taken up looking at open houses. He had called Claire, who seemed okay with the idea, even keen.

A full day in a full life.

"Mr. Thumps."

Chintak Rawat and Stas Black Weasel had somehow moved in on him when he wasn't looking, one on either side.

"Forgive the intrusion," said Rawat. "But we are curious as to the progress of house buying."

"There are many mistakes in purchasing house," said Stas.

"Structuring a mortgage," said Rawat. "Very complicated. Down payment, fixed term, variable term. Finding an honest lender."

"Many houses need repairs. Roof, plumbing, electrical, foundation. Do windows need to be replaced? Furnace? Air conditioner? Can be expensive."

"I'm not sure I'm interested in buying a house."

"Are you uninterested," said Rawat, "or disinterested?"

Thumps was sure he didn't want to answer that question.

"If you are uninterested," said Rawat, "it means you have little interest in buying a house."

"But disinterested," said Stas, "means you are impartial to idea."

"Many people think the two are the same," said Rawat.

"If I decide to buy a house," said Thumps, "I'll let you know."

"It is what friends do," said Rawat.

Al arrived with a steaming plate of eggs and hash browns. "Let the man eat his breakfast in peace."

"Thank you."

"If he's going house hunting with Ora Mae," said Al, "he's going to need all his strength."

THUMPS STOPPED AT the Cash and Carry to restock his house. Bananas, tomatoes, cheese, orange juice, chicken thighs, potatoes.

Stas and Rawat had had more to say about house buying, and before he knew it, Al had joined in. When he slipped away, they were debating the pros and cons of condo living as opposed to life in a trailer park.

The mangoes looked good, and he decided to take a chance on a cantaloupe from Mexico.

He took his time putting all the food away, arranging everything in its place. He filled the cats' bowls and cleaned their litter boxes. Freeway and Cookie weren't hard to find. They were on the sofa, staring at the computer monitor, waiting for the show to start.

"Cat videos aren't made for cats," he told them to no effect. "They're made for people who are trying to block out the world."

Freeway began yowling. Cookie joined in.

"It didn't work last time," said Thumps. "It won't work now."

Though now that he thought about it, the complaining *had* worked last time. And it wasn't like smoking or drinking or gambling. There were probably worse things than letting cats watch cat videos.

Thumps typed "cat videos" into the search bar. The first one up featured a bunch of kittens tumbling over each other, falling on their backs, and leaping about.

Okay, so they were sweet.

THE SHERIFF'S CRUISER was already in the parking lot. Duke had commandeered a table by a window, so he could look out and see the street. Atticus was sitting across from him.

"Did you know that Atticus here almost got to the big leagues?"

"Basketball?"

"Baseball," said Poe. "Pitcher."

"Triple-A," said Duke.

"Double-A," said Poe. "Fastball wasn't fast enough. Slider wouldn't slide."

"So you became a coin dealer."

"It was either that," said Poe, "or an underwear model."

Duke smiled, shook his head. "He's not kidding."

Fancy came over. "Looks like the gang's all here," she said. "These two rascals were waiting for yourself to arrive before they put in their order."

"Coffee," said Duke, "and a chocolate-coated."

"I will try one of your crullers," said Poe, "and a glass of milk."

"And Mr. DreadfulWater will have an unglazed old-fashioned and coffee," said Fancy.

"Please," said Thumps.

"You appear to be all serious and the like," said Fancy. "Is this a law-enforcement moment?"

"More a law-enforcement break," said Duke.

"And should I lock up the shop and turn off the microphones?"

"She's kidding," said Duke.

"I am, am I?" said Fancy. "I won't be bothering you. If you need a restocking of any sort, you'll have but to hold a finger in the air, and I'll come running."

POE TOOK THE envelope out of his messenger bag, slid it across the table to Thumps.

"I think these are yours."

"Keep them if you like," said Thumps. "I have copies."

Poe took the photographs out of the envelope and arranged them on the table. "Quite the rogues' gallery," he said, touching each photograph in turn. "Arkady Lukin, Boris Lukin, Otto Myers, Katheryn Souto, Emily Hunter, Nicodemus Eliopoulos, Hannibal Barca, and, of course, myself."

Thumps waited.

"Not a particularly good shot of Hannibal," said Poe. "But then he was not partial to cameras."

"You knew the Lukins," said Thumps.

"Everyone in the business knew the Lukins," said Poe. "I only met Arkady once. I knew the son better."

Thumps separated out several photos. "These were taken when both Arkady and Hannibal were alive. This is the only one I could find of them together. These two were taken of Arkady after Hannibal disappeared."

"If you say so."

"Here Arkady is on his own. And here are several with both Lukins together."

Poe used his fork to cut the cruller into quarters.

"This one is of Boris at a big gala just after his father died. It was taken about a year back."

Duke ran a hand over the photographs. "I'll be damned. Is that what I think it is?"

"Yes," said Thumps. "I believe it is."

"Maybe Mr. Poe would like to fill us in."

"Not sure what you're talking about," said Poe.

"This picture of Barca and Lukin Sr.," said Thumps. "There. On Barca's lapel."

"This stick pin," said Duke. "I'll be damned."

"Okay," said Poe, "it's a stick pin. As I recall, Barca did wear a stick pin."

"Enamel on gold," said Thumps. "In the shape of a tulip."

"Yes," said Poe. "I believe you are correct."

"And then Barca disappears," said Thumps. "And the stick pin disappears. In all the photos of Arkady Lukin after Barca's disappearance, there is no photo of him with that stick pin."

Poe put his fork down.

Thumps pushed a photo forward. "But after Arkady's death, here's Boris with the stick pin on his lapel."

"And you think that's the same pin." Poe sat back, crossed his arms.

"I do," said Thumps. "I saw that pin on Boris when he arrived for the show. Took a photo of him. Here's a blow-up."

"So, you're suggesting that Arkady had Hannibal killed and that he took the stick pin?"

"No," said Thumps. "I think Arkady and Hannibal were friends. I think the two of them didn't always agree, but they respected one another. I think Arkady was probably upset when Hannibal disappeared, especially when it was suggested that he had something to do with it."

"The meeting in New York," said Duke.

"The meeting in New York that Arkady was supposed to have arranged, but didn't."

"That's what Barca told me," said Poe.

"But now you know what happened," said Thumps. "You've known what happened for the better part of a year."

"Contrary to popular belief," said Poe, "gold-coin collectors are not clairvoyant."

"You knew when you saw the picture of Boris with the stick pin. You knew it was Boris who had killed Barca."

"I'm intrigued," said Poe. "If Boris did indeed kill Hannibal, why wouldn't he sport the pin immediately? Spoils of war and all that."

"Do you want me to guess?"

"I want you to guess," said Duke.

"Please."

"I think Boris wanted to impress his father. I think he wanted to get Barca's eagle. I think he used his father's name to set up a meeting. I think he tried to buy it, and when that didn't work, he threatened, and when that failed, he killed Barca. Maybe it was premeditated. Maybe he was enraged at being told no. Certainly, he would have been worried that Barca would tell his father about the deception. He couldn't allow that to happen."

Duke ate half his doughnut with one bite. "So he killed Barca and took the eagle?"

"No," said Thumps. "I don't think Barca took the eagle with him to the meeting. He trusted Arkady to a point, but he was a cautious man. I think he left it someplace safe. Just in case."

"The pin," said Poe.

"Right," said Thumps. "Boris took the pin, but he couldn't wear it. At least not as long as his father was alive. If Arkady had seen it, he would have known what happened."

Thumps moved a photo to the centre of the table. "But with his father dead . . ."

Duke nodded. "Boris felt safe."

"Well," said Poe, "that's as good an explanation as I've heard. It has a bit of the Poirot mystery to it, but all in all, it's logical and plausible."

"Thank you," said Thumps. "Now, all we have left is who killed Boris. And why."

41

Duke signalled Fancy for more coffee.

"I can bring more doughnuts, yeah? Serious conversation can wear you out."

"Coffee's fine," said Thumps.

"I wouldn't mind another doughnut," said the sheriff.

"I'll join you," said Poe. "Mr. DreadfulWater is very entertaining."

Thumps waited until Fancy filled the cups and brought the doughnuts.

"Where were we?"

"You were going to tell us who killed Boris," said Poe. "And why."

Duke broke his doughnut into quarters. "Well, seeing as I didn't kill Boris, and Thumps here didn't kill Boris, that seems to leave you."

"And why would I want to kill Boris?"

Thumps fished two of the photos out of the pile and set them together, side by side.

"I couldn't figure that one out until I discovered exactly who Hannibal Barca was."

Poe looked at the photos, touched each one in turn.

"Hannibal Barca was your father."

Poe smiled. "And you were doing so well."

"I asked Scoop Macleod to look at the two pictures. Dimples are inherited. So is nose structure, hairline."

"You are joking," said Poe. "If you haven't noticed, there's the little matter of race."

"It's a construct," said Thumps. "Your mother was from Barbados. Your father was from Russia."

"I guess we better do a DNA test," said Poe.

"No," said Thumps. "That's a non-starter. Unless we could find Barca's body, and I doubt Boris was that incompetent."

"So, all of this is conjecture."

"It is," said Thumps. "The rest of it is guesswork."

Poe spread his hands. "There's more?"

"There is."

"Am I going to need another doughnut?" said Duke.

"When Boris killed your father, he didn't find the double eagle because Barca had left it someplace safe. He might have left it with you. He might have left it with your mother. Safe enough because no one knew about you two. You were his secret family that he kept out of sight. He was a cautious man. He knew the points of vulnerability. Family being number one."

Poe stared out the window for a moment. "All right, let's play hypothetical. Let's say that Hannibal was my father. And let's say he left the double eagle with my mother. And let's say that Boris killed my father. Why would I wait all this time?"

"You didn't know," said Thumps. "Until you saw the stick pin, you didn't know that it was Boris who killed your father."

"All this on a stick pin?"

"A stick pin I'm guessing your mother made for your father. She was a jeweller. A very good one from everything I've read. The pin would have been precious to your father."

"That's a great deal of guessing."

"Now that you knew what had happened, you used the one thing that Boris desired to lure him out into the open. He was too hard to get at in Miami. So you sent him a postcard, offering the possibility of a 1933 double eagle. Barca's eagle. And you sent similar postcards to the other dealers for cover. It was, in many ways, the perfect ploy, the coin show the perfect time and place."

"We all saw the coin at the same time," said Poe.

"A recording you made," said Thumps. "The idea was the dealers would bid on the coin, the highest bid would take it, but it was never for sale. Then, after the video, you let Boris know he was the high bidder, invited him back to the room, and killed him."

Poe began a slow clap. "You should write crime fiction. That's a decent plot."

"When we found Lukin's body, the one thing missing was the pin. It wasn't on his lapel. It wasn't in the room. He was wearing an expensive watch, had over five thousand dollars cash in his wallet. None of that was taken. Only the pin."

"You can search me," said Poe.

"We won't find it," said Thumps, "and we won't find the double eagle. And we won't find the stun gun you used."

"No," said Poe, "I suspect you won't."

"Well," said Duke, "I'm impressed. I hope this is where you roll out the proof."

"No proof," said Thumps. "Just a bunch of guesses."

Poe licked his fingers, took a twenty-dollar bill out of his pocket, and slipped it under his coffee cup. "Those were excellent doughnuts."

"Nobody makes better doughnuts than Morris Dumbo," said Duke.

"What are you going to do?" said Thumps.

"Go home," said Poe. "My mother is in a long-term care facility. Whenever I return from a trip, I tell her about my exploits. She enjoys listening to my stories."

"I imagine she will enjoy this one in particular."

"Yes," said Poe. "I believe she will."

"We may have to arrest you," said Duke.

Poe took a card out of his jacket. "Doubtful, but if you have the urge, here's where you can find me. And if you do come to New York, please look me up. I'd love to show you the city."

42

Thumps left the photos where they lay. Duke cut the rest of the doughnut into thin slices and ate them in a slow, deliberate ritual.

"My theory," said Duke, "is that if you eat doughnuts in small amounts at a slow pace, the sugar won't hurt you."

"Interval eating."

"That's right," said Duke. "You should try it."

Fancy came by with the coffee pot. "So, your friend has off and left you, has he?"

"Not a friend," said Duke. "He's a suspect in a murder case."

"Really," said Fancy. "Seems like a decent chap."

"He killed a man," said Thumps.

"That the guy at the resort?" Fancy cocked her head to one side. "And you're not arresting him?"

"No proof."

"He have a good reason? For killing this guy?"

"He did," said Thumps. "Man he killed murdered his father."

"So it's not exactly as though he got away with murder."

"He did get away with murder."

"Yeah, okay," said Fancy, "but there's some sympathy to be found at the bottom of that bucket."

"Why don't you box up a dozen to go," said Duke. "Assorted with at least four chocolate."

"So, what are you going to do?" said Thumps.

"Try to figure out a way to get Amazon to unlock my account."

"Good luck with that," said Fancy. "Now there's a corporation needs a bit of discomforting."

Fancy went to sort the doughnuts in a box. Thumps and Duke stayed at the table.

"You going to tell Cruz?"

"Probably not," said Thumps.

"Might help," said Duke. "The FBI is getting ready to kick Benoit through the goal posts of life."

"Not sure knowing is going to do any good," said Thumps. "Benoit was supposed to be watching Lukin, and she blew it."

"She was drugged," said Duke. "Most likely by Poe."

"Needed to have her out of the way."

"Not sure FBI regulations make allowances for extenuating circumstances," said Duke.

"Think that's a good guess."

"Maybe we should tell them," said Duke. "Even if they can't prove that Poe was behind it, they could make his life a misery."

Thumps yawned. "You tell them. I have to go look at open houses."

CLAIRE AND IVORY were waiting for him at the first house. A 1950s bungalow on a large lot with a garage and workshop. Three bedrooms, two baths. The kitchen was knotty pine with a turquoise Formica and chrome countertop. One bathroom had a pink tub. All the bedrooms were off a long hallway with a floor furnace across from the linen closet.

"An all-original charmer" was how the listing agent described it. Thumps guessed that meant the place had not been touched since the day it was built. It might look dated now, the agent told them, but the style was on its way back.

The second house was an infill in a neighbourhood of other infills. Two bedrooms, two baths, all spanking new and up to date. The kitchen featured an induction stove. The refrigerator had French doors with a cold-water dispenser. The living room was spacious and bright in part because there were no window coverings, which, according to the young man showing the place, was a plus, as it would allow the lucky buyer to put their own decorative mark on the place.

Thumps and Claire and Ivory stopped after the second house to get burgers and fries at Skippy's.

Claire tried to look enthusiastic. "How many more?"

"Two."

"More open houses?" Ivory threw herself down on the table, as though she had been shot.

THE THIRD HOUSE was a front-to-back split-level. Thumps had never heard of the term but discovered it simply meant that the house was built on a slope and that you could walk out the basement to the backyard, which continued to slope down the hill until it plunged over the edge of an embankment and onto the railroad tracks that ran through town.

Thumps wasn't sure he liked the idea of a house on a slope. There was something precarious about the arrangement. The perfect arrangement for winter sledding, the agent declared, and Thumps could see the truth in that. The only problem being how you would stop.

Ora Mae was waiting for them at the fourth house, a one-acre property at the edge of town.

"It's a four-bedroom, two-bath two-storey, so you get a lot of room for the money. Later on, when you're old and worn out, you can sell it for a profit and move to a condo. Or you can leave it to your children."

"That's me," said Ivory.

"It's got a small barn, a garage, and a chicken coop. The perfect arrangement. Country in the city."

The house was solid and uninspired. It reminded Thumps of his place, just on a larger scale.

"Market is moving quick," said Ora Mae. "You going to do something, you better do something."

Ora Mae took them back to her office, where she explained the mortgage rates and the various options for financing a home. Thumps went numb after the first fifteen minutes.

"The question you have to ask," said Ora Mae, "is what will make you happy?"

THE DRIVE OUT to Moses's place was done in silence. Ivory went to sleep in the back seat. Claire leaned up against the door and watched the land fly by. Thumps kept his eyes on the road in case a deer or an antelope wandered into harm's way.

Claire sat up with a start. "So," she said, "what will make you happy?"

"With?"

"Life, I suppose. Roxanne thinks our relationship has stagnated," said Claire. "She thinks we need to move it ahead or go our separate ways."

"Roxanne tends to be rigid."

"Doesn't make her wrong," said Claire. "She gave me a lecture about mini-marts and what's on the shelves."

Thumps couldn't help but smile.

"I see she's mentioned mini-marts to you as well."

"She has."

"Are we stagnant?"

Thumps shrugged.

"Not an answer," said Claire.

"I'm not unhappy."

"Also not an answer."

Thumps turned off the main road and began the long, rutted descent to Moses's house on the river bottom.

"I think I'd like it if the three of us lived together."

"On the reservation or in town?"

Thumps eased the car through a small gully. "My place is a bit small. Your place is a bit isolated."

"Hence a new house for all of us?"

"Hence." Thumps let the car roll out onto the flat. "How'd you find looking at open houses?"

"Terrifying," said Claire.

"Me too," said Thumps. "But maybe we should give it another try."

MOSES WAS AT the kitchen table. Scoop and Cooley were sitting on either side, watching him intently.

"Hey," said Cooley, "you're just in time."

"Yeah," said Scoop. "You bring your camera?"

"The young people are making me nervous," said Moses.

Ivory skipped over to Moses's side, leaned over the plate. "What is that, old man?"

"It's Archie's specialty," said Cooley.

"It's specialty hard to eat," said Moses.

"Octopus," said Scoop. "I've never tried it."

"It's not bad," said Cooley, "but it's on the rubbery side."

"It reminds me of whale blubber," said Moses. "There was a guy from Alaska had a jar with pieces of whale blubber."

"Whale blubber?"

"You couldn't eat it either," said Moses. "You just chewed on it until you got tired."

"We looked at open houses," said Ivory.

Cooley and Moses stopped chewing.

"You guys are buying a house?" said Scoop.

"Together?" said Cooley.

"You should try some octopus to celebrate," said Moses. "Us Indians are great sharers."

"We just looked," said Claire.

"I'm okay sharing the whole thing," said Moses.

"One house had an extra bedroom for my horse," said Ivory. "And another room for Dog."

Claire walked Thumps to his car.

"Cooley and Scoop want to go over to the hot springs in Glory. So Ivory and I are going to stay with Moses for a couple of nights, make sure he's okay."

"Great idea."

"I think Cooley likes her," said Claire.

"I suspect she likes Cooley."

"Were we ever like that?"

Thumps pulled Claire in close. "Never too late."

"Aren't you the romantic."

Thumps looked out at the night sky. "Duke says we should go up the Beartooth Highway. He says you can see the Milky Way from the top."

"You know I'm a middle-aged woman with a six-year-old daughter."

"Almost as terrifying as house hunting."

"Could be complicated."

Thumps stepped back, pushed the hair out of Claire's face. "Then we best keep it simple."

43

The house was dark. Again.

The problem was simple. Thumps would leave the house during the day. Not the time to turn on lights. But he would get home after dark, when lights would be appreciated but wouldn't be on. Which is why coming into the house felt like stepping into a grave.

Maybe he should get one of those timers. He'd seen them advertised, and they looked to be handy. Maybe one of the mechanical ones. The electronic ones that worked off a microchip would take him most of a day to figure out.

Lights on. Home again. Safe and sound.

There was a box on the table. Gift-wrapped. Along with a card.

Pancho, thanks for the hospitality. Something to up your game with Claire.

Thumps opened the box. A T-shirt. A black T-shirt. There was a note in with the shirt.

Dry clean, cabrón. Don't even think about washing it.

At least the ninja assassin had gotten the right size, and, all in all, it was a nice shirt. Thumps checked the label. Silk. What the hell was he going to do with a silk T-shirt?

The cats were in the living room on the sofa. This is where Thumps had left them, and it appeared that they hadn't moved.

"If you think I'm letting you watch cat videos all day, you're out of your minds."

Freeway rolled over so he could rub her belly. Cookie jumped off the sofa and headed for the food bowl.

Thumps opened his new laptop and found the search bar.

Black ice was a thin coating of glaze ice on a hard surface. Black Ice was also a strong ice-filtered beer. And it was a 2022 movie, a documentary about the Colored Hockey League of the Maritimes in the early twentieth century. It had won the People's Choice award for best documentary at the Toronto International Film Festival.

The knock was light, and Thumps almost didn't hear it. But the cats did, and they vanished like smoke in a wind.

Thumps went to the door, turned on the porch light.

"Mr. DreadfulWater."

Atticus Poe.

"I hope I didn't come too late."

There were several people Thumps might expect to find on his porch of a night. Poe wasn't on the list.

"If it's inconvenient . . ."

Thumps opened the door. "No, come in."

Poe held up a Dumbo's Doughnuts bag. "I felt that I left things a bit unfinished this afternoon. I was hoping to remedy that."

"You want coffee?"

"Would you have milk?"

Thumps got plates and glasses out of the cupboard. By the time the two of them sat down at the table, the cats had come out of hiding to see who had come into the house.

"You have cats," said Poe.

"They have me is closer to the truth."

"Exactly," said Poe. "My mother had two Burmese. Much too smart. I've never had cats, but I seem to have inherited the pair. Tell me, do you ever get over the feeling that they might kill you in your sleep?"

"Your mother is in a home?"

"She had a stroke," said Poe. "I should have stayed in New York."

"But you had business here in Chinook."

"Yes, I did." Poe took the doughnuts out of the bag. "An unglazed old-fashioned, I believe."

Poe was wearing a wool sports coat. On the lapel was a tulip stick pin.

"You were quite correct," said Poe. "My mother did make it for my father."

"It's beautiful."

"That's why I've come. To tell you how much I appreciated the work you did. Quite impressive the way you put all the pieces together. I didn't expect it."

"Faint praise," said Thumps. "We can't prove any of it."

"But there are a few pieces missing," said Poe. "I felt you deserved to know the whole story."

"Can you wait until I turn on the tape recorder?"

"You don't need a tape recorder anymore," said Poe. "Your phone can record confessions just fine."

"And you'd like to see my phone?"

"Please."

Thumps put his cell on the table. Poe hooked a fingernail in the side of the phone and popped off the back. He quickly took the battery out.

"It's easy to put everything back together after we've finished."

"You took it apart," said Thumps. "You put it back together."

"Fair enough," said Poe. "All right, first off, I didn't lure Boris Lukin out here in order to kill him, though I can see where you would have thought that to be the case. You were right when you supposed that I didn't know what had happened to my father, until I saw Boris with the stick pin. But I didn't see it in a photo. Boris came to New York for a coin show. We even had coffee. Can you imagine?"

"He was wearing the pin."

"Yes," said Poe, "he was wearing the pin. I admired it, asked him where he got it."

"And he said he bought it at an estate sale?"

"Not quite," said Poe. "He said it had belonged to a friend, another coin dealer with whom he did business from time to time. The pin, he said, had been a gift."

"And the coin show?"

"Yes," said Poe. "As you guessed, the coin exhibition here in Chinook was the perfect opportunity. I knew that Lukin could not pass up the chance to acquire my father's '33 double eagle, so I dangled it in front of him."

"But you didn't want to kill him."

"No," said Poe, "I didn't. After everyone watched the video, I invited Boris back to the room, told him his bid was the winning bid, told him he could examine the coin in person."

"And he came."

"He had no idea that I was behind all of this, and I wanted to keep it that way."

"You were worried about retaliation?"

"The Lukins have a reputation," said Poe. "So I arranged for him to come to the room. He was to sit down at the table, where he would find a blackout bag that he was to put over his head. The coin would be placed in front of him. Then he could take off the bag and examine the coin. Afterwards, he'd put the bag back on, and I'd collect the coin, hold it until he had wired the money into my account."

"Beth found black threads on Lukin's shirt. I can't imagine he was pleased with that arrangement."

"He was quite unhappy," said Poe, "but greed will make fools of us all."

"But he was never going to get the coin."

"He was not."

"And then you killed him."

"Once Boris put the bag over his head, I came into the room . . ."

". . . and used a stun gun on him."

"Knock him out, take the pin, leave him face down in his own spittle."

"You didn't know about the pacemaker?"

"No," said Poe. "I didn't."

"So, his death was an accident."

"Well, that would be rather difficult to claim, given I lured him here in the first place. But the odd thing is, I don't feel apologetic for what happened. Truth be known, I'm rather pleased with how it all turned out."

"And now you go back to New York, look after your mother and the cats, and continue on with business as though none of this ever happened."

Poe reached into a pocket. "This is what it was all about."

The coin on the table was large and gold, with the warm lustre of soft butter.

"The 1933 double eagle," said Poe. "It was my father's."

Thumps broke off a piece of doughnut, ate it.

"Extremely rare," said Poe. "Extremely valuable. But it's not precious. What my father held most precious were his wife and his son. Do you have a family, Mr. DreadfulWater?" said Poe.

"More or less."

"Valuable. Precious." Poe smiled. "Don't ever think they're the same."

Freeway and Cookie wandered over and began to rub themselves against Poe's leg. He reached down and scratched each cat in turn.

"Do they puke on the carpet?"

"They do."

Poe picked up the coin, got to his feet. "I fly back in the morning. My mother gets upset if I don't stop in once a day. And the Burmese are unforgiving."

Thumps walked Poe to his car.

"It's a rental. If you're in the market for a new vehicle, I wouldn't recommend this one."

"Why did you tell me?"

"About Boris?"

"You didn't have to."

Poe opened the door. Then he shut it. "I'm not really sure. Maybe I wanted someone to understand what happened and why."

"Okay."

Poe got in the car. Through the windshield, Thumps could see the man start to say something. Then he pulled the car into gear and drove away.

There had been most of a doughnut on the table. Now it was gone.

The cats.

Thumps imagined them squirrelled away under a piece of furniture, trying to figure out exactly what doughnuts were, spending the rest of the night throwing up.

The coin had been impressive. He tried to imagine Archie's reaction when he told him. Except he wasn't going to tell him. If he did, one thing would lead to another, and there would be no end to it.

What he *was* going to do was drive out to Moses's place in the morning, take Claire and Ivory down to the river, show Ms. Monster where crawfish could be found. Later, he and Claire could sit in the cottonwoods and watch Ivory wave at the pelicans as they came out of the sun to skim the surface of the water.

Or maybe they would just go for a long walk.